WATER WITCH

G·K
Hall
&Cº

This Large Print Book carries the
Seal of Approval of N.A.V.H.

WATER WITCH

Connie Willis
Cynthia Felice

G.K. Hall & Co. • Thorndike, Maine

Copyright © 1982 by Cynthia Felice and Connie Willis

All rights reserved.

Published in 1999 by arrangement with Ace Books, an imprint of Berkley Publishing, a member of Penguin Putnam Inc.

G.K. Hall Large Print Science Fiction Series.

The text of this Large Print edition is unabridged.
Other aspects of the book may vary from the original edition.

Set in 16 pt. Plantin.

Printed in the United States on permanent paper.

Library of Congress Cataloging in Publication Data

Willis, Connie.
   Water witch / Connie Willis, Cynthia Felice.
     p. (large print) cm.
   ISBN 0-7838-8601-2 (lg. print : hc : alk. paper)
   1. Large type books. I. Felice, Cynthia. II. Title.
[PS3573.I45652W38 1999]
  813'.54—dc21   99-18831

To Ed Bryant and the Colorado Milfordians, without whom this book would have been full of stunning gaffs, and other stunning gaffes.

CHAPTER ONE

Radi came up onto the princess's gallery and strode for the courtyard. "Tell Sheria I'm here," he said brusquely to the guard, not bothering with the formalities. Sheria was only too well aware of the formalities, as this latest move of hers had proved.

The guard, almost as thin and delicate-looking as the princess she served, moved in front of him. "The Princess is holding audience. She is not to be disturbed."

Tell her anyway, Radi almost snapped, I won't be kept waiting on this. Then he thought better of it. Anger and highhandedness rarely had any good effect on Sheria. They only made her cooler and more distant, and he wanted an explanation, not a royal icebath. "Never mind," he said more civilly, and could see the guard relax at his decision. "I'll wait below." At least he would not give Sheria the pleasure of seeing him waiting in the courtyard like some common messenger.

He went back down the stairs to the narrower galleries that should have housed the lesser royalty. But there were no lesser royalty now, no families to live in all these rough-carved limestone chambers etched out of the walls of the

7

great red cavern. The old builders had not anticipated the rivalries, the petty disputes and plots
that would empty the royal galleries of everyone
but one slim girl, hardly fitted to rule the huge
City in the Red Cave, let alone to manage the
affairs on the surface of Mahali.

Radi leaned over the marble railings and
looked at the city below. From here it looked the
same as ever: the roofless dwellings and shops,
the glittering computer center with its masonry
walls of quartz and even rows of water grids that
formed the basis of the City's rule of the planet
Mahali. The elaborate computer-drawn grids
plotted every inch of Mahali's underground
water, the key to the wealth of a desert planet
where sweet surface water was almost nonexis-
tent. Mahali had an ocean, but it was laden with
heavy metal salts, and cripplingly expensive to
make potable, so the ancient City in the Red
Cave held sway over all of Mahali from its inviolate position underground. But Radi knew
things were changing.

The nomads, most of them, still feared and
depended on the City, paying their tithes and
housing the holy men and women of the City in
exchange for water, apparently unaware that
there wasn't a full-fledged water witch among
them. The computers and the grids made that
deception possible. It would take great abuses to
make the nomads turn against the City and face
the waterless desert on their own. But the foreigners from the distant planet Kalmar, and the

natives who clustered around their compounds, that was another matter. One Sheria refused to see.

Looking at the huge, complex city far below, Radi felt a stab of fear for the city. Sheria was, after all, just a child, a child forced into being princess because there was no one left to rule. It was her ambitious father's doing that there was no one of the true line left, that Akida and his infant daughter had fled the city. It had suited Sheria's father's plans to have no true water witch in the city, even though he made the claims of descent for his daughter. He had ruled with an iron hand with Sheria as figurehead for fifteen years, and he had not needed witching skills from her to tell him that the foreigners were a growing threat, that the City had to be careful to enlarge its navy and keep its location and water-knowledge secret in order to remain in control.

He had prepared Sheria to rule only when he knew his own death was imminent. His daughter did not comprehend the political intricacies any more than she understood the vast and complicated water grids on which policies were based. Her father's lifetime of experience could not be handed over to Sheria in a few short months. She looked the part of a ruler, standing cool and imperious behind the ceremonial cheek insets of a water witch. But this latest action of hers was obviously politically naïve. Remember how young she is and how unused to power in her own right, Radi reminded himself. If only they could marry soon so that he could assume the authority of the Red City as well as the responsibility. The City needed a true heir, one only he and Sheria could produce. He remembered Akida, shortly before the civil war that had caused him to flee the Red City, saying to him, "Remember always that the fate of the Red City lies in the continuation of its true line of water witches, not in its computers."

He heard voices above and automatically stepped back, even though he was feeling more kindly toward Sheria than he had when he'd come. The audience was over, apparently, and Sheria had come out into the courtyard with the supplicant, whoever it was. Radi could hear a man's deep voice and Sheria's high one.

"There was no reason to do that," the man's voice said. "They were only a couple of surface natives working a harmless swindle."

"Harmless?" Sheria said. "A pretender to the throne is not harmless. I didn't want to take any chances, and I don't want to take any chances with the mission either. I have worked it out and will tell you what to do, just as plainly as I told you what to do with the pretender." She hesitated a moment, then said, "You're certain we won't have any more interference from those natives?"

"Oh, yes. I didn't even have to convince the old man. He jumped at the escape I'd set up. I think he'd realized he was in deeper with the tycoon than he could handle. For a while I thought the boy would be a problem, but they took off anyhow. It's the mission I'm concerned about. He's determined to . . ." The rest of what he said was lost, for he'd apparently stepped away from the edge of the balcony.

"I've taken the necessary precautions," Sheria said, and then Radi heard firm steps coming toward him. He was about to step forward, so that it would appear he was just starting up the stairs, when he saw that it was Botvidi. The older man was in a hurry, scowling slightly. He did not look as if he wanted to meet anyone. Radi stayed well back in the shadow of the gallery and did not start up the stairs until Botvidi was well down on the next level. Perhaps he had been wrong. If Sheria had called an audience with the surface governor Botvidi, she must be concerned and if she were concerned, then Radi would have no problem convincing her to reassign the marines. It was troublesome to have to clear his every move with Sheria, especially now when he needed to be moving swiftly.

"Harubiki," he said to the guard this time, "can you announce me now?" He smiled easily at her.

She didn't smile back, whether because she was angry at his peremptory treatment of her before or because she knew he must have seen Botvidi. Probably the former. After all, Sheria would have no reason to conceal the visit from him. And he had acted badly toward Harubiki,

11

with whom he shared more than loyalty to the princess. Radi had been largely responsible for Harubiki's training as a guard. Fragile though she might look, she was well able to defend her princess or herself. Though Harubiki had never tightened her arms around Radi's neck except in passion, he had no doubt she would be a formidable enemy if she were defending her princess.

Harubiki turned on her heel. "Yes, sir," she said sharply.

He caught at her arm. "Harubiki," he said smoothly. "It is Sheria who angers me, not you. I'm sorry I spoke harshly."

She pulled his hand away with her fingers. "She is your princess, not your mistress, whom you can be angry with at will."

Radi dropped his arm, surprised. "Princess, of course. And soon to be wife."

"I will announce you," she said, and walked away. He followed her through the curtain into the receiving room. "The Princess," she said coldly to him and brushed past the curtain on her way back to her post.

Radi looked toward the dais where Sheria was supposed to receive her supplicants. She wasn't there. Then he saw her at the balcony that looked out over the lower galleries, her blonde hair in a coronet of braids. Now she saw Radi and stepped up on the dais.

"I am pleased to see you looking so fit and ready for your mission," she said, looking cool and beautiful as ever. Radi crossed the chamber and she extended her hand for him to kiss, ignoring his readiness to take her into his arms. Even this early she was wearing the white robes of a water witch and the fossilized gembone insets on her thin cheeks that were supposed to conduct water vibrations to the inner bone structure of the face and thence to the brain. Radi had rarely seen her without them, even though he knew she received no water messages through them. She betrayed her lack of water sensitivity in countless ways: her lack of awareness of weather changes, her reliance on the computers for the simplest of dousing tasks, and in the singing snakes she kept caged in her receiving room as proof of her station. Any true water witch would have kept the deadly snakes in her pocket. But Sheria was wise enough to realize she had no power over them.

But even though she did not have the gifts of waterwitching, she carried the potential for them in her genes, as did Radi. He must persuade her to marry him soon. But first he had to persuade her that the foreigner–Tycoon matter must be settled immediately.

"My mission," Radi said. "Which I suppose you expect me to carry out singlehandedly?"

"I've assigned you Chappa and a majini crew. Pelono's willing to go with you. And I'll send Harubiki with you, if you like." She turned away from him.

"Harubiki will hardly replace the contingent

of marines I was promised. Where are they, Sheria?" Radi said, giving into his anger. "They're not at the docks ready to go."

"I sent them on another important mission," she said, turning back to him and looking him straight in the eye. "You think these foreigners are the only problem on the whole world. You forget that I must deal with everyone, natives and foreigners, and there are just so many marines to order about. Yours were ready. I ordered them to take charge of the pirate at Sindra. He's been raiding the northern coast."

"A pirate!" Radi almost shouted, "A pirate's nothing compared to the danger the foreigners represent. We can't let this situation continue. The Tycoon's actually thrown a priest out of his compound. No one, foreigner or native, has ever done that before, and it sets a dangerous precedent. You should have sent me last spring when the Tycoon stopped tithing. Then this wouldn't have happened.

"Now he's thrown Pelono out, he's refusing to negotiate with Botvidi, and the compound's water is totally out of our control. If we have to realign the grids, it'll mean money and time. It'll also mean that the Tycoon will get away with his insolence for almost six months before the water can be completely cut off. In that time, who knows how many foreign compounds will defect, refuse to tithe. The power of the Red City will be seriously undermined."

"All he wants is more water," Sheria snapped.

"He was willing to pay for it, willing to pay a good deal. Is the City so rich that we can afford to turn down income?"

"Yes, the income's important, but the Tycoon shouldn't need any more water. His compound gets four times the allotted amount for a native settlement of that size. We can't risk depleting the water table so that the foreigners can waste water. And if he wants it for something other than those hot baths he takes, the City should know about it. You've talked to Botvidi. You know how dangerous the foreigners can be."

She looked up sharply. "I know nothing of the kind," she said. "I didn't know you were aware of his visit."

"I saw him on my way here, and I assumed that . . ."

She looked up at him, her expression softened, "I sent for him to begin the arrangements for our wedding. We will post the banns as soon as you return."

"If I return," Radi said sullenly, even though his heart had lifted at the news of the wedding. "We have no priest inside the compound, and we have no guarantee that the Tycoon will be willing to take water hospitality with us. Without the marines as a show of strength, I'll be risking the lives of the entire party."

"Surely no one would refuse water hospitality to a prince from the Red City."

"What does a prince mean to the foreigners? They've never seen the City nor challenged its

15

strength before. You would have done better to discuss this with Botvidi instead of wedding plans. He would have told you I need the marines."

"If you need them, get them. It won't take you more than a day if you take my majini. They're at Sindra. I'll tell them to stand by when they've taken care of the pirate. Then you can march south on the compound with all the display of force you feel you need."

Radi had misgivings. "Three days at least is what we'll lose, one getting to the marines, and two more marching south to the compound. And that's three days during which the Tycoon can learn of the march and strengthen his forces. We'll be coming from the north, over the karst. He could attack us anywhere in the narrow defiles and sinkholes of that wretched land, and it would be a slaughter."

"Radi, you're building a full-scale war out of a simple disagreement over water," she said, plainly displeased.

"Do I need to remind you," he said, "that all wars on Mahali have been fought over water?"

This was degenerating into an argument, one Sheria could carry on at length if she chose, and he had lost enough time with this change of plans already. She had kept him nearly an hour, debating something that should have been a foregone conclusion and would have been with her father: that the foreigners were a danger that had to be dealt with immediately.

"Still," he said, hoping he sounded properly convinced, "Things are as they are. The marines are at Sindra, and considering that, this is a good compromise."

"I thought it was," Sheria said.

"But once we're wed," Radi couldn't resist saying, "I will take charge of the strategic planning, from start to finish."

"Of course," she said, too quickly, and he wondered briefly if she wanted the interview to end, too, and would avoid an argument at any cost.

He hated to leave it like this. Because of their squabbling, he had not been able to ask her about Botvidi and the information he must have brought about the Tycoon. Now he would not be able to ask. And Chappa would be waiting by the boat, furious at the delay, more furious when he heard this new change in plans.

Sheria called in the guard. Harubiki already was dressed for the trip and carrying a backpack and a gembone-backed water-message device. So the offer of Harubiki's services had not been a spontaneous gesture, but something they had worked out beforehand. That meant Sheria knew how angry he would be at the change in plans and had prepared against it.

"Harubiki has promised to follow my orders without question. She will serve you as I have ordered her to. Isn't that right, Harubiki?"

"Yes," Harubiki said without smiling, "I serve the princess always."

17

"You said the majini was waiting," Sheria said. "You'd better go."

Radi hesitated, wishing she would dismiss the bodyguard so that they could have a private parting, but she made no move to soften the moment. It was hard to believe they would be making marriage plans when he returned.

"May the water hold you safely until I return," Radi said, reciting the old ritual of parting for those who had taken water hospitality together and wished to part in peace. Sheria made no movement toward him to clasp his hand and finish the ritual with, "And may we meet again where the water runs sweet." She stood perfectly still, waiting for him to leave.

He swept out of the room, and as he started down the stairs, he heard, barely audible from the receiving room behind him and still tinged with the coolness that had marked the entire interview, "Goodbye, Radi." He did not slow his steps. Harubiki followed behind him.

CHAPTER TWO

Deza waded gingerly into the water. Her skirts were tucked up into the narrow copper girdle so she wouldn't trip on them. The beach was treacherous here. Even before the sea had cut into this little inlet there had been water here, a mineral spring heavy with dissolved silica and calcium. The spring had poured out into a stream that flowed over sandstone in terraced steps down to the sea, leaving a smooth, polished layer of travertine on the wide steps. With the coming of the sea, the waves had deposited a layer of sand over the travertine beach, but underneath it was as slippery as glass. Deza placed each foot carefully, made sure of her footing before she took another.

The waves moved slowly, overlapping one another at the shore. Deza walked steadily into them until she was nearly waist-deep in the mineral-laden salt water, then stopped. She rubbed her fingers thoughtfully along the line of her cheeks.

— You're not far enough out for fish, daughter. —

Deza turned and glared at the figure back on the shore, on a step high above the water. — I can't go any deeper and you *know* that, — she

19

shot back. — My father would know it. —

— I am perfectly aware of your sensitivity to water, although I am not at all convinced it is the handicap you make it out to be. You are also, besides being too close to land, making much too much noise to have any hope of catching a . . . —

Deza cut him off. The fish slid slowly through the greenish water toward her, a large fish with oversized silvery scales. She netted her fingers together and bent over, her hands just under the water like a narrow channel for the fish to swim through. The fish touched her thumbs. She clamped down hard and yanked the fish high out of the water. — Too much noise, hey father? —

Her hands were suddenly full of flying feathers. She gasped and choked on a silver feather. The fish struggled wildly, like a wet and hysterical bird, only there were no firm legs or beak to hold onto. The tail was slippery. Deza tried to hug the fish against her chest and bring up her skirt to net it at the same time. That was even worse. The feathered fins beat wildly against her and flew into her face. Deza took the bottom of her skirt firmly in one hand and stepped forward to pull it over the fish.

Her heel dug through grains of sand, then skidded along slick brown travertine and went out from under her. The fish swam smoothly away, the treacherous silver feathers once more flat against its sides, as Deza went down. She slammed her arms down hard to break the fall, but the water blunted her effort. She went under.

Deza could swim. Her father had seen to that by pitching her mercilessly into the Agate Pools at Sindra, time and time again. She had cried. She had sworn to kill him. She had whined, "It hurts! The water hurts!" None of it had done any good. He had nearly drowned her, but she had finally known the mechanics of what to do, when she didn't panic.

She panicked now. The tight pain in her cheekbones became a slow throb that matched the rhythm of the waves. She felt overwhelmed by the power of the water, carried away by its dark, throbbing strength.

— Deza, come out of there this instant! — her father said.

She opened her mouth to answer. Water poured in. She choked on the bitter taste and spat, not wanting to swallow it. Her arms flailed as wildly as the fish's fins, and she went under again, still coughing. — I can't . . . swim. —

— Then stand up! —

She did.

— Marvellous, — her father said. — You have at least saved me the humiliation of telling people my daughter drowned in three feet of water. —

Deza waded carefully back to the shore, holding up her drenched skirt. — That would be a little difficult, wouldn't it, father? If you are

21

father. I didn't think mbuzim could talk. Or swim either. —

She came out of the water, hands on her hips, and stood beside the short black animal with the elongated goat's face and soft cat's body. It was lying down. It was always lying down, Deza thought, when it wasn't being carried by her with its stubby tri-cloven hooves banging limply against her collarbone. She had carried it for six days now, ever since her father died. She supposed she would go on carrying it until the bruises on her shoulder somehow cancelled out the bruises inside.

You know it's your imagination, she thought sadly, sitting down beside the mbuzi. Poor little thing, though, father or not, we're still stuck with each other.

The mbuzi and its mother had been in the stolen hovercraft with Deza and her father when it crashed. The beasts had been a gift from Edvar. She had accepted them because there was no time to refuse. Her father had insisted they be off. It had made no sense at the time; everything was going beautifully with the swindle. Edvar, the Tycoon's son, was enamoured of her, though still controllable. His foreigner parents had been suitably impressed by her father's claims, then suspicious, finally consumed with greed, all according to plan. Yet all at once her father had said, "We're leaving." And when she had tried to explain about Edvar and the gift of the mbuzim, he had said, "Now,

Deza!" And then, almost before she was over being angry with him for his highhanded treatment of her, the hovercraft was down in this forsaken place and her father lay beside her with his neck broken. And she, Deza, in her beautiful brocade skirt and copper girdle with its gembone buckle, she, Deza, the princess of the City in the Red Cave, complete with fake birthmarks and cheek-insets to prove it, was stuck in this stupid lime coastal village where the inhabitants were too stupid even to know what a princess was. They were the wildest kind of nomads, settled down in the barren cove for no good reason at all. They ate some horrible mess of worms and grass that turned Deza's stomach. They would not eat ocean fish. Those were holy messengers from the moon or something, whose flesh had been poisoned deliberately by some nameless divinity. It was obvious to Deza that they were not smart enough to cut out the heavy-metal gall and discard it, the deadly mercury and lead along with it. She had gone hungry for six dreary days while the winds out of the gritty mountains lashed the shore and whipped up huge, muddy waves. It looked like she would continue to be hungry. And wet. And miserable.

"Oh, poor father," she said aloud. "Why did you have to die?"

The mbuzi looked at her with his yellow, pupilless eyes. — Are you asking for a philosophical answer about the ways of time and fate, or do you want a practical answer? The practical

23

answer is that there is, as I have always suspected, a basic animosity that machines feel for people and which they manifest when they are sufficiently far from civilization to get away with it. —

It sounded just like her father. The mbuzi's thoughts, if that's what they were and not just her own grief-stricken imagination, always sounded exactly like her father. So far she had found no satisfactory way to prove it one way or the other to herself.

— Would you feel more comfortable if I had taken refuge in one of those dreadful little petrified bones people hang around their necks — her father said.

— I don't know. Maybe. — Although she had always been amused at the conversations people had with the "souls" of dear departed relatives who had supposedly taken up residence in the gemmified bone of a dead mbuzi, she'd recently learned that even well-educated foreigners, like the Tycoon and his family, seemed respectful of the living dead. At least the Tycoon allowed the mbuzim to graze freely inside his compound and paid his tithes to the priest from the Red City. — I don't know. Why did it have to be an mbuzi? It's so . . . stupid. —

— My very dear daughter, it was all that was available. We crashed very far from anything. Not even a worm-eating nomad could have inhabited that place. My soul was departing at an alarming rate for the far lands. I had to latch on to something. Be glad I didn't choose the mother. She weighed a good seventy pounds and had a very unpleasant aroma. —

It all sounded so like her father. And he knew things only her father could possibly know. Her father and *she* could know, she corrected. That was the catch. If he really was her father, he ought to know things she didn't, but if that were the case, how would she be able to test him about things she didn't know herself? Her lonely imagination could just make up something, anything, couldn't it?

— Why did we leave the foreigners' compound so abruptly? — she asked suddenly.

— There was danger there, — he answered promptly.

— What kind of dangers? —

He seemed to hesitate in her mind, then said, — The usual. There comes a point in any good swindle when the chances of being found out slightly overbalance the chances of success, and it is wisest to give up and try somewhere else. —

But that hadn't happened. Everything had been going perfectly. — What kind of dangers? — Deza repeated.

— If you are going to catch any fish, you had better do it now. The moon is already up, and you're going to have to eat your catch here or the nomads will have your head for devouring one of their "heavenly messengers." And since I have no desire to be out here on these slippery rocks after dark . . . —

Avoiding the issue was extremely like her father, too. And he, or her own subconscious, was right. She gave up on the problem and stood up. She unfastened the heavy brocade skirt at the waist and stepped out of it. Under it was a shorter muslin half-skirt that came just to her knees. She draped the longer one over a wide step of travertine to dry, then waded purposefully out into the water again.

She stopped when the water was barely past her ankles. She put her hands up to her face and frowned. — Father, — she said, — there's something wrong. Something on the water. —

— A cretin? —

— No. On the water. On the top of the water. —

She pressed her hands hard against the bone in front of her ears, feeling a definite vibration. — Yes, a boat. —

— A foreign boat? —

— No. It's a majini. There's something wrong! —

— Come out of the water, Deza. —

She didn't move. She stood, her legs slowly and dreamily splashed by the even waves, her hands still pressed to the bone on either side of her face. There was no motion of an approaching wake in the water. The green, graceful moon rose above the slow sea. The sky was blue and dark as lapis lazuli. Deza stood very still. She deliberately slowed her breathing and tried to sort out the sensations she was receiving.

26

— The rhythm is wrong, — she said at last, lifting her head. — It's going too fast. —

— The motor? —

— The motor. And the majini. Both of them too fast. — She squinted into the distance, trying to see to the far edge of the horizon. — Too fast. —

Deza stood in the water while the moon rose higher and lost its greenish color. Lumpy shadows formed in the placid swells, and swirls of moonsheen rippled around the snouts of jagged rocks. Lamps came on in the tent village out around the little headland. At last Deza came out of the water to sit on the brown travertine step. She lifted the mbuzi into her lap and held it against her. "They will crash," she said aloud. "It is too fast."

The little animal looked up at her but before it could answer Deza saw the spray of water from the majini as it rounded an outcropping of land and headed into the inlet. The body of the boat was dark-colored, as if its makers intended it to be invisible on moonless nights.

"Poor things," Deza said.

— Pay attention, — her father said. — You are letting yourself be hypnotized by the water. It's only a boat. —

— But it will crash. —

Of course it will. The submerged wings are badly stressed and it won't get much farther. —

— There isn't a proper channel, — she thought,

27

absently pushing the mbuzi from her lap.

— No, but there's you. And you wouldn't recognize good luck if it smacked you in the face. —

— Good luck? —

— You won't eat worms and you can't catch fish, but you can at least be first at the wreckage if you stop dreaming here. Perhaps the majini is carrying truffles to the foreigners or pokes of gembone fragments. Maybe even some gorgeous treasure smuggled out of the City in the Red Cave. Maybe you can even save the life of a fat and very grateful merchant who can carry you safely out of here. —

Deza gathered the mbuzi under one arm, snatched the damp brocade skirt with the other, and leaped to her feet. The majini was past her, veering away from the village headland, as she ran along the travertine steps. She had to have gold in hand when the caravans of barges came up the coast. Gold, gembone, even a ream of fiddler's lace would buy a seat on a sack of goods in one of the barges. Or maybe it would be the grateful merchant who bought her a seat and a pretty new dress when they got to one of the compounds upshore. Let the nomads have their glass beads and tin pots to tinker with over the cold winter while the grass and driftwood fires filled their tents with smoke. She would be in a solid walled house that didn't billow and shake in the wind, one with heat from pipes and running water. All she needed was to get there. Her wit would provide everything else.

Clear of the travertine, she ran across a ledge of fossilized sand dune, leaped down to the beach, then raced to the cove where the gentle waves would carry the debris.

CHAPTER THREE

Radi was not used to the majini. He usually rode in corsairs' barks or, if he wished to travel unobtrusively, hitched a ride in a caravan of merchant barges. Both the corsairs and the merchants owed their allegiance to the Red City, so there was not much need for the City to build ships of its own.

All that had changed with the coming of the foreigners from Kalmar. The wars that had cut Mahali off from the other civilized planets had been over for generations, and now Kalmar was ready to colonize again. At first they had expected to return as welcome countrymen. They didn't seem to realize that the City had reigned supreme in their absence, but now they were getting the sense of it. But they didn't give in easily. The Kalmarrans had tired rapidly of having their goods stolen by clever native pirates, yet instead of appealing to the City for help, they had imported hydrofoils from other worlds and mercenaries to run them, and they patrolled the shores themselves. The hydrofoils were much faster than the native barks and were independent of the wind. Even Sheria's now-dead father, a man more interested in computer programs that would convince surface natives and

Kalmarrans alike of the City's power over all of Mahalio had been alarmed by the foreigners' power over the coasts. He'd poured a great deal of the City's resources into developing the majini, an adaptation of the foreign craft with submerged wings pushing the hull out of the water to skim above the slow waves on an even keel. The City now had a small navy of the little barks on wings. They were faster than the foreigners' patrol boats, one of which they'd just outrun, and quicker to respond to the helmsman's commands in the treacherous shoals. The foreigners' crafts were designed for heavier seas on other worlds, and lacked many refinements in style. Their equipment, the motors and gyro-compasses, however, were more reliable than the native versions. Still, it was satisfying to know that they were placing orders for the majini with the native crafters, orders that were not likely to be filled now. The Tycoon had been showing far too much arrogance to the Red City lately. They would be fools to give him even more power.

Radi sat in the tiny cabin at the bow of the majini, taking a turn at steering the craft over the green waters. The moon was on the rise, climbing into the lapis lazuli sky like one of the foreigners' shiny ships, and he could see the distant shoreline in the moonlight. He headed closer to the shore. Out of sight of land, he felt uneasy, even though he knew the desert beacons and the predictable paths of the silverfish, as the

31

nomads called the constellations and planets. Even the fat greenish moon would show them the way back to the shoreline. Radi and his people were not seafarers. They had gaffs aboard, but unlike the corsairs or even the crews of the caravan barges, they were unskilled in their use. Radi would have given a lot to have the big harpoons that the foreigners were reputed to use when seeking the big sea-cretins. He did not feel comfortable with the swift majini. It seemed to be going almost too fast, skimming the easy waves with a speed that was almost reckless.

A shudder passed through the majini. Timbers creaked and planking rubbed noisily. Then as quickly as it started, the sounds stopped. Radi looked at Chappa, the young marine who had piloted the majini past the patrol boat and into these calm waters and then abandoned the command to Radi at Harubiki's request for music. Chappa was far more at ease than Radi. He was sitting tailor fashion by Harubiki's feet, just across the deck. His flute music barely skipped a beat as he shrugged. Harubiki smiled easily up at him, her feet tapping the deck silently in time to Chappa's music. Radi was glad to see her relaxed; she had seemed even more uneasy than Radi about the majini, insisting on wearing a flotation ring under her muslin blouse and hugging her water-message unit, pretending to listen for news from the Red City, but with such intentness that Radi suspected she was trying to shut out the reality of the majini.

There was nothing now. Pelono frowned, but he was a priest and at least partially a water witch and could be frowning about a distant rain squall. Radi leaned against the wheel, shoulders relaxing as he stared across the water to the shimmering beaches. They were travelling swiftly, making up time lost when they'd evaded the patrol. The Tycoon would know they were coming. The patrol would advise him on the airwaves. They'd also advise the Tycoon that the craft flying the City's red banner had refused to acknowledge both command and request to state their business in the Tycoon's waters. Entirely too highhanded. It was definitely time to show the Tycoon whose waters these were, whose world this was. He could not toss aside the priest from the City in the Red Cave as if he were a simple native shaman, nor could he command Radi's majini. He hoped there wouldn't be a foreign armada to deal with by the time he and the marines were ready to leave Sindra for the Tycoon's compound.

"Let me take the helm." Pelono's voice startled him despite its softness. "We're reputed to have a way with watery things," he said, his eyes sparkling.

"It was just an undercurrent we passed over," Radi said, but he handed the helm over to the old man and went to join the others for a few minutes of song. They were rounding the cape, and there were lights off in the distance, like yellow stars, that Radi knew were the lamps of a nomadic tribe's camp.

He took off his tunic with all its gold braid and gembone buttons and put it aside, then he sat down near Chappa and tried to think about the music. The majini veered smoothly and for a moment they seemed to be bearing down on the camp lights. Radi heard Pelono shout, but as the majini careened sharply and lurched with an ear-splitting sound, water engulfed him before he could answer.

Instinctively, Radi swam, well-muscled shoulders and thighs pushing against the weight of the entire ocean which at first threatened to keep him under. He kicked frantically, and though he knew it was his pants' legs clinging to his calves, he feared that he had somehow mired in a cretin's tentacles.

He broke the surface gasping with relief. He couldn't see the majini, then realized he was looking out to sea. He turned. The lights on the beach were hazy through a thick cloud of smoke issuing from the majini's wreck, burning on the rocks. He knew the craft had been travelling at full speed. Even so, he was shocked at the distance it had covered during the short time he'd been under water, and appalled by the growing fire. The fuel must be leaking. Damn lucky it hadn't exploded or there'd be no wreck to burn. Grimly he swam toward the smoke.

The burning majini was hung up on the rocks about a hundred yards from the shore. The tide was with Radi as he swam, and the same force was threatening to push the bark into deeper water. Radi thought he saw someone jump from the rocks, but it might have been only a burning brand, quickly quenched in the brine. At the top of the swells he saw that there were low crafts on the water, rafts being poled from the beach to the wreck. The nomads were coming to help. Heartened, Radi continued swimming strongly. All of his people could swim, but if they'd been burned or maimed, they might not be able to, and only the cautious Harubiki had worn a flotation ring. In the light of the flames, the survivors would be easy to see. The rafters could pick them up quickly.

When Radi reached the precariously balanced wreck, he had to swim around a pool of burning fuel in the water. The nomads had already lashed their rafts to the rocks and were bailing water onto the fire. He couldn't see any of his own people on the rafts or on the rocks.

"My crew!" Radi shouted as he heaved himself onto the rocks with the aid of a swell.

A startled villager turned, bailing bucket in hand. He swung at Radi without hesitation. The bucket glanced off Radi's shoulder to catch him soundly on the side of the head. Ear ringing, Radi fell back through a pool of flame into the water. The tip of a pole pushed him deeper, and Radi sensed that it was only his attacker's precarious footing on the rocks and perhaps the flaming water that prevented him from being run through. He dived deeper to avoid a second thrust, pushing away from the rocks at the same time. When he surfaced, his attacker had already turned his attention to the wreck.

As Radi struggled with pain to keep afloat, he saw that the nomads had the fire under control and were systematically loading the rafts with bedding, clothing, and food from the looted lockers. Bits of wreckage floated nearby, but he couldn't see the heads of his companions who might have been similarly rebuffed or ousted from the majini. More rafts were coming from the shore. Radi didn't dare call out. His head felt light from the blow, and his back was badly wrenched from the poling, making it difficult to swim. Dazed, he tried to move toward the beach. He hoped the tide would continue to carry him to the beach, for he had no strength to fight it. His arms moved slowly and it seemed as if his legs wouldn't move at all. When his knee scraped sand, he tried to stand, but a swell covered him and dragged him back as it ebbed. His necklace snagged on something, holding him fast. He groped, found two strong arms, the hands of which were grasping his gembone medallion.

With an outraged roar he tried to bring the person down. The stupid nomads didn't even have the decency to wait until he was dead before robbing him of his remaining treasure. But the sound he made was a lamentable gurgle, and it was he who fell to his knees, surf washing over him but barely making the other stagger.

He was pulled up rudely by his neck and hair.

"Come on," said a girl's voice. "You've got to try. I can't carry you, too!"

Radi swayed. The swell pushed his feet beneath him where they belonged, but when he stood he felt as if watery ropes were pulling him back.

"Lean on me if you must, but be careful of the mbuzi."

Slowly comprehending now that he was being aided and not attacked, Radi draped his arm around her shoulder. He thought he heard the plaintive bleating of a desert grazer, but it wasn't until she let him collapse behind a rock on the shore that he realized the furry and lumpy collar around the girl's neck was a young mbuzi. She let Radi lie where he fell while she lifted the struggling mbuzi over her head, cuddled it in her arms, and smoothed its damp fur. The little creature's legs galloped aimlessly as they dangled. Its eyes were wild, but finally the gentle cooing and reassuring strokes calmed the little beast until it only trembled from time to time. The girl's trembling matched the mbuzi's, especially when she looked back at the water.

"You nearly crushed him," she said to Radi, but there was no anger in her voice.

Although she was wet and disheveled, Radi could see that the girl's curly hair was plaited with silver ribbons and caught up in a torn wisp of fine fiddler's lace. Her teeth were white and even, like a Red City girl's, and she wasn't dressed in the flowing robes of the desert nomads. He guessed she was not one of the villagers, and though he wondered why a girl from the Red City would be here in this remote place, he touched the bit of gembone set in the gold medallion, dutifully giving thanks that she was here. The girl frowned at the gesture, or perhaps at the increasing sound coming to them from the beach behind the rock. The rafts were returning with their booty.

"We must hurry," she said, looking worriedly at him. "Can you walk now?"

"Hurry? Where?" Except for the tent village pitched along the shore and filled with the bloodthirsty and greedy nomads, there was nothing near enough to run to. Sindra and the marines were two days' march. The Tycoon's compound was closest, and that was still miles upcoast.

The girl shrugged. "Let's get away from here before the villagers find us."

Radi shook his head, winced as the movement sent shooting pains through his skull. "There were others with me on the majini," he said, sitting up carefully. He could move, but his back still ached.

"There's one person ahead of us on the rocks. The others probably were not so lucky."

"Only one?" Radi tried to peer around the rocks at the beach, but the view was blocked by mounds of fossilized sand dunes, sculpted by waves and eroded into grotesque shapes by the daytime winds. He looked back at the girl. "There were five of us."

"Shh," she said, furtively glancing the way he'd just looked. "If I saw him, no doubt one of those wretched nomads did, too."

There was a cry from the beach, an alarm perhaps, and the girl took fright. Hastily she pulled a long brocade skirt over her head, not bothering to fasten the laces or shake out the wrinkles. She bent over to scoop the mbuzi up, slinging it over her neck in a single motion, then extended a hand to help Radi up. Her eyes glanced over his clothes, as if appraising the damage his ordeal had done to them, then her fingers remained clasped over his ringed fingers just a second too long. She knew it, too, and with a rustling of skirts she gestured for him to follow, and scrambled up into the rocks.

Apprehensive now, Radi checked the hilt of his dagger, loosening the strap that kept it secure. If the way had permitted, he would have had the weapon in hand, but he needed his fingers to find footholds that his eyes could not see in the shadows. At the top of the rocks he was gratefully relieved to find himself in bright moonlight. For a distance he could see that the rocks were flat, nearly shadowless, and partially covered with slick-looking travertine. The girl was crouched over, running at an angle towards the back of the rocks, away from the water, cutting down the angle of vision between herself and the nomad-filled beach. Crouching made his back hurt, but Radi did likewise.

The girl disappeared over the edge of the rocks into shadow again, and Radi dropped to his belly in the moonlight, watching and listening, unable to forget the girl's more than casual inspection of him. The medallion was not large or valuable enough to attract most thieves, but he was leery of anything or anybody that was as out of place as this girl, in her copper girdle and fiddler's lace, so obviously was.

He thought he heard a sound mingled with the wind, perhaps furtive voices or maybe only the startled bleat of the mbuzi. He turned, heading far to the right of where the sounds originated, slithering across the travertine, uncomfortably aware that he was bathed in moonlight. He was invisible from the beach but easy enough to see in his bright yellow shirt if anyone had been curious enough to follow them up to the rocks. Travertine gave over to lumpy sandstone that caught on Radi's belt and laces, slowing his progress to the edge of the rocks. He pulled his dagger from the sheath, rested a moment, listening again. He could only hear the distant voices of the nomads over the sound of the surf lapping gently on the rocks behind him. He crawled, wanting to have his feet beneath him when he reached the edge. Cautiously he made ready to look over the side, poised to spring if the girl were alone, to leap away if she had secret companions.

Near Radi's feet, a man's arm snaked out of

the darkness to grab a tiny nub of rock. Radi had raised his dagger and nearly let it fly when Chappa's head and shoulders rose into the moonlight. The young marine saw Radi's feet, and as his gaze followed the wet brown legging up, a smile of recognition spread across his face.

"We thought you were dead," Chappa whispered. His tunic was torn and his cheek was cut. He hung wearily with his elbows hooked over the ledge, then his foothold must have slipped, for his body lurched. "This way, Radi," he said hastily. "Harubiki's with me." He dropped to what sounded like sand below.

Radi sheathed his dagger and followed, climbing down the rock, for though there was indeed sand below, he feared the jump might further injure his back and surely would set his head to throbbing again. At the bottom he followed Chappa to a niche in the rocks where Harubiki and the brocade-skirted girl were waiting.

"I only saw one survivor," the girl said, her bewildered glance going from Chappa to Harubiki.

Ignoring her, Radi looked around. They were in the shadow of tall rocks, protected by an overhang from being spotted from above but trapped by the protrusions if someone came from behind. Beyond the rocks would be some vegetation, watered only by the morning fog that drifted in from the sea. Beyond that was the vast Tegati Desert where not even surface natives

41

wandered. Radi gave Chappa two signs, tiny configurations with his fingers. Chappa gave no sign of surprise, didn't even glance at the stranger, but Radi knew Chappa's attention was on the girl. He stationed himself a little way from the niche where he could see anyone approaching their retreat, or attack the woman in a single leap. Finally Radi moved into the niche.

CHAPTER FOUR

Deza eased the shivering mbuzi off her shoulders to cradle it in her arms, uncomfortably aware that she was being scrutinized. Prudently, she kept her back to the wall of rock while she crooned softly and stroked the frightened animal. She had kept the animal nearly dry while she was in the water; she had also apparently scared it out of its wits. Its eyes rolled back into the head until only the green conjunctive showed. A bitter smell, emitted from the scent glands around the stiff little ears, was rapidly becoming evident in the windless niche.

— Father, — Deza called soundlessly. — Please, Father. I need your advice. I've rescued him but now I don't know what to do with him. —

— De . . . pri . . . cave . . . don't — Her father's voice could not get through the mbuzi's terror. It came to her in short, staticlike bursts, not even a whole word long.

— Shhh, — she thought at the mbuzi. — It's all right, it's all right, — she crooned. It was no use. The mbuzi was too frightened. Or perhaps it's me that's frightened, Deza thought.

She had been so busy keeping the mbuzi from drowning and the young man's head out of the waves that she had not thought about the water. Now its power rushed over her, and then, like an ebbing tide pulling grains of sand from the shore, it withdrew, leaving her weak in the knees. She reached a hand out to the gritty sandstone wall to steady herself. Her cheekbones ached. — Father, please. —

There was no answer. The mbuzi had fallen into a trembling sleep. She knelt, laid it gently on the sandy floor, and pillowed its head with the fiddler's lace she had worn in her hair, exaggerating her concern for the treacherous beast to give herself time to think before she turned to face the young man. The lace was no loss. Her hair was drying now in pretty curls around her face. She bent farther forward and with a deft movement loosened the drawstring of her blouse so that more of her bosom showed. Rescued by a pretty peasant, and a willing one at that, he would think. He could find out later that she was not all that willing, but not until she was safely inside a compound. She stood up, put her hands on her hips, and turned to face him.

"You're lucky I'm such a good swimmer," she said, smiling at him. "Maybe I'm lucky, too."

"Maybe," he said coldly. He was leaning against the entrance to the niche, dark eyes fixed on her. His wet hair was as straight as a foreigner's, and he was well-fed like them, too. But the telltale high cheekbones marked him as being from the City in the Red Cave, a renegade of some sort, no doubt, since he didn't wear any of the city's emblems. The younger man stood off to Deza's side, his arms casually folded across his chest. One of the woman's hands was hidden by a fold in her wet skirt.

Deza could not see any weapons, but she knew they were there, only a second's movement away. Their positions were too carefully studied to be real. One misstep and there might be a knife in her heart. One misstep . . . and she might already have made it.

— Father, come back, please. I don't think this con's going to be so easy to work. —

"Who are you?" the young man said sharply.

Deza flared. "My name is Deza. I saved your life, remember?"

"Why?"

The loosened drawstring, the prettily curling hair had been wasted on him. "I don't have the slightest idea. I should have let you drown," she said angrily.

"But you didn't. You led us here. Why? Are your friends waiting outside to strip us of the few things we have left?"

"I don't have any friends. And why would I put myself to all that trouble? I could have let the villagers kill you and taken your jewelry off you afterwards. I could have taken your necklace off you while we were coming here and you still wouldn't know it."

"I'm sure that idea crossed your mind."

What crossed Deza's mind was that they must be pirates. Who else could possibly have a

45

majini, or a need to fly across the waters at such high speeds? She stood stubbornly silent, head up, trying frantically to decide what story to use. She could hardly tell them she was from the City in the Red Cave and demand homage, not when they were pirates in the pay of the City. Or even worse, ones who were not! That was not a one-person con anyway. Her father had always been the one to inform people like Edvar's parents that she was the lost princess while she concentrated on looking innocent and unaware. Anyway, the whole thing was too complicated.

The best lie is the truth, Father always said. And since the high-and-mighty hero is not interested in sex, maybe the helpless little girl will appeal to him.

"All right, I'll tell you why I saved you." Her voice was still angry, but now there was a slight tremor in it, as if she were about to cry. "I thought you were rich enough to help me. Those horrid nomads wouldn't even help me go and get my . . . my . . . father!" She was about to burst into noisy tears when her father abruptly reestablished contact.

— It won't work, Deza. He's too smart. —

— It will. —

— It won't. I knew this boy's . . . just take my word for it. He won't fall for it. —

Deza tried to keep her face stubbornly brave for effect. — The others will. They'll believe me, and he'll have to go along with it. He won't want them to think he'd be cruel to a helpless orphan girl. —

She ignored her father's sharp and obscene remark in response to that, and she turned to the woman. "We . . . crashed in the desert, and I tried to get him out, but he was already dead!" She let the last word become a wail. The boy moved toward her. The woman looked uneasy.

"So I . . . came here. I was lost, and then those stupid nomads . . ." She put her face in her hands and sobbed. The boy put an arm around her.

"She's as stranded as we are," the boy said comfortingly.

"Chappa!" The arm left Deza's shoulder. "Go find out what those nomads are doing now. Harubiki! Stand guard for him." The woman and boy shuffled out of the niche of rocks, leaving Deza alone with the hard-eyed young man.

— I told you so, — Father said.

"Oh, shut up!" Deza said aloud, and then sat down on a rock.

"Well, well, what's happened to the poor little orphan girl? 'Shut up,' indeed. And where are your tears?" He reached a hand out to her cheek.

Startled by his touch, Deza looked up at the young man. I spoke aloud, she thought, horrified, and then, they mustn't guess. They mustn't know it's my father. The rest was reflex. As his fingers traced the tearless line of her cheek, she bit down hard on his nearest finger.

He yelped and grabbed her around the waist,

47

pinioning her arms. She kicked out at him unsuccessfully through her thick skirts and succeeded in unbalancing them both. She skidded off the rock onto the sandy floor with him on top of her. He snatched at both wrists and held them firmly to her sides, then grinned down at her. "You're lucky because I'm such a good swimmer," he mimicked. "Maybe I'm lucky, too."

"Shut up," she said again. "And let me go." There, she thought, satisfied. That should take his mind off my talking to my father, and I won't do it again.

"Not until I get the truth from you. What are you doing here? And no sultry peasant girls and no orphans."

"I *am* an orphan. My father and I had a hovercraft crash six days ago."

"Where were you coming from?"

"One of the foreigner's compounds. We . . . I worked there." She did not try to wriggle free. She lay still under his weight and tried to look truthful.

"Why didn't you signal for help?"

"I . . ." She wondered briefly if he'd believe she hadn't known how to work the transmitter, decided he wouldn't. "We had to leave in a hurry. There was a . . . we left in a hurry"

"Either you stole that mbuzi or you seduced the young man of the house."

"No!" Well, she hadn't. It was in the best interests of the con that she never quite seduce

48

anyone, and as a result, she was far more innocent than this young man would believe, but in
this case the truth was not nearly as good as a lie.
"Yes, and he was going to marry me, too, only
my father wouldn't . . . so here I sit, in this stupid
village, where all they eat is worms."

He laughed. "And when I came along I looked
like a good bet to get you to another compound
where you could work your wiles."

"Yes. I've told you the truth. Now, get off of
me!"

He laughed again. "Why don't you seduce me
instead? I mean, we're already here, so to speak,
and your father isn't. I'd even promise to marry
you, just like your foreign boyfriend. Besides, it's
a shame," he freed one wrist and fingered the
drawstring of her blouse, "to let all that careful
preparation go to waste."

That does it, Deza thought, and shoved with
all her weight behind her free hand. She scrambled up and snatched at a good sized rock. When
he stood up, still grinning, she had the rock
poised to smash his face in.

"No wonder they threw you out of the compound," he said.

"They did not. I left of my own accord. Now I
have a few questions I'd like to ask you," she
said, waving the rock threateningly.

"Fair enough."

"Who are you, and where are you going?"

"And will we take you with us?"

"Yes," Deza said. He seemed at ease now,

even amused, which infuriated Deza.

"My name is Radi and I'm a . . . humble priest. I travel as you do, from compound to compound, plying my trade, though perhaps not quite as dramatically. Because of my selfless devotions to the water of the world, I have been assigned . . ."

"You are not . . ." she started to say.

— Let it go, — her father said.

"You are not a rich man? You are a priest?" she said instead.

"I'm afraid so. But as for taking you to the nearest settlement, I can manage that as well as a rich man. The Tycoon's compound is only a few miles."

"I . . . oh, I didn't know that." She shouldn't have said that.

"Oh," Radi said, "and was it the Tycoon or his young son who got you into trouble?"

"There wasn't any trouble. My father was trying to protect me, but there wasn't any need." She was still trying to take in the fact that the Tycoon's compound was so close. She had been too angry with her father to pay any attention to where they were going, and when the hovercraft had crashed, she had been totally disoriented. She lowered the rock.

"I'm not sure the Tycoon will allow another priest into his compound," she said. Edvar's father had dismissed the last priest as if he were a shepherd, unceremoniously and without batting an eyelash. The surrounding community of

50

natives had been shocked, but if the Tycoon had noticed or cared, he hadn't shown it in his behavior or words. In fact, he seemed interested only in Edvar's courtship of "the lost princess," almost as if she, Deza, were more important to him than favorable countenance with the water witches in the City in the Red Cave. Certainly the surface governor, Botvidi, who came to ask after the ousted priest and to whom the Tycoon had made a point of introducing Deza had been annoyed at her being presented as a princess. It had been a tricky moment, for Deza's father had mysteriously fallen ill and was unable to present himself to Botvidi, and Deza was left on her own to decide on her behavior. She had used the charming and dumb routine, which was lost on Botvidi, who was interested only in talking about water. Deza and her father had left the compound that very night, but not before she'd heard the Tycoon also had stopped water-tithing, and that was yet another affront. She'd be a lot better off alone than in the company of a priest, real or not, if she wanted to get back into the Tycoon's good graces. She was in a real dilemma, though. She'd been lucky to find the sea after the crash, and the thought of facing the endless barchan dunes once again to return to the compound frightened her. She considered. "I guess I could get you into the compound."

It was Radi's turn to consider. No doubt that whatever means he'd intended to use to gain entrance into the Tycoon's compound had been lost with the majini. She was sure he wasn't a priest a few hours ago. Perhaps the majini had carried a load of contraband gembone, which the foreigners, including the Tycoon, always could be counted on to buy. Whatever it was, it had been lost.

"All right," Radi said finally. "We are both lucky this night. I will show you the way to the compound. You will get us inside." He took a step toward her.

Deza raised the rock again. "You promise to leave me alone?"

He stopped. "I promise the next time you find me on top of you it'll be because you invited me there."

"If you wait 'till then to pray on your beads, you will have forgotten how." She tossed the rock at his feet.

The man called Chappa slid in through the niche.

"Trouble?" Radi asked.

"No. They're still down on the beach. They've got the boat ashore, though, and they're looking at it with torches."

"I don't care about the majini so long as Harubiki has the water-message device."

"She does."

Radi thought a moment. "Deza, what'll the villagers do when they're through with the boat? Come after us?"

"I don't think so, not unless they think you'll fight to get your majini back. Did you have any alcohol with you?"

"Three barrels of wine, one of ale," Chappa said.

"Then they won't come after us, at least till morning. They don't have any alcohol here. They'll all get drunk."

Chappa nodded, but Radi still looked skeptical.

"Look," Deza said, "I've only been here six days. I don't know any more about the natives than you do. I'm only guessing, but my guess is that if we try to get out of here tonight nobody will care."

"Can you lead us around the village?"

"I suppose so. There's a moon. I don't really think . . ."

"Deza will lead us," he said to Chappa.

"Straight into the compound? Without . . ."

"I'm the priest, and that's all that's necessary."

Deza noticed Chappa's shocked look, and she smiled secretly. Even his companions couldn't see him as a priest. Dutifully, she hoisted the mbuzi to her shoulders. It still shivered in hiccuping spasms, but its mind was quiet.

"Are you taking that thing?" Radi asked.

"Yes," Deza said, her tone daring him to argue. But he merely looked curiously at the young mbuzi's hooves, and then nodded. She marched past him and slipped through the niche.

Chappa was helping the woman Harubiki up

the rocks to the door of the overhang. Radi whispered in Deza's ear, "Try your tricks on them and we'll leave you in the desert. Then you can work your cons on the wild mbuzim. Try seeing how you like stealing their gembone while they're still alive."

"I could do it, too," she hissed back.

"Of that I have no doubt."

The two others joined them silently, their hands once again carelessly close to the concealed knives. Deza thought a moment of what she knew of the terrain, remembered with what ease a path over the rocks had brought her stranded to a razor-sharp edge, and motioned them to follow her in an oblique line down to the edge of the water. When she found the mineral pool, she followed the trickle that flowed through a crack in the sandstone rocks, away from the sea. Beyond the narrow water-cut rocks was a gully that ran nearly to a grove of devil bushes that ringed the villagers' beach. Her companions froze a moment when they heard a singing snake's striking song, but Deza paid it little heed. They sneaked along the edge of the grove, being careful not to touch the sticky fronds that bent out seductively. Even so, a few creepers stuck to their boots and got in Deza's skirts, making her stop to remove them. It was too late for the stopping to do much good. Her skirts clung to her calves thereafter in clumps.

Past the devil bushes, Deza made straight for the beach again, even though they could still see the villagers' fires. The rocks, swept clean of sand by the evening wind, made an easy and silent path. She kept them as close to the water as possible, even where the rocks afforded good cover, for fear of getting tangled in a dead end. That was simple. She could feel the nearby water better than she could see it through the dark, sharp edged shadows.

"Stop a moment," Radi whispered when they were dangerously close to the water, standing on slime-covered rocks.

"Not here," Deza said, glancing nervously at the lantern-light patterns the villagers' fires made in the waves.

Radi ignored her protest and said to Harubiki: "Send the water message to Sindra."

"Sindra," Deza said, startled. "That's a pirate's nest these days."

Radi frowned her to silence. "Tell them to go south to the compound and meet us there."

Harubiki nodded, reluctantly, Deza thought, and then she stepped carefully down the slippery rocks and waded out into the water, pulling her gear off her back as she went. In a few minutes she was back, and Radi indicated that Deza should lead on.

The others followed so silently that Deza turned once to see if they were still there. Radi had taken up the rear, behind Harubiki. Deza led them over the last of the rocks, wading through knee-deep water in one place where the sandstone jutted unevenly into the water. She hesitated before stepping back onto the sand.

There was something troubling about the water, not like the tremors of the approaching crash earlier, nothing at all to do with the water and its power over her, but a nagging half-memory she could not quite get hold of. Something about the water. Finally she walked back onto the beach.

— What a success you were at fooling the young man. He was obviously taken in completely by the helpless orphan girl. —

— Be quiet, Father, — Deza thought, biting her lip to make sure she didn't speak again. The six days alone had made her careless, and fingers would not always be so easily available to bite down on and distract the listener.

— The whole episode was very good for you. I have always said a little honesty is good for the spirit, — her father said.

— Radi could certainly use a little of it. He's no more a priest than I am a —

— Than you are a princess of the City in the Red Cave, and both deceptions are better left unchallenged, I think, at the moment. —

— At least I'll be able to get back to the compound. Then maybe . . . —

— No. There can be no more swindles there. And definitely no princess. Not with these people around. —

— Oh, Father. — They were coming to the end of the stretch of beach Deza knew. At the end of it she had climbed to the top level of the rocks and stared out over the blank and colorless desert. I should have come at night before, she realized now, because even on the level of the beach she could see a pinkish reflection on the clouds above that betrayed the foreigners' well-lighted compound. And so much for my needing a guide. Anybody could find their way to that.

The others came up beside her as they left the beach and scrambled up the chunky rocks to the plateau. Radi sent Chappa back to reconnoiter, then questioned Deza.

"Are you certain you can get us into the compound?"

— Tell him no. Make him leave you here. You don't need him any longer. —

"Yes," she said quickly, giving the mbuzi a warning pinch on its right front fetlock.

Radi paused to brush sand off his boots, then glanced at the pink sky. The muscles in his neck rippled beneath silken skin. "Why are you help-ing us now?" he said suspiciously, looking at the beacon in the sky a moment before turning his penetrating gaze back to Deza.

— Yes, why? You can't handle it alone, Deza. It's more than any one person can . . . no! Deza, you can't have fallen for that hunk of sinew and flesh. Why, I've paraded the highest born boys of a dozen compounds before you, and you've never looked at them the way you're looking at him. —

Deza flushed. — Don't be silly, Father. The only thing I see in Radi is a marvellous opportunity to use him. —

— How? — her father said suspiciously.

"A priest in the compound who is indebted to me may be of some value," she said aloud, answering both her father and the suspicious pirate or priest or whatever he was.

Radi smiled. "I'll give you a wonderful recommendation to the young man of the house. From personal experience."

Deza lifted the mbuzi to her shoulders again and stood up. "I won't need any recommendations, thank you. And you certainly will not be able to . . ."

"Chappa's coming," Radi said, cutting her off with a wave of his hand.

The boy's head appeared over the edge of the scree slope. He didn't speak. He motioned the others to follow and set out at an impossible pace across the loose-packed dirt of the desert. Radi fell in behind the two women. Deza walked beside Harubiki, and then fell imperceptibly behind her, as if the mbuzi's weight were slowing her down.

— We're being followed and you decide it's time to dawdle back to exchange insults with your young man. —

— No. — Deza said, her thoughts distracted.

— What is it? —

— Remember when we went into the water? —

— Yes. —

— The woman. She didn't send a message.

58

She told Radi she did. But there was no message in the water. The pulses would still have been there when I stepped into the water. —

— What does that mean? —

— It means I'm going to walk just as far away from her and just as close to Radi as I can, and when I get to the compound, I'll . . . — She didn't finish her thought. The pace increased.

CHAPTER FIVE

Deza had halted the group behind a heap of broken, dirty boulders just in sight of the compound. The sea was not very far away, yet this was desert land broken in this place by massive outcroppings of rock and what had once been a tiny oasis with a muddy spring that trickled or not, as the City in the Red Cave pleased. Now Radi could see the Tycoon's new dam and reservoir in the rock ravine behind the compound, but Radi knew it held nothing but dust and a few thorny sutino plants in the shaded crannies. He wondered again what the Tycoon would do with all the water the reservoir could hold, and he wondered, too, why Botvidi had not mentioned that the dam was finished.

"What do we do now?" Radi said. "Go to the gate and beg admission?"

"Of course not," Deza said. "They've known we were coming for miles now. They've got sharp-eyed guards and I think machines from Kalmar that can track people."

"Then why are we hiding here?" he asked impatiently. Somewhere along the way he had ceased to be the leader of the party and Deza, stepping confidently through rockways and down stretches of sand, keeping them close to the water, had somehow taken over. Now she was making the decisions, too, and Radi didn't like it.

"We're not hiding. I have some preparations to make before we go any farther," she said stiffly. "Go ahead. Don't wait for me. I won't have any trouble getting into the compound alone, but you might."

"Oh, we all know how well-beloved you are in the compound. You've told us. Several times. But if you're the darling of the Tycoon that you say you are, why all these elaborate preparations?"

Deza didn't answer that.

She scrambled in behind a large boulder, still carrying the ridiculous mbuzi she refused to part with. Radi waited impatiently, watching the compound. It looked like any other, a huddle of native huts around the high wooden center house of the company representative. Even with the high sandstone cliff backing it, the house perched awkwardly against the desert background, like a feather-fish out of water. The foreigners were really ridiculous. Their attempts to bring their native plant with them were insane. They imported the wood and shingles on expensive freighters, imported workers, too, since the natives dissolved in laughter when they saw the plans and then wandered off to tell the good story to all their friends. The houses had steep-pitched, wood-shingled roofs and tiny windows, thick walls and fireplaces in every room, very sensible houses for Kalmar, where it snowed eleven months of the year. They built their houses and then suffocated in them, driven to all sorts of silly shifts to make them bearable in the heat and dusty dryness. Had they copied the natives' homes with their latticed roofs and wide low windows they would have liked their exile much more, Radi thought.

Radi could see activity in the square of the compound, but nothing unusual. People worked in the comfortable shade of their own front doors, women dipped jugs in the wide stone well-pool at the center of the square, then scurried off. They scurried a little too quickly for the heat, Radi thought, and then saw the reason why as the door to the house opened and an entourage came out, heading toward the gate.

Harubiki came and stood beside him. "They're armed," she said, and felt for her own dagger.

"Yes, but they also carry the water goblet with them."

"It looks like a basin," Harubiki said sharply. "The Tycoon is indeed a proud man. And a dangerous one. Yet we put ourselves in the care of a child-girl for the dealing with a man like that."

Radi ignored her. The basin-sized goblet told much about the Tycoon, though, since no real drinking was done from it, only the ceremonial sip that meant you placed yourself under the trust of the host's water-hospitality. That trust, on a planet where sweet water was the most priceless commodity, was inviolable. Even sworn enemies would not break it and were safe under each other's roofs. Provided the ceremony was performed. Provided Deza could get it performed when the Tycoon had expressly forbidden a priest inside his compound. They were bringing the basin, and that was a good sign. They were also, as Harubiki had noted, armed for battle. Radi frowned at the distant compound, trying to read expressions on the faraway faces.

Deza was back. "Oh, good," she said, squinting at the little group now almost to the gate. "It's Edvar and not his father." She turned to Radi. "I do much better with Edvar."

"I can imagine," Radi said dryly, and then stopped. Deza had run a brush through the tangle of curls, but they were as wild as ever. Her skirts were still draggled and her bare feet dusty, one of them bound up in some sort of bandage, yet one look at her told Radi she could indeed manage Edvar, or his father, or even himself, very well indeed. He had never really believed the story that she was an innocent serving girl the son of the household had become interested in. That she and her late father had been working some sort of swindle was obvious, and now Radi saw what it was. She was undoubtedly masquerading as the lost princess from the Red City. And no con in which she figured as a water witch from the City in the Red Cave could hope to work without the sign of her authenticity — the gembone filigrees. They were authentic. They fit her cheekbones perfectly, the delicately rosy gembone traceries carved to a fineness that had to come from his own people.

And they transformed her.

Insets made Sheria's already narrow face positively skeletal. She wore them at the ceremonials of water, and she wore them in her receiving chambers. Aside from Sheria, only the very old women who claimed direct water witch descent wore them all the time. But on Deza! They thinned and shaped her rather round face, the rosy gembone giving it even more color. She looked delicate and helpless and very pretty, a true princess. Even the tangle of cuds around her cheeks was appealing. If only Sheria had looked like that in them, but they served only to make her look somewhat imperial, and terribly thin.

"Where did you get those?" he demanded, angry at the disloyal comparisons he'd been making with Sheria.

"Stole them," Deza said cheerfully. "At least my father did. I could hardly be a princess without them, you know. And Edvar's father is the kind to check things like that out. You should have seen the lengths he went to to get them off me so he could have them analyzed. He'll check you out, too, so you'd better do your priest act right."

"Did he get them off of you, the filigrees, I mean?"

"Of course. *When* I let him. I know how to

handle him, thank you. My con has worked very nicely. I'm not sure yours will work at all. You don't even keep your hands in your sleeves. And priests are celibate, remember?" She turned to the others. "Ready?" she asked sweetly.

He could see the striking curve of the cheek and the curls brushing against it. Very, very flattering. And from her remark, she knew exactly what he was thinking. She was not only in control of the group, she was also starting to manage him.

Deza stepped out from the cover of the rocks and started firmly across the open space, then stopped before the others had a chance to follow. She looked thoughtful, alert, preoccupied for a long moment. Radi had the feeling she'd forgotten all about them. But perhaps that was part of her skillful maneuvering too. He did not ask her what was wrong.

She shook her head once, then again, then seemed to listen for another minute. "Oh, all right," she said at last. "But I don't think it's necessary. I told you, I can handle Edvar." She hiked her skirt up to reveal a long expanse of naked calf with a hidden pouch strapped around it. Rounded calves, he thought, making an even more unfortunate comparison with the thin Sheria and then feeling ashamed of himself.

There had been many women in his life, but only one princess. Sheria the inviolate. Sheria the incomparable. But he found himself comparing the incomparable with Deza, comparing

65

her to her discredit. Deza was maneuvering again. He could not believe, strange and disconnected as her remarks had been, that she would do anything without first measuring its effect on those around her, and that included lifting her skirts. Her con on Edvar, and even his father, Radi was sure, was based on her sexuality, which might or might not be withheld, whichever suited her purposes. He was almost sure that withholding suited her in almost every instance. It was amazing the power a woman could hold with just the promise of her favors, and how those favors once given, transferred the power subtly to the man. Get her in bed, and he would no longer be making comparisons with Sheria. Get her in bed, and the sooner the better. Radi smiled. That was definitely the answer.

Deza turned back to the group. "Sorry," she said, "I forgot something." She had taken something from the pouch and now held it loosely in her hand. Radi had not seen what it was.

She moved to Harubiki. "Would you mind carrying my mbuzi? I may have to move quickly if things . . . do not go as I've planned." She handed the limp mbuzi over, and Harubiki shouldered the animal. Radi wondered if she had done it simply to make it more difficult for the volatile Harubiki to get to her knife.

"All right," she said, "let's go." She led them across the burred and cactused desert to the gate, stepping lightly just ahead of the decorous Radi, who was remembering to keep his hands in his sleeves. The others followed behind with their heads reverently fixed on the sand.

"He has the water-goblet with him," Deza said. "That's a good sign." She did not turn her head.

"For you," Radi answered, barely moving his lips. "Let's hope he's willing to offer it to the rest of us, too."

"Just watch," Deza said and broke into a run. "Edvar," she cried, "Oh, Edvar!" She flung her arms around his neck.

Edvar was abashed, he was pleased, he was a little embarrassed in front of his men. He was everything Deza intended him to be. Simpleton, Radi thought, and then more observantly, young and innocent. He had the good sense to wear lightweight shirt and breeches, but they were the dark colors of Kalmar. Though his fingernails were decorated, his hands were calloused and tan and had the potential of a good grip in them. He had not gone native yet, but the symptoms were there, and Radi knew that he would be sent home shortly to marry, if he were not unduly distracted.

Deza distracted. "Oh, Edvar! He was dead, my own father! And I didn't know where I was and I walked and walked and couldn't find anybody and finally just as I was about to give up and just lie down and die, guess who found me?" She didn't give him a chance to answer. "Oh, Edvar, what luck that you'd just sent for another priest. I would have died out there all alone, just wandering and wandering till I dropped down dead if they hadn't come along, and I told them who I was and then they said that they were coming here and I was so glad because I was afraid I was never going to see you again!" She buried her tearful face against his shoulder. Real tears, too, Radi thought. She's good. Almost too good.

Edvar patted her awkwardly. "Well, Deza, I'm awfully glad they found you and all, but actually, Father didn't send for another priest. He had a sort of disagreement . . ."

"And they shared their food with me and bandaged my foot. See, it's only swollen a little and I honestly thought I was going to lose it at first, it was so red and puffy and then it turned this sort of purple color but I had to walk on it, because I just couldn't stay there. I couldn't bear to with my father dead, my poor father!" Edvar was being treated all this time to an enticing view of Deza's ankle, not swollen at all in the brand-new bandage. He hasn't taken her to bed yet, Radi thought exultantly, and look what a state she's got him in. I'll be like that in a few days if I don't get her properly subdued. "But they had some wonderful medicine and they were so awfully kind, and I know when your father finds out he's going to award them or something, though of course they'll probably refuse because he's a priest and priests are supposed to be kind for a living, but really they just saved my life and . . ."

Mistake, Deza, Radi thought. The reference

to the father was unfortunate. Edvar's face clouded and he raised his hand as if about to signal attack. "I know you're grateful to them and so am I, Deza darling, but I'm afraid you don't quite understand the situation. The priest my father had cheated him and he had to break off all relations with the local . . ."

She pulled herself abruptly away from Edvar and straightened up. The drawstring of her blouse had come undone and her breasts swayed tantalizingly before him. I've seen that trick before, Radi thought. "Oh, I see. You've been having some silly old political problem and that's more important than me. You don't care that they saved my life. You don't care that my bones could be out there right now, fossilizing."

"Deza, please, you simply don't understand how difficult this situation is. There are things about it . . ."

"Oh, I understand. You told me I was the most important thing in the world to you. Well, apparently you didn't mean that." She yanked the drawstring up to her neck and tied it firmly. The message was unmistakable.

Edvar was promptly at her mercy. "Wait a moment sweetheart. I'll work something out."

She still looked unappeased and Edvar flailed about, trying to find an answer that would please her and still not incur his father's wrath. "They *did* save your life. And my father does owe them his gratitude." He made a very slight motion with his hand and the servant carrying the water-goblet began edging a step at a time away from the group and back toward the safety of the gate. "I can hardly extend water-hospitality to them, but I can ask my father to give them an audience."

Deza looked somewhat placated. Radi was almost sure she had not seen the business with the servant. They could have an audience but without the protection of the water-ceremony, Edvar's father would be free to treat them any way he pleased. Throw them out, lock them up, have them murdered. Deza's charm would not be enough to get them out or reincarnate them.

"Oh, all right, I suppose," Deza said. "But after the audience, you'll do the ceremony, won't you?"

"Of course," Edvar said happily. He bowed toward Radi. "On behalf of my father the Tycoon, sovereign ruler, may I welcome you to seek an audience . . ."

"Oh," Deza said, sounding vaguely surprised, and collapsed onto the sandy ground.

For the mind of an mbuzi, Radi thought, annoyed. If she can't think of anything better to do than faint, I was an idiot to put my people in her hands. Even Edvar won't be taken in.

"Oh, Deza," Edvar said, half-placating, half-annoyed, and then, "Oh, my God! Water-bearer!"

The servant hesitated, well inside the gate, then came shuffling back. Everyone drew back horrified. "Hurry, for God's sake!" Edvar shouted at the servant. "It's a peketa! Hurry!"

Radi looked at Deza's arm, alarmed. The peketa bite was clearly there, a red dryish mark, swelling a little and beginning to blister. But where was the bug? If it bit her again, she would be in serious trouble. He glanced hurriedly at the tumble of her skirts, then at her exposed ankle. The bug was there, sitting boldly on the neat ankle that had so entranced Edvar, ready to bite again. Radi dived, smashing it with the flat of his hand, then pulling it off his hand with his fingers so that the drilling tail, which almost had a life of its own, would not work its way into his hand. He ground it into the sand and knelt by Deza.

Edvar was forcing water into her lips from the huge goblet. Her lips looked parched already, the skin of her cheeks under the filigrees tightening, or was that just his imagination? The bite of a peketa did not kill at once, did not kill at all if water in sufficient quantities could be given immediately to counteract the dehydrating effect of the poison. Deza would not be in any danger if the bug had only managed to bite her once. He examined the ankle closely, looking for the reddish bite mark, but could not find one.

Deza's eyes fluttered open. She hiccuped and choked on the water. "Oh," she said again in that surprised tone. "Did I faint or something?"

"No, darling," Edvar said, his voice tender. "You were bitten by a peketa, but don't worry . . ."

Idiot, Radi thought, that's not the way to tell

her. Deza struggled to rise, striking at her clothes with terrified hands, brushing hysterically at her arms and face.

Radi reached out and grabbed both of her hands in his. "It's all right, Deza," he said soothingly. "I killed the bug." He took the goblet from Edvar's passive hands and put it to Deza's lips. "Now, just take a big drink . . . that's it . . . and another . . ."

Edvar looked grateful for his interference. Radi held the heavy goblet under Deza's mouth again and met her eyes. She shot him a glance of fire and fury that almost surprised him into speech. He sat back on his heels, still holding the goblet in both hands, amazed at her reaction.

"I feel like such an idiot," Deza said, but there was an edge to her voice that indicated just who the idiot was, "to have interrupted everything like that, the water ceremony and all . . ."

"But we weren't . . ." Edvar began, and Radi finally came to, feeling like the idiot Deza had just called him. He hastily lifted the goblet to his lips and drank. "And I accept, as you give, the shelter of your water-hospitality and its trust," he said, and practically threw the goblet at Harubiki. The others passed it hastily among themselves, muttering the responses as if Edvar had actually spoken the welcome, instead of just standing there looking helpless.

"I have not . . ." he said.

"There's another one," Deza shrilled. "Oh, get it away, get it away." Her hands were in front

72

of her face, shielding it prettily from a harmless buifly. Her drawstring had come undone again.

"It's only a fly, Deza," Edvar said.

"Ohhhh . . ." It was a wail this time. "Please take me inside. I'm so scared it's going to bite me again."

He pulled her up and helped her through the gate. She leaned against him and favored her bitten arm, although Radi knew perfectly well that the bite of a peketa did not hurt at all, that its deadliness lay in its painlessness for the desert traveller, dehydrated and dying before he realized he'd been bitten.

Harubiki and his attendants followed, secure now even in the face of the men's weapons, safe under the inviolate protection of the water-hospitality. Radi hesitated a moment, looking down at the tumbled sand where Deza had fallen. He scraped at it with his sandaled foot, then stooped and picked something up. He put his arms in his sleeves, like a good priest, still holding on to it for future use, and followed the others at a slow and priestly pace. The sooner that girl's in my bed, he was thinking, the safer I'll be.

CHAPTER SIX

Edvar's father met the group at the front door. "They request an audience, Father," Edvar said fierily, then faltered. "They have passed water-hospitality with us."

The Tycoon already knew. His face didn't change from its stern pleasantness at all as he took in the sight of the priest, hands piously up his sleeves, the empty drinking goblet, Deza hanging on Edvar's arm. Deza tried to disentangle herself from Edvar's grip, but he was determined to hold onto her.

"Deza's injured," he said. "She has a twisted ankle, and a peketa bite. I will take her to her room."

"That won't be necessary, Edvar," his father said in a tone that allowed no argument. One of the servants appeared instantly at Deza's side and took her other arm. She felt pinioned like a prisoner between them, about to be led off to the dungeon. She was not at all sure that Edvar's father did not intend her to feel that way. He smiled broadly at her. "Welcome back, my dear," he said. It sent shivers up her spine. She wished she had not allowed her mbuzi to be carried off to the household's pens.

The servant led her off up the main staircase to

her old room. She could hear Radi and the others being disposed of just as rapidly below-stairs, told that an audience would come later, that it felt right and holy to have a priest in the house again, that he just now had important business to discuss with Edvar. Poor Edvar!

"Your room," the servant said, and shoved open the heavily carved wooden door.

"Thank you," Deza said, and sank carefully onto one of the fur-draped chairs, still favoring the ankle that was supposed to be twisted. She didn't want the servants gossiping that she really wasn't hurt. Servants could be your worst enemies in a con. Her father had taught her that. They saw everything, heard everything, knew everything in a household. They resented your elevated position because they sensed you were really one of them and would do anything to bring you down. "You may go," she said kindly, and smiled.

She waited a moment after the door had shut behind the servant, then raced through an inspection of the room. It was just as she had left it, the messenger's costume intact in the cache that fit neatly into the base of the fiti board, the dark stain for her hands and face, the razor for her hair: the getaway costume that her father had insisted on, but never had her use, even when they dived so frantically for the hovercraft. The cache had not been found, either. The spidery liquid she'd spread over it was intact.

She checked the room for listeners, then after

making sure the door was secure and cursing the fact that the foreigners' houses were so easily bugged, she slid the closet-back open and examined the slipspace she and her father had used. It too was intact, the web stretching across the dark door that Deza knew pitched almost straight down to the lower floors. Her father had managed to get the room below-stairs that connected with hers even though it had belonged to the priest. He had known, of course, which rooms had slipspaces between them before they'd come. He took infinite care with details and it always paid off. Her father knew how to work a con.

— Thank you, dear, — her father said suddenly inside her mind. — I wish I could say the same for you. —

— I thought you were out in the pens with the other livestock, — Deza said.

— I am, and not one of them that can hold a decent conversation, I might add. Not one of them with an ounce of sense, — he added pointedly.

— Including me, I suppose? I think I'm doing rather well, — she snapped. — I got us in, didn't I? —

— Oh, yes, and you didn't need the peketa at all, did you, daughter? —

— All right, I used the peketa. But I wouldn't have had to. It just seemed the fastest way out of a boring situation. —

— And now that you have gotten in and are

safely established in your old room, you will have no trouble working cons alone, I suppose. —

— I don't see why I should. I always did all the work, anyway. —

— Then you won't need my advice, — her father said stiffly, and went away.

— That's right. I won't. — She slammed the slipspace closed. She couldn't use it again until she found out who had the room below. A sudden thought struck her. It had been the priest's before it had been her father's. What if they stuck Radi in there now?

"It won't do any good," she said aloud. "He's too stupid to find it." And she was stupid to say anything aloud, even if she was almost sure there were no listeners placed. She added silently, fiercely, I can handle Radi. And cons. And all of them. I know a thing or two about a swindle, Father.

Deza dumped water in the bath from the copper vats overhead and shrugged out of her filthy clothes. That was the only good thing about these ridiculous Kalmarrans. They smothered in their airtight houses, dressed in suffocating furs and layers of itching wool, but they had marvellous ideas of what a bath should be like. They were wasting Mahali's water suicidally, but Deza didn't care. She sank up to her neck in the fragrant water, leaned her head back against the wooden edge of the bath, and breathed in the heavenly wet pine smell.

The foreigners all took hot baths for some

unknown reason, drenching the room in steam. This was the coolest Deza could get the bath by mixing from the vats, and the lowest. The Kalmarrans swam around in five feet of the water like boiled fish, turning red with the heat. Deza could not stand that much water around her, even though confined in the tub like this it did not have much power. Still, it made her cheekbones ache.

Deza unsnapped the gembone filigrees and dipped her face in the water, scrubbing with her hands to get the parched-look makeup off and then the peketa bite, which was fixed securely with glue. She let it soak a minute in the water, then gave it a good yank. She looked at it a moment and then laid it on the edge of the bath. It really was one of her father's best inventions. Even Radi had been fooled. The idiot! He hadn't even known what to do with the ceremonial water when she'd practically poured it on him. He'd been too busy taking in the charms she'd been working on Edvar, like some moonstruck boy. Well, that certainly didn't hurt, as long as he was safely below-stairs and didn't interfere with the con. He might even be useful to make Edvar jealous.

Deza stood up, dripping water and grateful for the cooling evaporation in the stifling room. She snapped the filigrees in place again, tried to drag a comb through her curls, now a hopeless frizzle from the water, and resignedly began to climb into the layers of clothes the Kalmarrans called, by some quirk of reasoning, their summer clothing. She was into the ruffled muslin camisole and the first two layers of linen pettipants when the door opened.

Deza went promptly onto the good ankle, holding the other one delicately arched, then was glad she had. It was Edvar's mother, in a bundle of clothes that made her look twice as round and short as she really was. She had fur around her neck and wrists, and a little woolen cap edged with more fur. She managed to look delighted and annoyed at the same time. "My dear Deza," she said sternly, "you should not be on that foot at all until it is rebandaged."

Deza hobbled obediently to a chair and sat down. The wife of the Tycoon, as she was called formally, or simply the wife, knelt before her with a large box of milkcloth bandages and ointments, and a huge flagon of water. "Now you must drink all of this, or you'll take fever from that insect bite, and that wouldn't do at all. Then you must tell me about your adventures. We were so dreadfully worried and had no idea where you were. Some awful place, I daresay. And your poor father. Edvar told me all about him. What a terrible thing for you, but at least here you are safe and sound after who knows what kind of adventures. I want to know all about them. Which ankle is it?"

"This one," Deza pointed, hoping the wife would not ask next to see her peketa bite, which was in the bathroom lying on the edge of the tub.

"Ouch," she said obligingly when the wife touched her ankle, and bit her lip. At least a twisted ankle didn't have to look like anything. "The natives were chasing me and I tripped on a rock. They had spears!"

"Spears! Oh, my dear, what an awful thing! You must tell me all about it. Drink," she said with an imperative look at the flagon. Obediently Deza swallowed some water. The wife deftly bandaged the ankle in an endless length of imported milkcloth, which, thought Deza, is not such a bad thing because at least I'll be able to keep track of which one it is. Only why is she here, kneeling at my feet, calling me her dear Deza, when she's never liked me at all? She had occupied her few meetings with Deza with references to Edvar's brilliant future on Kalmar, where Deza was sure she had someone appropriate all picked out for him. Deza, princess or not, had never fit into the mother's plans.

"I hope you weren't hurt some other way," the wife said suddenly. "I mean, those awful natives and all that time wandering by yourself in the desert . . ."

What was she getting at? Rape? What a peculiar thing to say.

"I mean," she went on, seeming almost embarrassed. She must mean rape. "You can still . . . do . . . what your father said!"

"I feel fine," Deza said carefully. "I just twisted my ankle." Of course I can still water-witch. But why on earth do you care? That's supposed to be your husband's concern.

"I wasn't able to hire anyone to go get the rocks before because . . . you understand my husband keeps me on a very strict allowance. But Edvar went out for me while you were gone. Poor boy, he was so lost without you and he had to have something to do. He'd heard of an area where there was supposed to be a deposit, and . . . well, I'm afraid there are rather a lot, but of course it won't take you long to tell them apart. Your father said . . ."

Deza knew exactly what her father had said. Had he been trying to placate the angry mother with hints of wealth to dazzle the folks back home, or simply bragging about his talented daughter to get the husband's interest? "Oh, my yes, and she can also spin wishes into water."

"Where are they?" Deza said weakly.

"Oh, outside in one of the barns. There simply wasn't room for them in the house."

Deza was afraid to ask how many there were. If Edvar really had found a new deposit, there would be a ton of the shapeless dirty brown rocks, from the size of Deza's fist to that of boulders, impossible to crack, uniformly gray-brown and unidentifiable.

"Of course I realize only a few will be orbs, but out of so many rocks, there will have to be at least . . . how many do you think? Oh, my friends back home will be so envious. Some of them have paid fortunes for an orb and then had nothing inside. But thanks to your lucky talent, I

81

shall have as many as I want." She twisted her little plump hands together anxiously.

She's trying to think of a nice way to ask me when I'm going to start finding her orbs for her, Deza thought, and I'm not about to help her. Orbs, the famous Mahali geodes, were rare not only because it took exact proportions of minerals, ground water, and time to create the jeweled core to be found inside one when its heavy rock outer cover had been cracked. They were also wildly expensive because of the impossibility of locating one in the heap of gray, unmarked rocks they were to be found in. Deza supposed her father had decided to embroider on her water-witching skills by saying she could feel the minute quantity of water trapped inside the orb. A marvellous but totally untrue boast, and if he had been drunk at the time, Deza would never forgive him.

"I think . . ." Deza said, going a practiced white, "oh . . . oh!" She sank back against the furs, breathing hard. "There was this funny stabbing pain in my ankle just now . . . it . . . oh! There it went again."

"Of course, my dear, I should have made you lie down in the first place, for you simply must take enough time to finish that water, and when you do, I'll have more sent up. I put a few drops of honey in it, that wonderful red honey they get at Sindra. Your ankle must get better, too. I shouldn't have talked business, but I just couldn't help thinking how wonderful it will be when my friends see the orbs I've got." She was helping Deza limp over to the large carved bed, heavy with its load of comforters and blankets. "But I was very inconsiderate, my dear. Just imagine, spears. You must tell me all about it." She held out the flagon to Deza, watched while she drank. Then she tucked Deza in up to her chin and waddled out. Deza stayed under the covers, her eyes closed.

— Father, — she said firmly. — This is all your fault. Come here. —

Nothing.

— I mean it. —

Still nothing.

— Father, please! —

The door opened. Deza opened her eyes and sat up in bed. "Edvar!" she said, and tried to pull the covers up over her revealing camisole. "Aren't you supposed to be talking to your father?" Edvar was not supposed to see her like this, in her underwear, in bed. He was supposed to be allowed one glimpse, one promise at a time.

"I talked to him," Edvar said carelessly, and came at her like a bull. Deza rolled out of the bed on the far side and went for the door, trying to remember to limp in case she needed to use the ankle as a last resort. "Edvar, you shouldn't be here. I'm not even dressed. What will your mother say? Or your father? Think of your father." Please, think of your father, and stop looking at me like you'd like to devour me.

83

"What about him?" He came around the bed, still speaking in that ominously careless tone. "And what do you care if you're dressed? You can go around naked from now on if you want." He seemed to savor that idea. "We're getting married."

Deza was backed flat against the wall. "When?" she squeaked, and put her hands over her chest.

"I told Father we'd get married when *I* said, not when he's finished with his crazy schemes to get water."

What crazy schemes? Deza almost asked, then decided it was safer to put a chair between them.

"I told him he could not dictate to me any longer, that you and I did not need him and his fancy house, that we would live in a native hut and raise mbuzim, that we would eat like natives, work like natives, without him. He has no domination over me. I like Mahali, it has a lot to offer me." He lunged for her.

Deza kept the chair between them, trying frantically to think, decided, and burst into noisy tears. "How could you?" she sobbed, sitting down on the chair. "Oh, Edvar, how could you?" She had taken her hands away from her chest and put them up to her face. Her breasts were heaving prettily with her sobs, but that should be no problem.

It wasn't. Edvar was instantly contrite. "Did I frighten you, my love? I wouldn't hurt you for the world. You're so charming and affectionate and . . . what a cad you must think me!"

"No, Edvar, it isn't that," she sniffled, coloring a little. "I mean, I know it isn't ladylike, but sometimes I don't want to wait either. But to cut yourself off from your father like that. You can't blame him for wanting us to wait. They say that waiting makes it better. And then we could live here. I don't think I could live like the natives when they eat . . . they eat worms!" she wailed, and released a new flood of tears.

"It's not all stuff like worms," he said, the words rushing. "There's game to be found in the morning mists by hunters who know the ways of Mahali, and there are fruits in the oases that are so good they're better than imported Kalmarran delicacies. I can take care of you, Deza. I would build you an airy hut, and keep you safe."

And out from under your father's thumb, Deza thought. "I . . . I want to live here! And have pretty things like . . ." She plucked at a ribbon on the camisole. "So you'd want me. You won't love me if I'm dirty and ragged and . . ."

"But Deza, it's not safe here," he blurted.

You're telling me, Deza thought. But what danger was he talking about? Had he realized that she wasn't a witch, that she couldn't possibly read the geodes? "What do you mean, 'not safe'?"

He frowned. "Never mind. I'll think of something. I have until tomorrow. In the meantime, don't do anything to aggravate my father. Just go along with his scheme until I can get you out of here."

85

What scheme is he talking about, Deza wondered. The geodes? Or something her father had cooked up with the Tycoon? But before she could ask, Edvar hurried out the door, slamming it behind him.

Whatever scheme he's talking about, I'm going to get dressed before there are any more interruptions, she thought, because I am getting sick and tired of standing around in my underwear trying to work cons I don't know anything about. She grabbed for a waistcoat and woolen overpants, and the door opened again.

"Well, well," said the Tycoon.

Deza stayed where she was, like a cornered animal, with the clothes up against her, breathing steadily. She was more frightened than she had ever been in her life. She had not looked closely at this man when she came in the house, leaning on Edvar's arm. She should have. She would have bolted and run right then. He had gone completely native since her departure. Where he had worn token robes over his own Kalmarran clothes, now he wore only the robe, brightly striped, and the cloth turban. His bare legs were short and heavily muscled. He was tanned, too, and his wide face was smiling pleasantly at Deza. Danger, every nerve in Deza's body told her, danger.

"I dismissed my priest because I had you," he said casually, "but then I had neither. Now I have both again. I cannot seem to strike the proper balance."

Deza watched him silently.

"It's difficult to know which way to jump, you know, whether to trust that you will not take off again or to resume negotiations with the new religious man. On the whole, I think you are the better bet. Don't you agree, Deza?"

She didn't answer.

"The priest might leave. He's taken water-hospitality. Who knows what else he might take? But you, Deza, you're not going anywhere." He put his hand against the door. He could flatten me with that hand, Deza thought. "I'll see you at dinner, Deza dear. I trust you'll be recovered by then."

Deza did not move until he had been gone a full five minutes. I am in trouble, she thought, I am in trouble here. Now I know why father left in such a hurry. This is not a con that either of us was working. That's why we ran like a couple of scared rabbits. Well, I'm ready to run again.

— Father . . . — she yelled, then aloud, not caring about listeners, "Father!"

No answer.

"You stupid mbuzi," she shouted to the room. "You got me into this mess. Now you can get me out!" She stepped angrily out of the top layer of pettipants and flung them against the wall. "I want out, father, right now." She unsnapped the filigrees and threw them, too. "You come talk to me, right now!"

"You want to talk, Deza?" a voice said from behind her. Deza whirled. Radi was standing in front of the closet, the slipspace yawning open behind him. He was holding the fake peketa in his outstretched hand, and like everybody else in this forsaken place, he was smiling. "What a nice coincidence! I want to talk to you, too."

CHAPTER SEVEN

She stared at him, mouth agape and eyes wide, as if she couldn't believe what she saw. She seemed transfixed by the peketa in his hand, yet managed to be an appealing picture of distress, if he could believe it, with her skin scrubbed pink and her wet hair mingling with the ribbons on her bodice. Ever the actress, she'd received the Tycoon in her underwear looking as vulnerable as a hatchling gull and as foolish as one, too. Now she looked totally stunned by Radi's sudden appearance and bewildered by the thing in his hand. But Radi saw something else, an aspect in her eyes that if not new was suddenly plain to him: fear. Only a hint in the pretty green eyes before she composed herself, but he knew he was not mistaken. Did she think he was going to expose her trick? He tossed the peketa to his other hand and closed his fingers over it.

"A bit of warning and I wouldn't have been so clumsy out there," he said, "but I thank you just the same. Well done."

"I told you I could get us in. I'm not quite so sure I can get me out, which is something I'd like to do right away." Her voice was a bit thin, and her eyes darted to the open slipspace behind him.

"That won't do," he said, gesturing to the slipspace. "It only leads to my room, directly below-stairs."

"Is your door unlocked?" she said.

"Not at the moment. I didn't want anyone walking in on my, um, devotions. I bolted it before I came up here."

"But you can unlock it from inside? You're sure?"

He hadn't tried the door before throwing the inner lock. He noticed now that Deza's door did not have a similar device. He crossed the room to try the handle. It turned, but the heavy wooden door did not open. When he looked in the slender space between the door and jamb, he could see the shadow of the thick bolt holding it shut.

"Why would the Tycoon lock in his son's betrothed?" he wondered aloud. "He can't know the truth about the peketa, and if he did, he'd surely send you packing, not lock you in." As he turned to Deza for an explanation, he held up the peketa, twisting its rubbery form between his fingers. Visually, it would fool anyone, including himself as it had indeed for awhile. Only the rubbery feel of it when he'd smashed it into the sand had induced him to pick it up before they left, for a gorged peketa would have popped and crunched. He hadn't wanted to leave a fake peketa round for a shuffling guard or servant to find on the very spot where Deza had suffered her attack.

Deza shook her head. "He doesn't know about that, but he knows something else."

"What?"

She shrugged helplessly. She was still glancing at the slipspace, no doubt wondering if she dared use it. "I don't think I should stay around to find out. I'll be found out when the wife gets hold of her geodes anyway."

Finally Radi smiled. "They think you are not only a princess, but a water witch as well?" He'd heard that the foreigners believed the water witches could tell a geode from a rock, and in fact, he knew a few priests who claimed to be able to make the distinction. He also knew that performing the trick took elaborate preparation — cementing geodes together so perfectly that the crack could only be found with a magnifying glass, marking the geodes in a fashion no one but the initiated could see or feel, then distributing the geodes in a likely place so they could be found, seemingly discovered, at will. Likely, Deza's father had always made these preparations for her, since he could probably have moved about freely while his daughter kept the household's attention.

"I could arrange for a few geodes," he said. She looked doubtful. "I can have them marked, say with a mound that will fit the palm of your left hand and a dent you can feel with your right. I'll have Harubiki do it."

Finally her attention came away from the slipspace, and she looked at him suspiciously.

91

"Can you also arrange something for the Tycoon, like a fatal accident?"

"I'd rather not," he said, walking thoughtfully and slowly over the fleecy pelt on the floor before the bed. "You see, he wants something that he can get either from you or from me. Perhaps we can get him to tell us what it is at dinner."

"You overheard?"

"Of course. Edvar, too, though I'm sorry I missed the beginning of that scene. Was it true what you said about it being better if you wait?"

"I'm not sure that I should," she said. She fingered the woolen overpants lying on the end of the bed.

"If you blood that young whelp, he'll not be satisfied with one taste. And he's not smart enough not to get caught when he comes sneaking back for more," Radi said, wondering why his voice had risen with anger.

"I meant, I don't know if I should stay for dinner," Deza said sharply. "I can handle Edvar. He's the least of my concerns."

"Well," Radi said gruffly. "I can handle the problem with the wife for you, so you only have one left to cope with: the Tycoon himself."

"He's the big one," Deza said, sitting on the edge of the bed. "Did you see the way he was dressed?"

Radi nodded. "Full ceremonial robes, right down to the gembone necklace. I half expected to see cheek insets."

Deza nodded thoughtfully, fitting her own

insets along her cheekbone. They were intricately carved with the pattern of the royal house, as fine as Sheria's own. "He used to wear Kalmarran clothes." She turned to look at Radi. "Why do you suppose he'd do that, change his manner of dress? It can't suddenly be the heat. He's been here for years and the heat never bothered him before."

"Empire-carving, I'd say," Radi said seriously. "He's decided he's here to stay, no longer planning to go back to that frigid planet he came from. That's not hard to figure out. What puzzles me is why Mahali suddenly looks so attractive to him. And so easy. What's made him think he can get away without tithing to the City? He must have some plan for getting water or he wouldn't risk the City's wrath."

"And one of us fits into the plan somewhere," Deza said. "And since empire-building is a little beyond my scope, I think I'll let it be you by being gone before dinner." She grabbed the woolen pants and swung her feet into them.

"Wait, Deza, where would you go? You have a lot of time invested here, and it can still work out well for you, if you'll cooperate with me."

"How?" She pulled up the overdrawers.

"Just find out what he wants, then I'll make sure he knows I can supply it better, or more cheaply, or more quickly than you."

"And if you can't supply whatever it is? Then where am I? Up to my neck in his plot, that's where, and in yours. I think I'd better stick to my own plots. I'm leaving."

"Deza, if it gets dangerous, I'll get you out. What's the difference between sneaking out now and waiting a week or even a few days?"

"No dinner and those natives who eat worms," Deza said wistfully. Idly she tied the drawstrings around her waist. "I ought to at least build up my strength. Anyway, I think he's watching me too closely right now to try and get away. He might lock me in so securely even I can't get out. Besides, I can't leave without the mbuzi and I don't even know where he is."

"Then it's settled?" Radi said.

"How do I know I can trust you?" He thought she looked as if she wanted to, and ordinarily knowing would have made him prey on her hope like a vulture. The circumstances did, after all, call for anything that would work. But that hint of fear had returned to her eyes, and he didn't like seeing her afraid. He sat next to her.

"You don't know for sure, but I swear that you can trust me." It was exactly what he would have said if he were lying. The difference was that he meant it and he knew he meant it. He would see her safely away from the Tycoon's stronghold, if only to have her to himself.

She regarded him a moment, then nodded.

He took her hand, and she seemed surprised. "I just want to measure the size of your palm so that Harubiki can mark the geodes." He turned her hand over to run his fingers over the mound

94

of her thumb into her palm. Her skin was rough and scratched from her days along the shore, but she hadn't come by the firm flesh beneath them in so short a time. "Good," he said, quietly releasing her. "A bit smaller than she would fashion for herself, but not too much."

"You know that from memory?"

"I know Harubiki's hands well," he said, remembering how skillfully they could encircle an enemy's neck and how tenderly his own.

"Oh," Deza said. "Well, don't reacquaint yourself too well during the after-dinner punch. I may need to make Edvar jealous."

"Won't Chappa do? He's younger."

"That's precisely why he won't do. Edvar will worry about a mature man in ways he'd never consider worrying about a boy who seems his own age, especially one who's nothing more than a priest's lackey. But the priest himself, that's a different matter. There are enough stories around about priests and the girls in the households they served for him to make the connection. If there aren't any stories, I'll see that there are."

Radi nodded. "I'll be properly attentive to you, Deza dear, and you may rest assured that my intentions will not look at all proper." He flicked a curl away from her breast. Those certainly were not rough or scratched. Her skin looked smooth, her flesh soft. "Well, now," he said, restraining himself, "where do you want me to put the rigged geodes?"

"In the barn. The wife's got a mound of them waiting for me. Put them at the lower edge of the pile. To the right as you face the door of the barn. There're bound to be guards," Deza added worriedly. "They always watch the breeder animals carefully, and with the added value of the geodes, there may be even more guards than usual."

"A few guards won't bother us," Radi said casually. "But, why would they guard a few mbuzim? Why in the world would anyone want to breed those smelly beasts? They're not very good eating, and the pelts never quite lose that distinctive odor. The only useful part of them is the skeleton, and that only when it's properly fossilized into gembone."

"I'm sure I don't know. He's determined to build up his herd. They must be useful for something. Perhaps he's found some use for them off-planet."

Radi thought a moment. "No," he said slowly. "If that were the case, they'd have been shipping them off Mahali, even if only in small numbers. So far as I know, the only mbuzi parts they're buying from the nomads are the fossilized bones, and it's true there's a small off-world market in gembone jewelry, but not enough to justify his interest. The supply is too limited. I don't think even the Tycoon would make investments that can't possibly pay off for half a million years . . . unless, of course, he had access to ground water, but the City will not sell him that. No, it's got to be the mbuzim themselves, not their fossilized relics."

The overhead light flickered and went out. Radi felt Deza's hand on his thigh as she jumped.

"It's all right, Deza," he whispered. "They'll come back on in a moment. Harubiki has interrupted the power so they won't be suspicious when they find their listener tapes disabled. They would have had a power-off signal etched right into the tapes, and they'd have known someone tampered with them. This way they'll just think it was the power failure."

"Then there are listeners in here?" Deza said, sounding frightened again.

"Yes, but they were off before I came up here. The Tycoon won't find out about your conversation with Edvar. Or me."

The lights came back on, dazzling them for a second. Radi put his finger across his lips, indicating that they couldn't talk any longer. That glint of fear was back in her eyes, and this time it didn't disappear. Yet she nodded solemnly, smiling slightly. She hadn't struck him as being foolishly brave, nor innocently trusting. She'd been through too much in her life not to have shed temptations like those long ago. So why was she trusting him now? She must realize he could get the Tycoon's plan from her and then abandon her to whatever fate might bring. Unless, of course, there was something she saw in his eyes that responded to the fear in hers. It was foolish to wait for another time when she wouldn't be afraid. There was plenty of time before dinner, right now. But before he could even touch her, or gesture towards the bed, there was a knock at the door.

"What is it?" Deza answered quickly and loudly.

"I've brought you some water and come to help you to dinner," replied a timid voice.

"I don't need any help," Deza said. "I know the way."

"But your ankle . . . The wife said . . ."

"Oh," Deza said. "Just a minute." She gestured toward the slipspace, indicating that Radi should go.

Impulsively he put his arms around her and whispered softly in her ear, "I'll be back later." He tried for a quick kiss, but she was pushing him away, hurrying him to the slipspace and making ready to close it behind him. He glanced at the door, then at Deza, and finally ducked out. He heard the gentle *snick* as the paneling moved back into place.

CHAPTER EIGHT

Deza watched the slipspace close, smiled at it a moment, and then hurried to empty the flagon of water into the tub before she opened the door. The servant slid the bolt and edged in, hardly opening the door. She was a young girl who looked at Deza with large eyes that were filled with awe and almost a touch of fear. Whatever for? Well, at least take advantage of it.

"How long is it until dinner?" Deza asked her, limping with dignity back to her dressing table. "I had not thought it was at this early hour." She sounded a little too imperious even to her own ears.

The servant girl quailed. She was holding a huge decanter, twice the size of the flagon the wife had left. "Oh, no, miss, not for another hour, but they said to come. They said you might need dressing. They said . . ."

What the servants had said about her was obviously very impressive. It had this poor child tongue-tied with fear. And it was all very surprising. Deza's father had always said the servants were the key to a household, that to ignore their influence and feeling was to court disaster because, in spite of appearances, servants knew everything. The question was not how to keep them from finding out a con, but how to arrange their allegiance so they would not tell what they knew.

Their awareness had worked to Deza's favor when she went after Edvar. After all, it was a typical enough situation. They hated the lady of the house with her high-and-mighty foreign ways. They were glad to see her brought down through her son. But they had not had any particular allegiance to her. They knew her for the part she was playing. The pretty trollop out to seduce the naïve son. They had stood by and watched, amused and a little contemptuous. In fact, Deza was still convinced that one of the servants had precipitated their sudden, disastrous departure. So why were they reverent now? Even frightened of her, if this girl was any indication. There was no time to question the girl. Besides, she might faint from sheer fright if Deza spoke harshly. No, better to make her an ally for now and find out more about this mysterious change later.

"I . . . my ankle hurts so much I'm afraid it makes me rude," she said, abandoning the regal tones for a pretty forlornness. "I had hoped to go and find my mbuzi before dinner. He cannot bear to be away from me for long. But I don't know where they have taken him, and with my ankle I can't go running about the compound looking for him." She didn't mention the locked door that also prevented her from running about.

"Oh, but I can," the girl said eagerly. "I can

find out for you. If, I mean if that's all right. I could dress you and then go and fetch it for you." She waited, poised for flight.

Deza frowned. This was no good. The girl would bring her the mbuzi and she would know no more than she had before except for what her father could, or would tell her. She needed to use the mbuzi as an excuse to explore the place herself. She also needed to get rid of this girl so she could wrap her ankle and collect her confused thoughts before dinner. Events were still skidding away from her at an alarming rate.

"Where do you think they might be keeping the mbuzi?" she asked, careful to smile at the girl.

"Oh, with the others probably. In the grazing pens behind the lower stables."

But there aren't any grazing pens below the lower stables. And if there are, I need to see them for myself. "Run and see if it is there," she said thoughtfully. "My mbuzi is very sensitive. It may not let you carry it." She didn't say what the girl should do in that case, which Deza was fairly sure would be the way her father would react. The girl's hesitation in deciding to leave it and fetch Deza, or to struggle with the sharp-hoofed animal herself should give her enough time to follow the girl and see things for herself.

"It is so nice to have a helpful friend. I envy you your swift legs and strong feet," she said wistfully. That had the desired effect. The girl was off like a shot. Deza eased the door shut after her and hurried back into the bathroom, remembering to take the decanter with her and to empty it promptly. Anyone with a peketa bite would have to consume ten times the body's normal liquid requirements, else succumb to the fever, dehydration, and quite likely death. It was turning out to be a terrible bother to pretend that she was suffering from a peketa bite *and* a turned ankle. She should have used only the peketa, then groaned inwardly as she remembered that was exactly what her father had recommended.

With the door unbolted, she had no time to spare, but it could not be helped. She never would remember to limp unless she bound her ankle again so there would be no forgetting. She hurriedly slipped on the wide-sleeved yellow blouse and tied the turquoise wool waistcoat over it, bound up her hair with a strip of rose wool, and then sat down again on the edge of the tub to rebind her foot.

She fumbled through the bath sack looking for something sharp, remembered the peketa that Radi had confiscated, and smiled again. That was an area, at least, where she could keep pace. So he wanted to get her into bed, did he? Well, she just might let him succeed. She had watched him weighing the advantages of the moment. He had seemed to think they were on his side. She had done a little figuring herself. And decided . . . well, she hadn't decided, but she was considering some intriguing possibilities. It was all a question of whether he would be more eager to help her before or after she was bedded. Edvar, of course, was simple. He could be staved off forever, for he was far too inexperienced to know that his peculiar noble pride was being manipulated, and he was much more useful that way. She was not sure Radi would be so easily put off. It was obviously a game to him, a question of conquest and surrender. Deza was inclined to agree with him, though she was not sure they had quite the same thing in mind.

She smiled again, and abruptly pulled her finger out of the bath sack and sucked on it. Something sharp was in there after all. A rough, bristled sponge, more suitable for the scrub bucket than the bath. She tore off a corner of it, pushed the rough edge against her bare ankle, and began tightly rewrapping the ankle and the leg. The slight bulge would be noticeable only as a little swelling from the sore ankle, and with the sharp bristles digging into her skin, she would not forget again that she needed to limp.

She put the sponge back in the bag, put the bandaged foot into one of her own sandals and the other into a fleecelined boot, and hurried out of the room and down the side stairs that led to the back of the enclosure. Since there was no one on the long straight enclosed staircase she risked running and didn't slow her steps until she was nearly to the lower stables.

Servants were about, grooming the horses and tending the lumpish, sweating draft animals the Tycoon had insisted on bringing from his home planet and nearly killing with the heat. They were kept here, in the hollowed-out sandstone caves, away from the blistering sun and the most intense heat. It was still hot and dusty, though, and the animals looked uncomfortable in the gloomy stalls.

The servants looked up as she hobbled past them, head held high so that her insets would catch the lamplight. There was a slight sibilance that followed her passage, whispering among them, and an echo of the girl's expression on their hardened faces. She looked directly at one of them, and his head dropped to his work. She would at least not be forbidden to go to the grazing pens. She wondered if there was any servant even brave enough to question her right to be there.

Behind the stables, the girl had said. Deza could still not believe she had heard right. The last of the stalls butted up against the low over-hanging sandstone roof, and the final yards Deza was crossing to them were solid rock with only a fine dusting of dirt, obviously the far reaches of the dugout. Come to think of it, though, a servant had mentioned rough storage rooms clawed into the solid sandstone where they kept cheese and butter. Perhaps the mbuzi was there, though Deza could not imagine why, and the servant girl had distinctly said, "with the others." She had thought there were only those few that grazed in the compound's irrigated green with the Tycoon's ponies and Edvar's pair in the barn.

The servant girl suddenly plummeted from behind the last of the wood-supported stalls. She stopped short in front of Deza and dropped a hasty curtsey. "I was coming for you," she said, wide-eyed. "Oh, it was just as you said. The mbuzi wouldn't come at all." The girl's hands were covered with sharp scratches.

"Where is it?" Deza said.

"This way." The girl darted in front of her. Deza followed, wishing she had put a gentler reminder in the bandages. Her running had shifted the sponge slightly so it dug savagely into Deza's ankle at every step. The girl ducked suddenly behind the last of the stalls and then ran back for Deza. "I forgot about your ankle. Forgive me," she said, and grabbed Deza's arm. Her idea of helping was worse than useless. Deza now had to put her full weight sideways on the sharp bristles with every step.

They skirted the rough backs of the stalls, which were almost flush with the dark sandstone wall, only a narrow path between them. The roof dipped sharply, and they ducked under it and through an even narrower space and then abruptly were in the open. The girl had not exaggerated. There were certainly grazing pens behind the lower stables. Twenty, no, fifty of them, each the size of Deza's room or larger, stretched back into the darkness, lit only by occasional lamps on tall poles. And each was filled almost to overflowing with mbuzim. Deza shook off the girl's arm and turned to look behind her. "Is this a natural cave?" she asked.

"Oh, no, miss, the Tycoon had it dug." Her tone implied the question, didn't you know? Deza decided she could not risk any more questions. But she could certainly see for herself. She would never have suspected this vast domed cave lay below and behind, yes, behind and to the west, she supposed, of the enclosure. It must stretch almost half a mile toward the karst plateau on the west. If the Tycoon had dug much farther he would certainly have encountered natural caves. She had a new respect for the Tycoon. The mbuzim would not care where they were stabled. They did not require the sun. All they cared about was food and water. And . . . Deza suddenly put her hand up to her cheek, as if to catch a thought. She pressed her hand flat against the inset, trying to feel the rock around them, the dusty sandstone that was over and under and on all sides of them.

"Here he is, miss. Oh, he's not glad to see me at all." The servant girl was kneeling by the pen that held Deza's mbuzi. He was hardly recognizable — his matted hair had been clipped and curled, his hooves polished so that the patterned gembone shone in the dim light. He was lying in the accustomed heap, but his hooves kicked out reflexively as the girl put out a hesitant hand toward him.

— Stop that, father, — Deza said. — You're being childish. —

— Churlish. There's a difference. —

— None that I can see. Let her carry you. We're going to dinner and I have injured my ankle. —

— Daughter, — he said sternly. — There is such a thing as carrying a con too far. The peketa is a simple trick, but a sprained ankle is another matter. And there is the limp, a difficult thing to remember to do in conditions of stress. —

— I can remember — Deza said sharply. — And I quite agree, father. There is such a thing as carrying a con too far. Or working too many at one time. —

To the girl she said aloud, "I think you can pick him up now. He won't fight you now that I'm here."

The mbuzi allowed itself to be picked up without a struggle. The girl hoisted the animal over her shoulders with a practiced shrug and started off at her breakneck pace the way they had come before.

"Oh," Deza said, clutching at her ankle.

The girl stopped and whirled around, concerned. "Are you hurt, miss?"

"No . . . oh," she said, rubbing the bandage, "is there any other way out of here?" She hoped the question sounded logical and not over-interested.

"None that I know of, miss, except the opening onto the karst plateau where they bring the water in, and that is farther, not nearer." She reached out that over-helpful hand to Deza. "Here. I will help you back to the house."

"No, that's all right," Deza said, and the girl took off again. Once in motion, nothing could stop her, and anyway, Deza wanted to be early for dinner.

There was no one in the dining room. Deza had time to brush any telltale dust from her clothes and to instruct the girl to place the mbuzi by her chair at the already-set table. She hesitated a moment, wondering which chair she should pick.

— I take it from your concern over position that yours is not a position of strength, — her father said.

— It will be when this dinner is over. — She said sharply to the girl, "Seat me there. Between Edvar and the priest and facing the lady of the house."

— You should sit facing the Tycoon directly. He is your adversary. —

— They are all my adversaries, thanks to you. You might have told me your plans. —

— And you might have listened when I told you this place was dangerous. Since, however, you will have everyone under your thumb by the end of the meal, you do not need my advice. — The mbuzi sank into a heavy, snoring sleep.

"Deza!" Edvar said, "Darling, you shouldn't have come down alone." He helped her to her chair.

"Our Deza is a resourceful girl," said the Tycoon behind his son. He heaved himself into the chair at the head of the table. "She will get

108

where she wants to go, injured ankle or no, I think." He laughed. "Isn't that so, Deza?" There was no laughter under the surface of his voice.

What did that mean? Had she been shadowed on her way to the grazing pens? Father was right. The stupid ankle was going to be her undoing. Deza looked sideways at the Tycoon. "I am a poor orphan girl with no kind father like you to guide and help me. If I do not make my way in the world, who will make it for me?"

"Make it you shall. I have every confidence in you."

Deza blushed gracefully. "With your kind help, my lord, I am sure of it."

The Tycoon smiled humorlessly at her for a moment and then raised his arms in the signal that the meal was to begin. Thank goodness. Deza felt weak from the encounter. Sparring with the Tycoon was no easy task at any time. Now, when he held all the cards, it was tiring and frightening. She hoped Radi knew the Kalmarran customs well enough to realize that conversation was for after the meal, not during it. She needed the respite to gather her defenses for the second round of battle.

Radi kept his head piously bowed over the endless courses of steaming food. In spite of the Tycoon's sudden embracing of native dress, it was obvious that he had not changed his life style significantly. Either that, or the iron-handed lady of the house had refused to relinquish her kitchen. The food, like the clothing, was desperately inappropriate to the climate, but after a week of hunger, Deza was not about to complain about the hot feather-fish, hot soup, and boiled vegetables. And she had to smile each time the servant refilled her water goblet after each sip. It would have been easier to pretend to take one draught of antivenom, if only there were such a thing for peketa poison. Even Kalmarrans, who claimed to be more advanced than Mahalians, had not managed to develop such a thing, for when there was a Kalmarran peketa victim, he did the same thing every Mahalian did — drink enough water to flush the poison. Deza was beginning to feel as if she were floating away.

The Tycoon sighed a hearty, relaxed sigh at the entrance of the pitcher of hot bitter Kalmarran cider. Deza breathed a long breath, too, but not of relaxation. She took a long look around the table, as if it were a battlefield, and exhaled, slowly, carefully. She was determined to have the first word, determined to set the conversation on the proper track at once. In this she knew she had the advantage. The Tycoon would not speak until the steaming drink had been poured all around the table, but she was under no such rule of etiquette.

"We were so sorry that Pelono was called back to the City in the Red Cave," the Tycoon said as soon as she opened her mouth. "I trust he is well."

Radi arched an eyebrow. "Very well," he said blandly.

Deza sat quietly. Radi was not doing badly for a first encounter, but he was no match for the Tycoon, who'd just neatly dismissed the entire issue of the priest's dismissal, and would now turn the conversation to his own ends. But it was Radi who spoke, smiling easily at Deza.

"You have your mbuzi again, Deza-child. A prettier sight than during our dusty trek."

The mbuzi, as if on cue, tottered to its feet at her side and nudged against her ribs. She trickled water from her crystal finger bowl into the mbuzi's open mouth. "My servant went after him for me," she said, careful not to lie directly. "The stableman has improved his appearance considerably."

"It's the male of a matched pair," Edvar said. "The other is mine. My female is not as large, but just as pretty."

Radi leaned over Deza and lifted one of the mbuzi's feet. The unsteady animal toppled farther against Deza's side, nearly knocking her off her chair. "The fossilizing has progressed quite far in this animal. This is beautiful stuff," he said, looking curious and sincere. "Where did you get these animals?"

Edvar shot a sharp look at his father.

"They were a gift from a traveller," the Tycoon said, "a traveller who wanted water protection."

Radi took the mbuzi's hoof in his hand to examine it more closely. Deza fumed, pinioned between the two young men. The mbuzi, now totally unable to keep its balance, was practically in her lap. The Tycoon smiled benignly at her.

"Then the traveller paid dearly," Radi said. "I suppose you know what these are worth. This is some of the finest gembone I've ever seen on a live animal."

"The traveller promised us that the offspring would be even more valuable, have even higher quality gembone," the Tycoon said, a little too quickly.

— Move over, — Deza said. — You're digging into my ribs. —

— Quit fidgeting and listen. —

— How can I listen? I can hardly breathe. And these two idiots are bent on suffocating me between them. —

— You want to get control of this situation. You need information. Stop behaving like a spoiled child and listen. —

"I'm afraid the traveller deceived you there," Radi went on. "Gembone has nothing to do with genetics. Unless you can graze your animals on land fed by ground water or feed it to them directly, there won't be any fossilization. The water is the key. The mbuzim that drink it, and it has to be ground water from far down, Maundifu river water that has a tremendous mineral content, do fossilize. Their bones, even to some extent the cartilage tissue, turns to gembone. But the process only continues as long as they have access to ground water."

"Oh, really? I know little about mbuzim," the

Tycoon said, drinking deeply of his cider and looking a little bored. "I suppose I shall have to give up my hope for gembone on the hoof. That, or find some ground water."

"I'm afraid that's impossible," Radi said.

"Oh?"

"It's found a few places in the far south as surface water. Perhaps that's where the traveller was from. There are a few artesian wells on the karst plateau to the west of you, but most of that area is uninhabitable. There would be nothing there for mbuzim to graze on even if you could find water. I'm afraid you'll have to be content with your pair of mbuzim as they are."

— Listen to what? — Deza said. — I don't see what all this . . . —

— The water is the key, — her father said.

— And the grazing pens open onto the karst plateau. — Her hand went almost reflexively up to touch her insets. She hastily put it back in her lap, hoping the Tycoon hadn't noticed. That was what had seemed wrong about the grazing pens. There was no water in the sandstone cave. The dry dustiness had told her that, but so had her water sense. No water in the rock. All those mbuzim. And an opening onto the karst plateau, where there were only a few scattered wells. It made no sense.

"Your cheek . . . decorations are made of gembone, aren't they, Deza?" the Tycoon's wife said.

"What? My insets? Oh, yes, they are."

"That's an example of what makes gembone so valuable," Radi said. "A gem that can be sculptured like soap into a filigree pattern like Deza's insets would command a high price on any planet, although jewelry is necessarily a limited market. Have they found some other use for gembone on Kalmar?"

The Tycoon frowned at Radi's question and said abruptly, "I understand some of your people believe there's a religious significance to the gembone."

— Change the subject when someone gets too close to the truth for comfort, — Deza's father said. — He's a wise man. —

— That gembone's valuable? Everybody knows that. — Her father was being absolutely maddening tonight. He wanted her to listen, but then he kept interrupting with these cryptic comments.

"Oh, yes," Radi said, "there's a tradition that the spirits of the dead, deprived of their own bodies, lodge in the gembone. You've seen the large filigreed amulets many of us wear. Those are to provide a place for relatives to lodge in case of need."

"But what if you wanted to be rid of the relative? What if he had hung about your neck in life? Would you allow him to hang around your neck in death, too?"

Radi laughed. "And what if your relatives did not get along? Would you have to listen to their bickering?"

"Yes," the Tycoon said, "I've heard of people who claim they converse with the spirits. I can't imagine what I'd talk to the dead about. Religion, perhaps."

"Or how they wished you'd died instead," Radi said.

"Deza," Edvar said. "Your insets, are they full of ghosts?"

"Oh, no," she said lightly. "My spirit resides in my mbuzi."

That brought a general laugh. "And do you talk to it?" the Tycoon said.

"Oh, yes, all the time."

"About what?"

"About you, my lord." That brought even more laughter. "My spirit is that of a poor dead lady. She is quite in love with you."

The Tycoon roared with laughter. "And is she pretty?"

"She says she is, my lord. But saying and being are quite different things."

"Indeed, Deza. Saying and being are different things, but easily found out."

"How, my lord?" Deza said, wishing she had not gotten on such difficult ground and not quite sure how she had gotten there.

He looked steadily at her. "Oh, there are ways, Deza." Then he said lightly, "Tell the lady that I have a wife, and that even if I hadn't . . ." he stopped and raised his arms again in the signal that the dinner was over. "I could not bring myself to kiss an mbuzi."

115

And thank goodness, dinner was over. Radi and Edvar fought nicely over who would take her back upstairs and ended by both taking an arm. "I shall need someone to bring my mbuzi," she said sweetly. "Radi, you like pretty ladies. Would you bring it, please?" Edvar blushed with pleasure and Radi looked annoyed, both of which were good signs. But Radi should be looking worried, not annoyed. Dinner was over, she felt less in control of the situation than ever, and she needed to talk to Radi as soon as possible.

The Tycoon had talked about gembone as if he were an innocent, even though Deza knew full well her father had told him all the legends surrounding it when he presented her as a water witch, with ground water fossilizing in the thin bones of her face and making her sensitive. A traveller had not given them the mbuzim. They'd been a gift from Botvidi, the priest, and everyone at that table except Radi knew it and had not batted an eye. And what had made the Tycoon suddenly change the subject? And make such threats to her, barely veiled from the rest of the company? "There are ways to separate the saying from the being." He was not afraid of her at all. His attitude was what the servants, had been before she left, contemptuous and amused. Now they were frightened to death of her, and he was . . . playing with her as a cat plays with a mouse before it devours it.

"My ankle hurts," she said to Edvar. "I want to lie down."

"Of course." He shot a glance at Radi behind them. "I'll come in and see you settled."

Radi obediently deposited the mbuzi at the foot of Deza's bed and left the room without an argument. Deza did not dare look at him. Come to me, she thought earnestly. I'll get rid of Edvar immediately. He started to pull the door shut.

"Oh, Edvar, I'm sorry, but it really hurts. I just want to be alone."

"I could rewrap it for you. The bandages are too tight, perhaps."

"No, I . . ." she put an appealing hand on his arm. "Please. I just want to lie down."

Edvar finally nodded and managed to smile. Before he left, he poured water into a cup from a fresh pewter pitcher. The empty flagon and decanter had been removed. Then Edvar left.

Deza heard them both down the hall and their boots' first steps down the front stairway. She put down the cup, then hurried to the slipspace. Please, please come. And hurry.

— Waiting for someone? — her father said. — Or is that your peculiar way of celebrating your astonishing success at dinner? —

— Oh, shut up, — Deza said.

— Really, you were marvellous. Had them all eating out of the palm of your hand. Especially the Tycoon. —

— What is he up to? — Deza said frantically. She came and knelt by the mbuzi. — You have to tell me, father. I'm afraid of him. —

— I don't know, Deza, — her father said in a

curiously flat, defeated tone.

— How can you not know? You were the one who set it up, weren't you? —

— I set up a charming little con in which you played water witch to keep mama occupied until you had the son in a compromising position. I kept papa occupied with interesting stories about Mahali, in which I think now he was far too interested but which at the time I was grateful for since it gave you time to work. When the son was duly compromised, I stood ready to get a nice fat sum in return for the promise that we would go away. That's all. —

— That's all? That can't be all. — She stood up. — Look at those pens under the stables. All those mbuzim and no water. And the pens open onto the karst. He knows all about the karst. —

Her father's voice suddenly sounded almost like Radi's. — Gembone could command a high price on any planet. —

— But where's he going to get the ground water to make the gembone? Does he expect me to dig for wells in the karst? —

There was a faint scratching inside the wall. Deza stood looking at the mbuzi a moment longer and then went to open the slipspace.

CHAPTER NINE

It had really irritated Radi that he should have to carry Deza's mbuzi, as if he cared how the damn thing got up the stairs into its mistress's bedroom. The episode was nothing more than a well-executed step in Deza's plan to compromise young Edvar. The boy was practically salivating at the edge of Deza's bed, helping her into it because her poor overused ankle wouldn't let her get into it alone. Oh, it was cute the way her pants hiked up over the well-turned calf as she leaned back, but Radi didn't believe for one second that her bodice ribbon had just happened to come undone *again*. She'd let the tortured boy close enough to see forbidden flashes of flesh, to smell her perfumed pillows, all of which would have Edvar imagining what it would be like to lie there with Deza. Too bad Edvar didn't know his way around the slipspaces. He could have come back the way Radi had now. He made a soft noise, like a mouse scrambling somewhere in the walls. Deza didn't keep him waiting.

Deza looked about to burst with speech, which Radi silenced with a kiss. He hadn't dared to risk a second power failure to turn off the listeners. The listeners were on, and the kiss, the quick kiss to keep the words behind her tongue did more to take his breath away, for her mouth was sweet and he lingered there. She slipped into his arms, her body fitting neatly against him, and she made a noise deep in her throat. Radi was too much the soldier to forget the listeners. Reluctantly he pushed Deza away, signing to her for silence at the same time. She nodded.

Radi brushed her lips with his own before tiptoeing across the room to the heavy drapery where one of the listening devices was certain to be hidden. He had little trouble finding it, for the off-world wool was weighted at the bottom hem with real anchors that were similarly shaped but heavier. After he had extracted the listener, he went into the bathroom and put it in the bath sack. He threw a frilly petticoat over it. He wondered if there were a second device here in the bathroom, perhaps there in the eye of the sea-nymph tapestry that looked at the empty tub. He hung a towel over the wall hanging, wondering if it were only a listener or if somebody besides Edvar had lusted after Deza. He turned on the faucets, letting the water run noisily into the wooden tub.

In the bedroom a single flambeau coiled over the dressing table cast a mellow light over the room, making soft shadows of Deza against the curtains as she struggled with a stubborn closure. She took a pin from her hair, stepping aside to catch the light better, then jabbed the pin through the fabric, twisting the closure hems together and cutting off the view of her bedroom from the courtyard.

The mbuzi stumbled out from between Deza's legs, its half-fossilized hooves sparkling even in the dim light, only a hint of how radiant they would become when the fossilization was complete. Deza, finished with the drapes, swept the mbuzi into her arms before she tripped over it again. The creature's ears shook and it looked at her dolefully while she settled it into a nest of cushions on the bed. The creature's nervous tremors made a gembone hoof clatter against the bedpost until Deza adjusted the cushions.

"What's the matter with it?" Radi whispered. "It certainly can't be cold in here." With the night breeze cut off by the closed curtains, the bedroom already was stuffy.

"It's frightened," Deza said, poking another cushion behind the mbuzi and looked around for yet another, as if the creature's comfort were her greatest concern. "The Tycoon thinks I'm a real water witch . . ." she turned, still looking for a pillow, her face more frantic than the task could possibly warrant. If the mbuzi was frightened, Deza was terrified.

"Deza," Radi said, catching her hand and pulling her close to him. "You managed dinner perfectly. Why so fearful now?"

"I didn't handle it well at all. I still have no idea what he wants. And I think he knows all about me. My instincts tell me to leave. The con isn't going right. I should have stayed away."

"The con's going fine, both of them," Radi

said. "Tomorrow the wife will take you to her pile of rocks and you'll select a few geodes for her. Once you get the wife off the Tycoon's back, he'll pay less attention to you, too."

"I don't think so," Deza said.

"Of course he will. All this undue attention is because of her appetite for rare native treasures. Once she's satisfied, her husband will be, too, and you'll only have young Edvar to deal with. I know you can keep him at arm's length until we leave."

"Leave?" Deza said. She looked away from the mbuzi and straight into Radi's eyes. "You mean together? You and me?" She spoke as if the thought were new and startling. The strange thing was that it was precisely that to Radi, for it just now occurred to him that he would, that he must take Deza with him when he left, that he must not let her go, that he could not take the chance of never seeing her again.

"Yes, we'll leave together," Radi said impatiently. "You don't really want to marry Edvar, do you?"

"I never marry any of the marks. But how soon can we leave? I'm afraid to wait."

Radi had been thinking of a dignified exit, *after* the marines had arrived and camped outside the compound, *after* Radi found out what value gembone and mbuzim had on Kalmar, aside from a component of jewelry. "I didn't mean we'd bolt tonight, Deza."

"But, Radi," Deza said, cutting him off. "I

don't think you understand. The mbuzim must be given groundwater if their bones and hooves are to fossilize, and . . ."

"I know that. The Red City won't give him Maundifu water, not until it knows what he wants it for. Perhaps not even then. If gembone suddenly has become important off-world, Sheria can have her own herds."

"Sheria?" Deza said. "Who is Sheria?"

He couldn't resist. "The princess of the Red City. The real one. Oh, don't worry, I haven't said anything to the Tycoon. Besides, your con hasn't been to impersonate Sheria, has it? I thought you were some dispossessed princess thrown out like Akida's daughter and trying to get the throne back."

"What?" Deza said, but it was as if she were not really listening to what he had said at all. She sat down on the bed next to the mbuzi and put her arm around its neck.

"There's no reason to be jealous. Sheria may be my betrothed, but, what's the matter, Deza?"

She had put her hands up to her head as if it suddenly ached. "I don't know," she said curiously. She tried to rise, holding onto the bedpost, and nearly swooned. Radi caught her up in his arms. He lifted her onto the bed, setting her down gently on the coverlet. "Deza, tell me what's wrong," he said again. He didn't believe for a second that she would attempt one of her silly tricks on him, as if he were no brighter than Edvar. She really had swooned. Her skin was clammy and pale, her muscles limp. Even the mbuzi knew something was wrong, for it stood up and bleated pitifully, staring at its mistress all the while.

"Deza," Radi said, stroking her cheek with his hand. Her facial muscles felt like steel beneath the silken skin, tense and taut and clenched. But her eyes opened and focused on him.

"I thought you were a pirate," she said. "I never even made the connection. I should have. I remember . . ." She leaned back and closed her eyes again.

"I'm sorry I wasn't honest with you in the beginning," he said, genuinely concerned. "I suppose I assumed you saw through my disguise the same way I saw through yours."

"Disguise," Deza said, as if it meant something very different from what he had said. "Why didn't you march straight to the compound under the red banner instead of sneaking in like pirates?" She did not sound like she even cared what the answer was.

"We planned to until the majini was wrecked. The priest was killed, and we'd lost all our weapons. We had no way to pick up the marines we planned as a backup. It seemed wiser to come in the back door." He chafed Deza's cold hands between his own. "After the reception we got, I can see it was the only way in. We of the Red City are grateful for your assistance and in your debt."

"That is a thing I never thought to hear a

prince of the Red City say to me." She closed her eyes again, smiling faintly. The mbuzi bleated in Radi's face, and Radi pushed it aside to pour water into the cup, really alarmed. Could she somehow have been poisoned at dinner? She sounded so strange, almost drugged. And her skin was so clammy, as if she were in shock.

She was still deathly pale, but her eyes were open and truly looking at him. He tried to dab her with water, but she put a hand up to stop him. "Not water," she said, "I don't need any more water."

He stopped and sat down on the bed. "What happened?"

"I think . . . it's hot in here. I have on heavy wool clothes and about twenty layers of underwear. I think I got a little overheated."

He continued to look at her. Whatever had made her so distressed, even ill, was over now. She lay looking up at him, the color returning to her cheeks, her eyes smiling at him almost impishly.

"I need to get undressed," she said, with a subtle emphasis on the word *need*.

"Let me help you," Radi said, reaching for the waistcoat laces.

"I wondered when you'd think of it," she said, smiling openly now. Her fingers were quick to part the fold in his priest's robe and slip inside the garment. Her hand was warm against his flesh, no sign of the cold that had come over her just moments ago. Radi leaned over to kiss Deza, easing her out of the waistcoat and blouse and tugging at the resisting ribbons of the camisole.

"Why is it these drawstrings are untied at all times except now?" he murmured, nuzzling at her ear.

"Here, let me help you," she said, nimbly untying the laces that she so often used as bait. She was not teasing now. She loosened the drawstrings and sat up, still pressed against Radi's body, to lift the camisole over her head.

The mbuzi stumbled from its cushions and stood staring over Radi's shoulder at her. She stopped cold, her arms poised to pull the camisole off, and waited as if she were listening. For a moment, Radi was afraid she was getting ill again. Then she bit her lip and smiled at Radi.

"We seem to have an interested audience," she said. "It's staring."

Radi looked over his shoulder. It was indeed staring at them through its slanted, pupilless eyes. "Let it," he said, and reached for her. "I get to see you. Why shouldn't it?"

"No!" Deza said, and then more softly, "Put it in the slipspace."

Radi got up, took the mbuzi by the scruff of its woolly neck and deposited it on the narrow landing behind the slipspace. He shut the door. Deza was tossing pettipants into a fluffy heap until she had to feel as cool as custard in the hot room. As he turned, she lifted the camisole over her head and stepped out of the last pair of pantaloons.

There was one nice thing about priests' robes. They came off completely with one shrug. Radi remembered thinking briefly of young Edvar as Deza moved smoothly into his arms. Deza and her father had been wrong in thinking that the boy's devotion could only be held by keeping the promise of Deza out of reach. Radi was with Deza now, and having her was not going to lessen his feelings toward her. But they were right in knowing the promise was not going to compare with the reality. Nothing, no one could compare with Deza.

CHAPTER TEN

Deza came abruptly awake. For a moment, she thought her father was pressing gently on the side of her neck to awaken her to danger. She slowed her breathing to the even shallowness of sleep and listened. She could not hear anything, but she had the distinct feeling that the sound that had brought her awake had been close. The slipspace maybe.

She fluttered her eyelids and turned over, murmuring. The quick glance had shown her that the room was dark, but nothing else. She couldn't tell whether the slipspace was open or not. No light was leaking through, but she was not sure it would. The slipspace was very steep. She lay still, wondering whether to risk Radi's name.

There was the nearly inaudible closing of a door and then a murmur of voices. A man and a woman. The servant girl? Edvar's father? Surely Radi had not been fool enough to leave her room by the door. The woman was whispering, but the man spoke in a low even voice. It was not much louder than the woman's whisper, but Deza recognized the timbre of the voice. Edvar. Edvar at her door? Edvar and the servant girl? Edvar and the girl and a plan to get Deza out?

128

Despite the subdued way Edvar had acted at supper, Deza's brain was sending her sharp negatives. No. The sound that had brought her awake had come from within the room or possibly from the room below. Maybe Edvar and whoever was in the hall with him had scared the intruder away or merely into the cover of the slipspace, and the sound of its shutting was what had awakened Deza. Whatever, the voices she was hearing now had nothing to do with it. Deza was glad she had not risked a whispered name. Radi would hide from others but not from her. She turned over again, sighing and tugging at the covers, until she was up against the wall, near her knife. She quieted her breathing to nothing and waited.

No one in the room. Or someone in the room as skilled as she. Deza slid her hand down beside the wall for her knife. The voices were clearer now, the woman's whispering petulantly. "When will she do it? You know what your father has planned for her. That could take days."

"He won't like your doing this, Mother."

Mother. What if Radi hadn't told Harubiki last night? He would not have anticipated the planted geodes would be needed so soon. Perhaps he had intended to wait until morning to tell her. Even if he had told her, she might not have had time to doctor the geodes and return them to the heaps Edvar's mother had collected. Nothing in this waterforsaken place was working like she'd planned.

Deza had a sudden impulse to bolt through the slipspace and out the back door. She stifled it, listened hard a few more seconds, and got quietly out of bed. She felt her way to the door through the dark room. There was a little grayish light coming through the heavy wooden shutters. It must be close to dawn. The fire had gone out. Deza shivered in her thin bedshift. She put her ear to the crack by the door jamb.

They were standing no more than a door down from hers now, still arguing, the wife in that sulky whisper, Edvar in the slow, reasonable voice that actually made Deza wonder if he had more sense than she gave him credit for.

"It won't take that long. Her father said she just picks up the orbs and holds them to her cheek and she can tell if they're true or not."

"But why can't it wait until they get back? Deza has enough to think about without you bothering her with this silliness."

"I would hardly call orbs silliness when they cost a great deal more than you have ever made with your mbuzim. Certainly Deza has a lot to think about. She is trying to think how to dangle both you and that young priest."

"That isn't fair, Mother, Deza is . . ."

"A little slut. It breaks my heart to see the way she manipulates you when you could have any girl back on Kalmar that you wanted. She doesn't care for you at all. She's probably had a hundred men, maybe even in her own bed in our house, maybe at this very moment there's a man in her bed. But I've put up with it for your father's sake, so he could be king of this horrible planet or whatever it is he wants. I've put up with it, and I should get something for it. I consider the orbs small payment for the pain she's caused me."

"You're just as bad as Father, always thinking what you can get out of Deza. She's a person, Mother, not just something to use for your own ends. That's why . . ." There was a pause before the mother started in again, and Deza had the feeling that he had intended to say something and been stopped, not by his mother's whining, but out of his own better judgment. Deza wondered what it was he had been going to say.

"Using her? What do you think she and that father of hers were doing if not using us? They hadn't been here two days when that awful man came to me asking for money, money mind you, so that she'd leave you alone. Of course I refused. I knew your better judgment would prevail in the end and you would see her for the hussy that she is."

Refused, indeed. She had practically begged her husband for the money. Deza's father had been sure that she would get it in only a few more days, especially if Deza continued to go about with her blouse untied. But now Deza wondered if her father had been right. The Tycoon might already have been plotting this scheme that would what? Surely not make him king of Mahali. There was no such thing, unless he planned to take over the City in the Red Cave, and Deza would surely be no help to him there. She was positive her father had never claimed an intimate knowledge of the city's defenses. That would have been far too risky even for him, and besides, that would have been a scheme he might have tried for himself, but since the story was that Deza had been banished as an infant from the Red City, she could hardly be of any use. And it was Deza he had wanted even then, before her father died.

"She's not a hussy," Edvar said patiently. "And there's no point blaming her for her father's greediness. He's dead. She's all alone, without protection, and I intend to see that you don't manipulate her."

"All I want her to do is look at a few orbs. I hardly see how that can be called manipulating."

They had been walking steadily, a step at a time, toward Deza's room as they spoke. Deza had been concentrating on what they were saying. She realized with a shock they were nearly at the door. Disagreeing about her honesty and virtue or not, they would both find her with her ear to the door.

She hurried back to the bed just in time to hear the even quiet knock that had to be Edvar's "Deza," he whispered in a softer voice than he'd used through the whole interchange with his mother. "Deza, wake up."

She murmured something sleepy-sounded, pulled a wool robe around her shoulders, and shuffled to the door. "Oh, hello, Edvar," she said, stifling a yawn, "what time is it?"

"Early," he said. "My mother is with me. May we come in?"

"Oh, hello," Deza said blinking sleepily, and will you kindly take notice of the fact that I didn't embrace your precious son or invite him into my bedroom in the middle of the night with no questions? "Umm, I guess so." She yawned again. "How early?"

"I'm terribly sorry, my dear, I know it's early, but would you mind doing those orbs for me?"

"Now?" Deza asked, shielding her eyes against the light Edvar turned up. "It's so early." She sank down on the bed. "Couldn't we do it later?"

Edvar's mother looked unhappy. "But later you'll be gone and I don't know when you'll get back."

"Gone?" He must not be taking her out to the desert to murder her or Edvar's mother would hardly mention it to her this directly. Deza wondered if she could maneuver her into telling more.

She could. The wife opened her mouth, ready with a sulky explanation. Edvar took hold of his mother's arm. "I really think you should come with us, Deza," he said quietly.

Something in his tone made Deza think suddenly, "He's going to get me out of here." She stopped protesting the hour and the inconvenience, and shoved them out of the room so she could get dressed. As soon as the door was shut on the two of them, she grabbed up her clothes and ran to the slipspace. "Radi," she whispered, "Radi." No answer. She hesitated, wondering whether to risk the steep slipspace in darkness, wondering whether to risk Edvar's finding an empty room if he got impatient and stepped in to hurry her.

— Trust him — her father said. — He knows more than you think. — The mbuzi was staring at her with its large yellow eyes from the foot of the bed. Radi must have put him there when he left. She caught a sudden image, not clear enough to form words, of the empty courtyard, the near-dawn darkness, the closeness of the gate.

She nodded at the animal and hurried into her pettipants, camisole, and a light set of pants and shirt. She started for the slipspace again, pulling on her sandals as she went.

— He's not there — her father said.

— Then where is he? —

— Gone. Danger, — the mbuzi said, haltingly, as if it were drugged.

— Where has Radi gone? Who's in danger? Radi or me? —

— Danger. Trust Edvar. —

— Where has Radi gone? —

The mbuzi gazed placidly at her. She lifted its limp shoulders and glared directly into its glazed eyes. — Where has Radi gone? — She gave the unresisting animal a shake. — Tell me. — The mbuzi closed its eyes and slumped into sleep.

She scooped it up and swung it over her shoulders, then started for the door. She walked halfway across the room, stopped and listened as she had before, and looked back at the slipspace. Edvar knocked on the door. She opened the slipspace and deposited the mbuzi inside, laying it in a quiescent heap just inside the door, above the top of the steep ramp. The slipspace was totally dark. Not even a thread of light showed from Radi's room below. The mbuzi did not open its eyes. She slid the slipspace shut, grabbed her dark blue cloak, and opened the door of her room.

Edvar's mother was waiting for her at the foot of the main stairway. Edvar had gone past her to open the heavy wooden front door. It was nearly dawn. A thin gray light softened the gaudy northern colors of the main hall. Edvar held the door open for them. Deza pulled the hood of her cloak up over her head and followed the small woman out into the chilly courtyard.

The geodes were piled in a huge disorderly heap in one of the outer barns. It was, as Deza had hoped, very near the gate of the compound. There was not a guard in sight, although Deza was sure one was there. But most of them were Edvar's friends, preferring the personable young man to the Tycoon with his military blustering. Surely . . . she looked at Edvar, who was standing between her and the gate, holding one of the geodes and looking anxious. She felt the sudden clutching of doubt. He won't be fast enough, she thought. He means well, but he's no match for his father. Father's wrong. He'll be no help at all. Should I make a run for the gate now or chance the geodes?

Edvar's mother knelt at the edge of the pile, right hand side facing the barn's door, and plumped one of the rough stones into Deza's hand. "Oh," she said, wringing her plump little hands. "I *do* hope you can do it."

So do I, thought Deza fervently, as she felt over the gravelly surface of the stone for Harubiki's promised notches. They were there, a little too obvious even, and Deza sighed gratefully. At least Radi hadn't completely lost his head last night, although perhaps that was a bad sign. She had certainly lost hers. But right now she was grateful that he had remembered to tell Harubiki and that Harubiki had carved the necessary marks, even if she'd used too heavy a hand. Thank goodness Edvar's mother had been too eager to examine the rock herself.

"This holds a gem," she said, and handed it to Edvar. Edvar looked questioningly at her. She smiled and nodded, and at her signal, he bent down over the orb and thwacked it squarely on the markings. It resounded dully and then cracked. Uh oh, Deza thought, and stopped herself from raising her hand in protest. Might as well go through with it even though she could already tell the result.

Edvar hit the rock again. This time it split down one side, revealing dark uneven rock veined with black. Edvar hit the larger piece, but Deza already knew there was no gem in the rock. The piece merely splintered into smaller chunks of the veined rock.

The wife's eyes went wide and hurt with surprise. You aren't any more surprised than I am, Deza thought, picking up the largest chunk of the geode. She dug her fingers into the deepest groove. The wife was waiting for an explanation, wringing her little hands and looking fretful. "I . . . the cold makes my insets insensitive to the water in the metallic compounds. Maybe if we waited until it was warmer."

The grooves were definitely carved and not an accident of nature. The smooth edges had been made by a knife like the one Harubiki carried. She couldn't have been mistaken, either, marking a geode wrongly because she didn't know what was inside. This geode had already been split with something more sophisticated than Edvar's hammer. Deza could feel the fine line, close to the center, where the halves had been cemented together again. And the grooves had fit her hand exactly as Radi had measured for them. No mistake. There was no time to follow the thought through to any logical conclusion. The wife was looking both disappointed and belligerent.

"The sun's nearly up," Deza said. The gate won't be dark and unguarded when the sun comes up, Edvar. Are you listening? "Perhaps we could wait till then. Or I could go back inside

and warm the insets. They're picking up moisture from the air that's interfering with my abilities."

"No," the wife said and looked anxiously
behind her. "No," she said more softly, "it has to
be now."

Deza shrugged and reached for another of the
treacherous geodes. She rummaged under the
pile this time, as anxious to get one this time that
the treacherous Harubiki hadn't doctored as she
had been to find one of the prepared orbs before.
She brought up a small one. "I can't promise
anything for sure," she said, holding the geode
up to her cheek. "I'm quite sure the night air is
causing the problem." What had her father told
the wife she did in magically testing the geodes?
Read the orbs for the tiny amount of water
caught inside when the crystals formed? Deza
pressed the geode hard against her insets, not
really hoping for anything but a little time to
think things out. Her father had always had more
faith in her waterwitching abilities than she had.
She could read a simple water message, of
course, but . . . Harubiki hadn't sent one.

Deza tried to fit that with the treachery of the
orbs and failed. She had assumed that the girl
had been jealous of Radi's attentions to her and
taken a petty revenge. She would want to ruin
Deza, and Radi would have given her the perfect
chance to do so. But the water message was
something else entirely. It had nothing to do
with Deza at all. Who was Harubiki trying to

ruin — Deza or Radi? And what other subtle sabotages had she set up?

"Is that one?" the wife said anxiously.

"Yes . . . no . . . I'm not sure," Deza said. "You really will have to wait for dawn if you want me to do a good job."

"But by dawn we'll be well on our way," said the Tycoon. She whirled around to face him, still holding the rock. The Tycoon was dressed for desert riding in native breeches and a long white tunic. Behind him, a servant led two small ponies. The Tycoon put his arm around his wife's shoulder. "My dear, you should have let our guest sleep. It is a long and arduous journey to the karat."

"The karat?" Deza echoed.

"I'm afraid you'll have to go as you are. The ponies are ready, and we don't want to be caught by the midday sun. You should have dressed more suitably for the desert."

"The wife has asked a favor from me. After all her kindnesses to me I can hardly leave that favor undone."

"Silly games. Our work is more important."

"Perhaps you would explain it to me then. And to your family, so we can judge its urgency for ourselves." Do something, Edvar, anything. This conversation is not getting me anywhere.

The Tycoon patted his wife's arm. "All right, then. One more stone, my dear, and then we must be on our way."

And if it isn't one with crystals, Deza thought,

perhaps he'll give up his dreams of my witching the karst into a waterland for him, or whatever it is he wants. Deza carried the geode she was holding to Edvar.

"This is one, lined with golden citrine crystals of rare size," she said confidently. Under her breath, she said to Edvar, "Get Radi. I cannot go out on the karst." He knelt poised over the rock, looking up at her questioningly. "I cannot witch water. When your father finds that out, he won't bring me back. *Get* Radi." Stupid, stupid, why had her father ever said to trust him?

"Finish it later," the Tycoon said. "Deza, come."

"In matters of water the priest should consult," Deza said desperately. "A witch is not authorized to douse without a blessing from a priest."

He handed her the reins of the smaller pony. "The priest, unfortunately, is no longer with us. He has left without our blessings. Why should we ask his?"

"Left?" Radi gone.

"With that henchwoman of his."

"Harubiki," Deza said.

Edvar brought the blunt-nosed hammer down with a crash. The geode split evenly into two hollow halves. The yellow citrine crystals caught the first gold light of dawn and reflected onto Edvar's worried face.

CHAPTER ELEVEN

The cursed mbuzi had dashed between his legs the moment he opened the slipspace, nearly upsetting Radi and sending him headlong into the dark stairwell. He hadn't known the beasts could move that quickly unless they were in blind panic, and he'd never seen one leap successfully as this one did from the polished wooden floor to the place in Deza's bed that Radi had just vacated. From its still-warm nest, the mbuzi stared at him until he closed the slipspace.

Downstairs, Radi made the mouse signal on the entrance to his own bedroom, and waited for Chappa to answer that all was clear. He'd left the young marine sleeping in his place so that if any of the servants ducked into the priest's chamber for confessions or to buy dispensation they'd find him asleep and leave quietly to return at a more convenient time. No one wanted to deal with a sleep-grumpy priest, for penance and prices were steep enough from cheerful ones.

Radi signaled again, and when there was still no response, he put his ear to the panel, listening for voices for a long time. He heard nothing, so he opened the slipspace, gingerly at first. The room was empty but for Chappa's form under the bedcovers, apparently sound asleep. No doubt the bed was more comfortable than the desert rocks they'd rested on the night before, and Chappa more tired than he'd been for a long time.

"Well, I'm pleased to see you do your alignments so well, but this one's over, my friend. We'll miss morning prayers if we don't hurry, and everyone will think I'm a sloppy priest," Radi said, entering the room and pulling a fresh robe from the closet, which the Tycoon thoughtfully kept filled with holy garb. He'd selected a dun robe with City-scarlet trim and pulled it on, then noticed that Chappa had not yet stirred. Somewhat vexed, he walked to the bed. Had Chappa brought a servant girl into the priest's quarters and stayed up half the night involved in a little tryst of his own? Damn foolish risk if he had; his companion had only to mention that the novice was alone and everyone would be wondering where the priest had been. But the moment Radi shook Chappa, he knew the young marine had not dallied with a mere servant girl, he was dead, a knife buried in his back up to the hilt. The protruding grip was native-carved, of a size the Tycoon might carry under his flowing robes. Radi shook his head. He knew it wasn't likely that the Tycoon did his own dirty work; he'd bought too many henchmen on Mahali to bother soiling his own hands. But Radi didn't doubt for an instant that the man was responsible. No wonder he'd been so amiable at dinner last night; he had no intention of ever discussing tithing at all, let alone paying a fair price for some additional water. Well, Radi thought angrily, the Tycoon would discover that a priest of the City in the Red Cave could not be murdered any more easily than one could be thrown out of the compound for long. Chappa's death would be avenged.

Radi's scalp prickled as he suddenly became aware that he was not alone in the room. He whirled and was relieved to see Harubiki standing at the slipspace, staring at him wide-eyed.

"And where were you when the desert rats slipped in?" he said. Her room was next door, she slept lighter than a chumacat perched on a limb.

"I . . . I was hung up . . . in the barn. There were more guards than I expected. I couldn't get out until minutes ago."

"Did you get the geodes marked?" he said, too sharply. His mind was filled with misgivings over the Tycoon's unexpected ruthlessness, and from learning that stealthy Harubiki had had difficulties moving in and out of a common barn. The thought of Deza having difficulties with the geodes added to his consternation.

"Oh, yes. The rocks are well marked. The little witch won't have any trouble finding them."

Radi grunted and turned back to the slain marine, fighting the remorse that would be so easy to give in to. But there were other things to think of, like a Tycoon who not only refused to tithe but who murdered as well, and what Radi must do next to forestall the man for one more day, until the marines arrived from Sindra. Finally he reached over to pull the strong linen sheet around the body. "Help me wrap him up so we can carry him," he said to Harubiki.

"Carry him where?" she said. "There are guards all over the place. We'd be better off to sound the alarm and act innocent, as of course we truly are."

Radi stopped and frowned, watching Harubiki a moment. He was not accustomed to having his orders questioned, not even by Sheria's hand-maiden. And yet, somehow Harubiki's status had become elevated, little by little, apparently without his noticing until now, when she questioned instead of jumping to obey as she once would have done. Since Sheria began her reign, there had been many small changes. He shook his head, not wanting to deal with all of them at once, just wanting to do what needed to be done. "It's obvious the Tycoon's assassin mistook Chappa for me. If he'll violate the water hospitality to be rid of me, do you think he'd hesitate to accuse me of murder, as well? There's bound to be a dozen people prepared to swear that's my knife in Chappa's back, and I can't very well ask Deza to tell where I really was. That would be just as damaging; just isn't priestlike. We'll use the slipspace to evade the guards, take him well away from the compound to bury him."

"You won't just be late for morning prayers,

you'll miss them," Harubiki said, "and that isn't very priestlike either." Despite her protest, she crossed the room and started to help with the body, forestalling the sharp reprimand just behind Radi's teeth.

"We'll be back by evening prayers," Radi said instead, "and he won't be expecting me then either. That's no doubt the hour he'd insist on sending someone to check on me."

"What if he comes sooner?" Harubiki said, pulling out the knife and tossing it into the sheet to be carried away with the body. "He'd surely expect me, or Chappa, to set up a wail. When that doesn't happen, he may become suspicious."

"And do what about it? Call Botvidi to tell him that he had the priest murdered last night, so would he come to discover the body, please?"

Harubiki looked at Radi sharply as he shook his head in answer to his own question.

"He may be in suspense," Radi said, "but I suspect he'll arrange to be far away from the compound today."

With no trace of remorse in her beautiful face, Harubiki secured the sheet by tying it several times around with the curtain sash. When she was satisfied that nothing would come undone, she gestured for Radi to pick up the corpse from the shoulders. Together they carried him to the slipspace.

Chappa dead seemed heavier than Chappa

alive could have been. Even so, Radi might have managed to carry him over his shoulder if the overhead clearance in the slipspace passages hadn't been so low. With a great deal of difficulty in simultaneously maintaining their holds on the body and pocket-flares, they finally made their way off the solid wood stairs and into the caverns beneath the house. They went past the slipspace to the control room where Radi and Chappa had halted the computer-controlled listeners only last night. Now Harubiki took the lead, for she had explored these caverns more thoroughly than he when she found her way to the barn.

"If we can get this load into the loft," Harubiki said, "we can lower it outside the compound wall with the block and tackle they use to haul up fodder bales."

"You said there were guards." Radi paused in the passageway.

Harubiki was looking at him impatiently.

"I got out, didn't I? Surely my teacher in the arts can equal my feat in reverse."

"Should have taught you the art of civility, as well. I don't like what we're doing any more than you. Chappa is entitled to a more honorable burial, but I don't doubt for one second that he'd understand the necessity of this and approve of it, if he but could."

"I do not care how we dispose of Chappa, only that we do it quickly and quietly . . . so that we may return before evening prayers," she said, then added solemnly, "It must be dawn already."

Radi sighed. She'd always been hard, a quality he remembered admiring. But she'd been loyal, too, and that he had always thought included respect for friends, dead or alive. It seemed he was wrong in that, but at least he could count on her to carry her end of the burden without complaint. They moved along, trying not to trip on the rough-cut stone.

"I smell mbuzim," Radi said, wrinkling his nose as they turned out of a chiselled corridor and into a natural one.

"The barn's just up ahead, and I do mean up," Harubiki said, tugging at her end of the corpse and shining her pocket flare up a steep tunnel to show what she meant. The tunnel had been blasted through the wall of the cave.

"I smell mbuzim here," Radi said, tucking the dead man's knees under one arm so that he could shine his light around the walls. He spotted exactly what he expected; a rope ladder leading to a trapdoor above him. "Just a second. I'm going up to take a look."

"Radi, we can't wait."

But Radi had already set down his burden and was halfway up the ladder. At the top, he eased up the trapdoor a crack and peered into a well-lighted stable. The smell of horsedroppings and fresh wood-chips assaulted him, but not the stinging musk of the mbuzim. There were two ponies in the aisle crossties, their cream-colored hides curried and brushed to a high gloss. One was saddled with ordinary leather tack, the other with the appointments of a high-ranking nomad chieftain, complete with browband of inlaid gembone, braided reins, gem-studded breastplate and colorful martingale. The saddle was a heavy, plain-skirted one padded and lined with tissue-thin leather, with flask and sandwich-case fastened on the front. Plainly the Tycoon was going for a ride in the desert, which didn't surprise Radi at all. The man wouldn't, after all, care to be around when the priest's body was found. What did surprise Radi was the number of ponies still stabled. Each of these foreigners' households had stout ponies for every man, and perhaps a cob or two for the ladies of the house or for servants' use. But this stable was huge! There were more than forty stalls on this aisle alone, twice the number he would have guessed from the outside of the stable. Most of it was underground, hidden; from his perch on the ladder he couldn't see how many more aisles there might be. What ever could the man be doing with so many ponies? No wonder he needed more water than the City could account for; each pony probably consumed fifteen or twenty gallons a day.

Radi was sorely tempted to crawl through the trapdoor to see just how many more ponies there were and if their number was, indeed, great enough to account for the Tycoon's water demands when a groom came scurrying around the corner from the end of the aisle.

"He's coming," the man shouted to companions unseen by Radi. Instantly Radi heard the sound of running footsteps coming toward him. He hadn't even closed the crack when a heavily booted foot hit the trapdoor and did it for him. He dropped down the ladder to the passageway below where he found Harubiki glaring at him.

"This way," she hissed, then took up her end of the corpse again.

The passage floor was suddenly slick, almost as if it were heavily used and the smell of mbuzim stronger, or maybe he just noticed the smell more because he had to breathe so deeply; the way *was* steep, the load heavy. It seemed an eternity before they reached the higher passages again and he saw the familiar slot that indicated a slipspace. Harubiki stopped.

Radi opened the slipspace just in time to see the creamy flash of a pony's tail that was braided with the same bright colors as the martingale on the Tycoon's pony as it was led out of the barn. He thought he'd seen the wife's silhouette in a shadow, and he closed the slipspace to wait for her to follow the ponies outside. When Radi opened the door again, the barn looked empty. He motioned for Harubiki to help him ease the shrouded body through the slender notch, and once inside the barn, he hoisted the whole load to his shoulder.

The barn was as it seemed from outdoors. There was just enough room for two dairy cows' stalls, a manger where two mbuzim as pampered and showy as Deza's were tied, and a feed bin filled this morning with tons of rock. The wife hadn't stinted on the rocks in hopes of finding her geodes; curious now, Radi took a few steps toward the bin when he heard Harubiki's warning hiss. He dove behind a water trough, banging his knees but managing to keep his burden balanced. Harubiki was only feet away from him, crouching behind grain sacks, her fingers pressed to her lips for silence. He kept silent, but he heard nothing. He kept his eyes on Harubiki, knowing she must be able to see some danger that he could not. When minutes had passed and his feet were getting numb, she finally gestured him to the loft ladder. This time Radi made no detours.

The loft floor was shiny, polished by fodder bales and sacks of woodchips being dragged to and fro. The loft door was open to the brilliant desert sky, a welcome sight. Even so, Radi stepped cautiously to the opening, watching carefully for signs of guards or servants as the scope widened with every step. The way was safe, empty. There was a track that meandered in from the desert, branching to the little barn at the edge of the compound where carts were unloaded by a block and tackle. There was no ladder down to the desert floor, and it was too far down to jump safely. Yet Radi was surprised to find the Tycoon's compound exposed as much to determined penetration as to motivated exit.

"They keep this place guarded," Harubiki said, helping Radi put the body down. She shook a strand of silken hair off her cheek and smiled. "But it will be a long time before they find out what happened to the morning guard." She gestured to the rafter-high bales of fodder behind her. "If you're careful, you can pull out the bales from the bottom and the upper ones remain in place. I tunneled in about eight bales." She didn't seem to be able to help her self-satisfied grin, and Radi couldn't help but smile, too, even though he knew that the inevitable stench from the dead guard would demand investigation long before the cows and mbuzim would have eaten enough hay to cause discovery of the body. It was possible that Harubiki just didn't know; a body secreted in the remote caverns of the City in the Red Cave was mummified in the cool, dry air. Life was different on the planet surface, and though Radi had arranged for Harubiki to spend time with a band of nomads, he knew now that she had not learned everything there was to know.

When they lowered the body out the door, it was shrouded in dun-colored gunny sacks. Once it was down on the dust and rocks, Radi got ready to climb down the tackle rope. He hesitated when Harubiki rolled a wheelbarrow out from behind a pile of grainsacks they had raided for Chappa's new and less noticeable shroud. "What are you doing with that?" he asked.

"Would you prefer carrying the body on your

151

back out to the desert?"

"Of course not," Radi said, really getting irritated with her arch tone. "I had already decided that it was your turn."

With that, he slid down the ropes a bit too fast, burning his hands. He unfastened the hook from the sacks around Chappa and stood by as Harubiki lowered the wheelbarrow. He also looked on while she struggled to get the body into it, and he certainly didn't offer to take one handle when it finally was time to go. He just pulled the hood of his priest's robe up over his head to protect him from the sun as he walked along the dirt track.

Outside the compound as they were, Radi was not particularly concerned about being discovered. Guards on the masonry wall surely would see them, but they weren't worth more than casual notice. At this distance they'd seem nothing more than a couple of natives walking away from the compound. There were true surface natives, one-time nomads who had built houses right outside the compound walls and gratefully accepted the water the Tycoon doled out. When one of them was about to pass too close, he and Harubiki simply stepped off the path and turned away, as if they were resting a moment. But while the presence of natives made it easy to pass through the vicinity of the compound unnoticed, it did, he realized, present another problem. They couldn't go terribly far into the Tegati Desert on foot; even if they pushed on until late afternoon with all possible speed, they couldn't be positive they'd not be observed while digging the grave. Anyplace they could walk to within half a day of the Tycoon's compound would have some people about, even if it was a simple shepherd child watching over a flock of clipwinged guli birds while they picked mites and other insects off the sparse and tough vegetation. They should have headed for the karstlands, he realized too late, where few people ever went. But those were on the far side of the compound, and he couldn't risk a trek around. Radi shielded his eyes against the quickly climbing sun. There were occasional stands of rocks, and they might use the cover those would offer while they dug. But rocks exposed were, he knew, usually just the tops of even bigger rocks, covered by sand and dirt. A clump of trees, stunted as they were in this area, was best; they'd give cover and provide soil soft enough to dig deep. But any within walking distance to the compound was likely to be at least temporarily inhabited by natives combing the waxy green vegetation for kala nuts and asetely berries. Digging out in the open was out of the question. No one would stop them; but anyone who happened to see them at their labors was sure to come back after dark and dig up the valuables. He'd just about decided to hide Chappa's body high in some rocks instead of burying it at all when Harubiki stopped short in the road.

"What's that?" she said.

"What?" Radi asked. He could see only a clump of shrubs and devil bushes off to the left and the promising rocks beyond.

"Listen," she said.

Then he heard it. A sound something like the wind, but too high-pitched and far more unnerving. His skin popped goose flesh just as soon as he recognized it. "Singing snake," he said.

"Here?" she said.

"Where do you think the snakes in Sheria's receiving chamber came from?"

Harubiki mopped her sweating brow with the back of her hand. "I never heard those make a noise before."

"That's its striking song."

She looked so unconcerned. It was becoming obvious to Radi that he should have seen to every facet of Harubiki's training himself, even her surface training. This woman who did not have enough knowledge to fear a singing snake was the person to whom he had entrusted Sheria's life. True, he was certain no one would live to enter the princess's chamber unwanted, and Sheria was not likely ever to need to leave the City. But the City's ruler needed a bodyguard who could cope with any situation, one without limitations.

"The singing snakes Sheria keeps are worms compared to the ones that live in the wild," he said. "The big ones have enough poison to kill a chuma cat. The death is painful, and agonizingly slow."

"The death may be slow, but so is the snake. I am quick, Radi, too quick for one of them."

"Sheria's pets are always torpid because the caves are cool. Up here the singing snakes move swiftly, even quickly enough to catch you, my quicksilver friend."

Finally Harubiki frowned. "How big are they?" she asked looking at the thicket with considerable respect.

"No longer than my arm, and no thicker than your little finger."

"That's not so large; it couldn't eat a chuma cat. A cave bui is swift and its poison can kill a man, but at least the bui eats its prey . . . and its children eat, and the children's children."

"No one ever said a singing snake was ecologically efficient. They happen to be attracted to anything warmblooded, frenzied, really. Usually anything bigger than a mouse is smart enough to keep clear of the song."

"You'd think it wouldn't sing, so that even a mouse wouldn't know it was coming."

Radi looked at her gravely. "The singing snake *never* comes from where you hear the song. The poison is deadly, but it's listening to the song that kills you. The snake has air sacks that open to where it has been rather than ahead, and the whipping motion it makes with its tail distorts the sound." Even as he spoke, the snake's song had moved to the far edge of the grove, but with nothing in between, no time, no gradation of sound.

"Are you thinking, Radi, that if everyone fears this singing snake, no one will be in this grove?" She smiled slyly.

Surface experience or not, Harubiki's mind worked like Radi's. She too was worried about being seen burying the body. "We should fear the singing snake, too," he said.

"I do not," she said, turning the wheelbarrow purposefully toward the grove.

"Harubiki," he called. She stopped and looked back at him. "We'll take turns guarding." She nodded and continued.

In the grove, they found a patch of clear and slightly loose ground. Radi started digging, regretting that making Harubiki push the wheel-barrow gave him first turn at the shovel. "Watch high and low," he warned her. "And remember especially to keep your eyes away from where the song seems to be coming from."

"It seems to be coming from everywhere," she said, sounding a little hesitant for the first time.

"I know," he said. "That's what makes it so deadly." Doggedly he dug and pitched aside spadesful of sandy loam. He noticed that Harubiki had produced a laser handgun from somewhere inside her loose blouse; he was surprised. He hadn't realized there was one among them, believed they'd all been lost with the majini. But its presence in her hand made him inclined to dig a little longer than he might have

156

otherwise. Harubiki was better with a laser than he, her aim more precise whether wide beam or narrow, and he was stronger and therefore better suited to shoveling.

When Radi was standing in a hole up to his thighs, Harubiki said, "That's enough, Radi."

"Agreed," he said, gratefully standing the spade in the pile of loose earth. He was reaching for the handgun, oddly just completely unable to react with anything except confusion when he realized the sighting tube was aimed at him.

"Don't bother to step out," she said, her voice as deadly as the whistle of the singing snake. "Just sit down and get the feel of the grave you have dug for yourself."

Her steely eyes took away any doubts that he had, but not the confusion. "Why? What possible motive could you have for wanting to kill me? I know that you, of all people, have not sold out to the Tycoon."

"Turn around," she said, "and stop talking. You know that tactic is useless on me. I can't be distracted from the job at hand; my teacher saw to that."

He turned slowly, wishing he'd been a little less thorough. He couldn't remember anything he hadn't taught her about a situation like this, except, perhaps the singing snake. "The song is distant again," he said. If she had replied, he might have taken his chances in jumping for her, but she merely pulled a rope from beneath her blouse and clenched one end between her teeth.

With a single hand, she tied his wrists behind his back in the very fashion that he himself had taught her. It would take hours to wriggle loose.

"Sit down," she commanded, pulling his pocket flare and dagger from his belt.

Reluctantly he did so, and with proper caution she bound his legs as well. Not completely satisfied, she arranged a few slip loops around his neck so that any violent struggle would choke him. It was little comfort at this moment to realize that she probably did not intend to kill him right away, for when she started kicking dirt onto him, filling in the hole, he decided she must mean for him to die of suffocation.

"How will you explain your betrayal to Sheria?" he said.

"If you had died on the majini as she wished, you would have saved me more explanation than I shall have to do now."

"She? Who has bought your loyalty and made you betray the City?" he demanded.

Harubiki pushed more dirt onto him with her foot, not speaking again until he was buried up to his neck. Then she said, "My loyalty is where it always has been, with the princess."

"I don't believe . . ."

But Harubiki cut him off. "It is she, with my help, who will make the City strong, and no place for debauchers like you. Did you believe that she didn't understand the amount of power the foreigners like the Tycoon could hand over to her? Did you believe she'd stand by helplessly while you interfered in her plans?"

"Harubiki, you've misunderstood her. She knows my loyalty to her is complete. She has only to order me and I will obey." Harubiki had gone mad. Her obsessive loyalty to Sheria had made her see betrayal in him.

Harubiki laughed. "Then die. That is her order. She did not say how to kill you. She wanted it quick, final, as it would have been if you'd slept in your own bed last night."

"You killed Chappa?"

"You'd have been happier to die last night by my dagger than you will tonight by the singing snake. Agonizing, did you say? Almost frenzied into attacking anything warmblooded? I wish I had time to stay and watch, but Sheria is expecting me to attend her when she meets the Tycoon this evening."

"You're lying. Sheria is not on the surface; she would not leave the Red Cave."

But Harubiki held his eyes with hers, shaking her head and smiling a thin, cruel smile. "Oh, no, Radi. Not one word of it is a lie. Why do you think the marines were not available to you? Because she misplanned? You underestimate her. She'll have the marines as her own escort later today. She'll exchange ground water for guns and ammunition, and turn the guns on the Tycoon and the other foreigners when she's ready. Then she'll control not only the source for turning the mbuzim herds into gembone on the hoof, but the means for exporting it as well."

"No," Radi said. "I don't believe any of this. It's not worth it for the price of gembone trinkets; there's nothing to gain."

Harubiki reached into her pocket, then knelt by him in the dirt, fingers holding a gembone-backed water message device. In the moonlight it glowed, pearly green. "It looks just like the ones your water witch ancestors fashioned, does it not, Radi? But there's no magic to this one, no lost art. This one was made off-world; the only thing the Kalmarrans could not duplicate was the gembone; and substitutes will not work. Do you know how many oceans there are in the galaxy? And did you know that communication between worlds is more reliable than communication under their surfaces? Sheria has known for months what you with your rigid Red City ways could not have guessed. The market for gembone is as vast as all the galaxy's oceans and richer than anything that has come before, and Sheria will control all of it."

"Sheria could not, would not . . ."

But Harubiki stopped him from saying more by stuffing a gag into his mouth and binding it into place with his own silken sash. "And did you believe, Radi, that she loved you? That she actually wanted your hot hands on her body? Believe it to your death, if you will, but if you do, you are a complete fool. She hates you, Radi, and she never would submit to you. It's for that reason I will not let you die easily. When you're agonizing, when your vitals are boiling with poison, think of how she must have felt when you put your hands on her."

With that, she rose, turned on her heel and left, disappearing into the early evening shadows without so much as looking back.

He still didn't believe Harubiki, not about Sheria. If she were on the planet surface, she'd been lured or badly advised. Surely she loved him. It was Harubiki's insane jealousy of her princess that had warped her thinking into the disturbed story she had told him. By now Sheria would know that he had not met the marines as planned. Perhaps she was coming to see why not, and to bring the marines herself.

The song of the snake suddenly leaped across the pit, more distant now, which could very well mean that the serpent was close by. Whatever else he didn't believe, of one thing he was certain. He believed in the presence of the singing snake.

CHAPTER TWELVE

The Tycoon's ponies moved surprisingly fast. If they had gone straight to the karst, they would have been in its tangled contours in a matter of minutes. From the gates of the compound, Deza could see the low morning fog from the sea covering it. Instead, the Tycoon took a circuitous route that swung several miles north, through a native village, and north again before turning to the bluffs that rimmed the karst. It was much narrower here and rougher, and Deza could see no reason for his choice of route, but she was grateful for the delay.

She wasn't sure why the Tycoon was bringing her here, and not knowing made her feel helpless. She did not underestimate his determination to get what he wanted — she was through with underestimating him — but her new awareness of his ruthlessness was not going to help her now. She examined their loaded saddles for some clue to the reason for their journey. Her own pony was carrying food for just a day and a couple of metal helmets, the kind miners used when they excavated rubble-filled sinkholes, looking for fossilized mbuzi bones. The Tycoon's was slung with coils of rope. She could not see what was in his saddlebags, but the helmets made her guess they were stocked with carbide lanterns or magnesium pocket flares, though why he would want to descend into one of the treacherous sinkholes of the karst was more than Deza could fathom. Her father might conceivably have told him Deza's water sense could distinguish waterfilled orbs, but even he would have been hard-pressed to justify her finding an underground treasure trove of mbuzi bones, and anyway, she was quite sure her father never would have suggested the karst. He always had avoided the karst, even though it meant travelling into places with far less cover and far more danger of discovery. Only once, because of some soldiers pursuing, had her father relented to so much as skirting along the bluffs that rimmed a karst area. That time they had gone no more than half a mile before he had stopped, taken a long look at Deza who was by then feeling peculiar, felt her forehead, and then headed straight out into the arms of the soldiers. She had not felt ill, and the pressure on her cheekbones had been no worse than usual when she was surrounded by that much water, but she had felt oddly detached even when they were captured. Deza still was not completely certain how her father had managed to obtain their release; it took her days to recover her sense of reality.

She had tried to contact her father before they got out of reach of the compound this morning, but couldn't. She had no idea what "out of reach" meant. Telepathy, if it was telepathy, should not be bound by distances, yet she had been unable to raise her father when he was no farther away than the mbuzi pens. When the Tycoon stopped to water the ponies at the native village, she slid off her mount and while he was preoccupied at the well, tried again, mentally shouting to waken the sluggish mbuzi. Deza was glad she had put him in the slipspace. No one knew about the slipspaces except Radi, and quite possibly the Tycoon, she amended. Assume the Tycoon knows everything, she drilled herself. It's too dangerous not to. But the Tycoon was here, so the mbuzi should be safe. And able to pick up her messages. She sent out one last call and went to sit on the edge of the well, shivering in the warm morning sun. She pulled her cloak about her.

The Tycoon looked at her curiously, and then turned abruptly back to the ponies, as if he saw artifice in her every move. He doesn't underestimate me either, she thought, and waited for the shock of cold fear that thought should have brought with it, but it was too much effort to keep her footing in the deep sand. She put out her hand for balance to the well's edge and stumbled.

The Tycoon was consulting a map. Deza wondered where he had gotten it. It was small, on thick folded paper, crossed with elaborate black grids and blue wavery lines. The Red City made that, she thought. I wonder who gave it to him? Some part of her mind told her that the map was a clue, but she could not hold the thought. — Father, — she thought again, and grasped the smooth rock edge of the well with both hands. It was cool to the touch, smooth, with water-carved ripples in the surface of the stones. She closed her eyes.

She was climbing the rock, trying to get to the top. The rock was smooth and cool beneath her little hands, with water-carved ripples in it, and it sloped steadily upward to a thin line of light. Her father was behind her, crawling up the same cool slope of rock. The steep slope was hard to climb. Her hands and knees were numb with the chill of the rock as she crawled. She was not crying, but her father behind her kept saying, "Only a little farther, Deza. Just a few feet and then we're free of it. Just a little farther, darling, that's it. Don't you want to sit in the nice sunshine, Deza? That's it, sweetheart." Some part of Deza that was standing in the full sunlight holding onto the edge of a well, thought, "He's talking to me as if I were a child," and that same part answered, "You were only three years old." Her father's encouraging words droned softly on. She could hear them distinctly, and at the same time catch his worry, his haste, though there was no sign of either in his quiet voice. The rock floor was rippled, as though water had flowed over it, and there was water somewhere near. Deza pulled herself up in the animal-like crawl of the very young while her father groped behind her for the few fingerholds the rock offered. Up, up, and Deza could see the sun and the jumbled landscape of the karst beyond, bright shapes against a brilliantly blue sky. But that's impossible, Deza thought; I have never been on the karst before.

"So your father informed me," the Tycoon said. "But I trust that will make your powers all the sharper."

Deza blinked at him, trying to shake the fragments of the vision. She must have spoken aloud. Careless, Deza, she thought, and tried to feel alarm, but she couldn't seem to muster any feeling at all, only a vague surprise at the vivid memory. It had to be a memory, didn't it? Or was it a waking dream, brought on by her fear?

"I've never been on the karst," she said again.

"So you said." The Tycoon stood grimly over her. "I trust you are not thinking of using that as an excuse."

"No," she said, blinking at him as if he were the blinding sunlight at the mouth of the cave. "No, but . . ." Her voice trailed off uncertainly. How odd. She could not remember what she was going to say. "I haven't ever been in the karst."

And now when she said it, she knew it was a lie. That she and her father had stood at this very well — no, he had lifted her up and sat her on the well's edge and scooped up drinks of sweet water for her in his hands. Deza was suddenly afraid.

The Tycoon was watching her impatiently, as if he suspected a complicated plan to unfold.

Deza stood up very straight and let go of the well's edge.

"I'm eager to see this karst of yours," she said clearly, and watched his frown deepen. By concentrating very carefully she was able to walk to her pony and mount it without stumbling once. The Tycoon stood by the well, watching her. She smiled at him. "Let's get on with it, shall we?" she said.

The Tycoon led the horses single file away from the oasis and into a narrow defile in the bluffs. Deza's pony followed easily, sure-footed on the loose rock. The way was lined with yellow sandstone that rose almost to cliffs on either side of them as they climbed through it, winding left to block and conceal the way they had come and to form the northern barrier of the karst.

The defile narrowed until the flanks of the Tycoon's pony brushed the sides, and then the way abruptly widened out to the karst plain. It was walled on three sides by bluffs, open on the fourth to the Tycoon's compound with its empty reservoir and the distant sea. A faint, disappearing mist still clung to the ground here this late in the morning, mist that had been fog in the pre-dawn hours, an eerie and almost frightening sight on a world where there were rarely any clouds and only occasional thunderstorms in the distant highlands.

The mist was now no more than enough to blur the jumbled boulders, dry lake beds, and threatening sinkholes of the karst. Water had formed the landscape, but not water that ever had been seen here except as the evanescent mist. The water was far below, in the complicated water table that formed the underlying life-support grid of the desert planet. Here, in the limestone and dolomite underlying the sandstone crust, the water had eroded and dissolved the ground from beneath to form domed caves, vast underground lakes, and complex passages with delicate roofs that collapsed under their own weight into treacherous sinkholes and pits. The sandy floor of the desert here was interrupted by sudden dry canyons and sharp ledges that stepped off into nothing.

The Tycoon went slowly, glancing back fearfully at Deza from time to time, as if he thought the ground might suddenly collapse under them. As well it might, Deza thought, not feeling any particular fear or comfort from the idea of the Tycoon pitching, pony and all, into a sudden sinkhole, but only a kind of detached interest at her first view of a karst.

Far away on the bluffs at the southern rim she caught sight of a turquoise lake, set like a gemstone in the red-gold sandstone bluff and spilling over its rim in a froth of white that fell away into the rocks below and disappeared. Otherwise there was no sign of water in the whole brown and gold landscape. Deza knew it was there, far beneath the surface, though oddly she was not feeling its pressure that much. In fact, she felt light-headed, as she did sometimes in the desert when there was no water for miles around, and yet its presence was belied by the mist and the circle of dazzling blue. Perhaps the ground water was too far separated from her by the empty limestone caverns and dark passages she knew lay beneath her feet, and the mist probably did not contain enough moisture to register on her delicate cheekbones. Even so, she should be feeling the presence of the lake.

It was hot in the airless bowl. The high rimming bluffs seemed to catch the sun as in a lens and concentrate it there. Deza swayed a little, feeling suddenly desperately thirsty.

"Could I have something to drink?" Deza said, and fell off her pony onto the rocks.

"It's very hot," the Tycoon said. "Come into the shade." He picked her up — gently enough — and led her into the abrupt shade of an overhanging rock, as if there were nothing disgraceful in having fallen off a perfectly tame pony going no more than a few steps each minute.

It was suddenly dark out of the sun. Deza stood perfectly still, waiting for her eyes to adjust to the shade, and the Tycoon waited with her, still loosely holding her arm.

"I can't see," she said. It was dark, darker than anything else she had ever experienced. She put her hand out in front of her face and could not see it. "It's dark," she said in a childlike wail. "It's dark, Daddy."

And out of the darkness, far too close, so close

she had to be able to see him and couldn't, came her father's patient voice. "Just a little farther, Deza, and then we can have a light. It's not safe yet." Abruptly her father found the hand that she had been holding practically up to her nose and grasped it firmly. "Would you like to have a picnic? A picnic underground? That would be nice, wouldn't it? It's just a little farther and then we'll have our picnic."

"I can't see," she said stubbornly, and that other Deza, watching her, said, "Hurry, you little brat. Can't you see they're after you? Of course you can't see. And they can't see you either. That's the whole idea."

Her father's voice, unendingly patient, said, "Come along now, Deza. You know the way. Toward the water." His words had a calming effect on the child. She did know the way. She shook free of her father's hand and put both hands up to her chubby cheeks to feel the pressure along her cheekbones better. Then she reached for her father's hand as confidently as if she could see it. "This way," she said, and led him down into darkness.

She opened her eyes. The Tycoon was bending over her, looking . . . she could not tell if it were fear or a kind of gloating she saw in his heavy face.

"You went into a trance. It's the karst, isn't it?" he said, unable to contain his delight. "He said it would have that effect on you." He leaned over her eagerly. "What did you see? The water?

170

The source? Does the Maundifu still flow?"

Deza said, "Could I sit down?"

The Tycoon eased her back down onto the sand with her back against the steep sandstone wall and went back to the pony for a flask of water for her. He was practically running in his excitement. Deza wondered vaguely what was making him so happy. Whatever it was, it meant her life was safe for the moment and she could continue to sit here in the shade leaning against the rough sandstone and straining dry sand through her fingers like water. She pushed the Tycoon's offered flask away with one hand. He didn't protest.

"The Maundifu, Deza," he said, breathing heavily. "Can you lead me to it?"

"Certainly," Deza said. She called silently to her father. — Oh, Father, wherever you may be, you told him I could lead him to the Maundifu, so I must be able to. Whatever you say, Father dear. Onward to the wonderful Maundifu. — That same part of her mind said sternly to her, "You sound drunk," and anxiously retraced her actions of the morning and the night before, searching for anything drugged she might have eaten or drunk. "How can I be drunk?" the rest of her responded gaily. "There's nothing here to drink. Just sand." She trickled some through her fingers. "There's water in the karst, but it's a long way down where nobody can get it. Nobody. Not even the old Tycoon."

"Certainly I can find the Maundifu," she said

171

aloud. "Wherever it might be." She attempted to get to her feet. "Certainly. I can do anything."

Except get on her pony. She had to have the Tycoon help her up, giggling a little as her hands skidded off the dry leather of the saddle. He settled her roughly, and then, after another piercing look into her face that made her giggle again, he tied her hands to the saddle horn. She didn't protest, but slumped easily forward over the horn.

"Wake up!" that part of her mind, now almost hysterical, screamed at her. "Wake up! Radi hasn't come, you're heading into the center of the karst with a man who's going to kill you if you don't tell him where the Maundifu is. You let him tie you up, and all you can do is giggle like a drunken child. There's something wrong with you. Wake up!"

"Which way?" the Tycoon said, and when she only smiled sleepily at him, he gripped her tied hands in his strong one and shook them in front of her threateningly. "Tell me where the Maundifu flows or I'll leave you here. You won't be laughing then. *Where is it?*"

"That way," Deza said, gesturing with her bound hands. She had no idea of what direction the Maundifu lay, but she had to answer him so he would leave her alone and she could go to sleep. She was really very sleepy.

"Are you sure?" he said, and jerked her upright by her hair. "So help me, if you're lying

172

to me, I'll kill you and throw you down one of these pits!"

"I'm sure," Deza said, giggling again for no real reason except that he was hurting her. "I'm a water witch. I can spin water out of wishes. That way. Toward the blue lake."

He let go of her hair, and she fell forward onto the pony, resting her cheek against her tied hands on the pommel of the saddle. He mounted his pony and prodded them forward across the broken ground.

The jarring movement of her pony against her cheek roused Deza a little. She sat up awkwardly and tried to untie her hands. The Tycoon had tied them with a red scarf, and that seemed important. As she struggled with the scarf, it covered both her hands in a film of red.

It was dark again. It was not the same dark as that other blanketing dark. She was clearly above ground and running through the rooms of some building because she could see dim outlines of walls and corridors. She was running through the dark, calling someone. "Vira, Vira," she called, as if it were a game of hide-and-seek. She was not afraid of the dark, but there was a growing uneasiness in that other conscious Deza — a feeling of dread that grew and grew as the little girl ran through the darkened rooms calling.

There was a thread of light. A door and a lighted room beyond and the end to the game. "Don't, oh, please don't," the conscious Deza said to her, but it was too late. She was through the door already. "Vira," the little girl said one more time, and squatted on her short legs by the woman's body. She shook her by the shoulder and her hand came away covered with a film of red.

"Where is it, you little liar?" the Tycoon said. "Time is running out." He had slapped her, Deza realized by the way his hand was pulled back to strike her again. She was off the pony again and lying on the ground and the Tycoon was standing over her, looking as if he would kill her. Like Vira. Terror overwhelmed her. She struggled to get away from him, and his hand came down across her face with all the force of murder.

"I'll kill you," he said, and yanked her to her feet. "Tell me where it is or I'll kill you!" She swayed against him, and he held her up by the force of his own body, his hands digging into her arms. "TELL ME!"

"I can't tell," she said. "They'll find us if I tell. My daddy said they'll kill us if they find us."

"*I'll* kill you, you liar. Lead me all over the karst like one of your love-sick suitors, will you? 'Certainly I'll take you to the Maundifu. I'm a water witch, aren't I? Certainly.' You're no water witch at all, and you've used up my last precious day to find the Maundifu with your stupid charade. How dare you lie to me?" His hands were crushing her arms, but she was grateful for them. They were all that kept her

174

from falling, from disappearing into the eternal darkness under the karst, from falling and falling and falling until everything was covered with red.

Deza didn't like the red stickiness on her hands. She tried to shake it off. She rubbed at the blood with her other hand, and it came away red, too. She squatted a moment longer, looking at the still woman and the red stream of blood at her throat. Then she was up and running again through the darkened rooms, but silently now, running without making a sound. That tiny part of Deza that held to consciousness tried to rouse herself to warn the little girl running through the dark, to tell her not to run, to tell her to hide, to hide before the hand came out of the darkness to stop her headlong flight. The hand that was so sudden that her neck would be jerked back and the breath knocked out of her so she could not even scream. "Deza," she called helplessly to the little girl, but the large hand was upon them both, smothering them and dragging them down into darkness.

CHAPTER THIRTEEN

The thicket-splintered shards of sunlight on his grave softened and gave way to starlight and the nearly full green moon rose, and still Radi heard the whiffling song of the snake. The dirt packed around him was sun hot and leaching sweat from his body; no matter that he could smell the sea mist starting to blow across the desert dunes; it brought scant relief with only his head above ground to feel it. He could move his fingers — just barely — but it was to no avail, for they filled with dirt, not rope that he could worry away from his wrists. His chest heaved against the packed earth as the snakesong faded again. The serpent was on the prowl. Twigs and sharp sand stung his neck every time he turned his head, like the nips of a thousand peketa; those might be here, too, attracted by the sweat dripping through the tight band of the gag. A few peketa bites might be a blessing over the terrible death from the snake's poison, but he was not ready to die, not while Sheria was in need. Not heeding the bite of the loops around his neck, Radi struggled against the grave.

The rustling of parched fitala leaves halted his movement. It wasn't the snake moving in, couldn't be. He'd never hear its silent advance.

No, something else was in the thicket. Barely breathing lest the sound of his own breath mask a softer noise, Radi listened. He heard only the distant chirp of a desert locust at the far side of the oasis, no other sound. Silence. His heart thumped beneath the grave; if the snake was so close that he could not hear its song, it must be poised to strike. He stared through a jungle of moonlit grass blades off to the right, certain they'd part when the snake made its thrust, fangs bared. So certain was he that the grass concealed the snake, he cried into the gag when a solitary blade moved. When the expected stab from the trident fangs did not come, he opened his eyes to see the soft leather of a desert boot rise over the grass and come silently to rest beside his cheek. The Tycoon's whelp stared down at him, leather flagon and bulging pouch dangling from his belt.

Edvar knelt and pried the gag from Radi's mouth. "I waited until she was over the horizon," the youth was saying. "I don't think she'll double back, but . . ."

"Snake," Radi tried to say through his cottony mouth.

"What?" Edvar said, reaching for the water flagon at his belt. He trickled some wine over Radi's lips, which Radi sucked at greedily.

"Singing snake in the brush," he rasped, and drank some more.

"Oh, sure. I disposed of it. Wouldn't do to have it bite me on the arse while I dig you out."

Radi stared at the boy with new respect; few

desert hunters could successfully stalk a singing snake, hardly a skill he would have expected a pampered foreigner to have mastered. Edvar scooped dirt away from Radi's neck, exposing the coils of rope. Then he gently sliced through the twine, and continued scooping away the dirt.

"I was afraid she'd killed you, or that the snake had gotten you."

"How did you know . . . ?"

"Deza sent me to warn you about Harubiki. I thought it was too late when I saw Harubiki in the barn, but when I realized she wasn't alone, I guessed it was you she was with. The marine wasn't in on it."

Radi looked at Edvar sharply. "What marine?"

"Chappa. Don't bother pretending. I know you're no priest, and so does my father. He knew who you were the minute he saw the princess's messenger."

"What princess's messenger?"

Edvar sighed and handed Radi the flagon of wine again. "Have some more. The heat has slowed your thinking. There's only one princess on Mahali who is of any consequence, the Princess Sheria. Her messenger is Harubiki, your travelling companion and would-be murderer. She was sent to replace the old messenger who kept my father and the princess in contact when Botvidi wasn't around. Pelono was to have been replaced soon in any case by electronic communications. But my father had to turn the old priest out before he was ready. The old man

178

wasn't quite as senile as he'd thought, and he feared he'd broken the code of the messages he was required to send. He was supposed to just disappear in the desert. He did — really, I mean. The next thing we knew, Botvidi arrived to say the old man had made his way back to the City."

"Through the caves," Radi said, amazed. "He'd be one of the few old enough to remember the way, but I, too, thought he was rambling." Radi shook his head regretfully.

"Botvidi said Sheria would send a replacement. When Harubiki arrived with her water message device, we thought she must be the witch."

Radi shook his head. "There are no more witches. We use the message devices crafted from gembone by the old witches. No one can make them anymore."

"They can on Kalmar," Edvar said, and Radi nodded bitterly. There had been some truth in Harubiki's wild tale after all. Edvar continued. "The witch was supposed to arrive alone, so I had no clue that Deza was more deeply involved than she was before. I thought that as long as Botvidi was gone, she was not in immediate danger. I planned to take her away with me, but," he added forlornly, "she wouldn't go."

Radi remembered now that Harubiki was the only one in the majini to wear water wings, and she might very well have arrived at the compound alone had Deza not been on the scene to keep Radi's head above water. Pelono had not been as fortunate. The old man rambled a lot, but his water sleuthing had made him valuable to the City and apparently to enemies of the City, as well. But only for so long as he could be kept ignorant of the contents of the messages he was sending. His drowning, Radi was certain now, was more of an execution than a mishap. "And now," Radi said, "your father needed to be rid of me, too, and so he used Harubiki to do it."

Radi's shoulders were free now and he struggled to lift his hands high enough so that Edvar could cut the rest of the ropes, but the dirt kept caving in. Edvar continued scooping it away.

"Oh, no," Edvar said. "I don't think my father much cared about you. He's a businessman, not a murderer, at least, so far he's not."

"He turned an old man out into the desert, and he's engaged in treason."

"He's a citizen of Kalmar, not Mahali, so it's just business to him, not treason. He could have had Pelono killed in the compound instead of turning him out. He didn't murder him, your people did," Edvar said stubbornly. "Furthermore, he doesn't really want to deal with your treacherous princess. He'd much rather succeed on his own, without her help. That's why he took Deza out to the karst to have her douse for the Maundifu flow that he needs for his mbuzim herd before they eat his entire investment. Deza will fail, of course. I've always known she was no princess of the Red City, that she and her father were working a swindle. I didn't mind exactly."

He looked at Radi. "It's rather nice, even when you know she doesn't mean it. I don't think my father believed in her either, not until Botvidi came with orders to murder her. I tried to warn her, but she'd already escaped in the hovercraft with her father, which was just what Botvidi had planned, I'm sure. That was when my father realized that if the Princess Sheria considered Deza a threat to her plans, Deza might be useful. My father decided that perhaps there was some truth to the crazy stories her father told about her being a princess and water witch. By now he's found out that she's a fraud, and he'll know that he has to deal with your princess." Edvar looked at Radi. "So far he hasn't hurt anyone, not really. He won't hurt Deza, will he?"

"He's *your* father," Radi said, quite unwilling to engage in defending the Tycoon, who was every bit as deeply involved in treachery as he was coming to believe Sheria was. Still, the boy looked so troubled that he added: "He'd have nothing to gain but your ill will if he harmed her. Besides, Deza can take care of herself."

Reluctantly, Edvar nodded. "But maybe this time, she'll need me. They already tried to kill her once, and succeeded with her father. She's only safe because my father didn't tell Botvidi that Deza was back when he came to the compound last night. When Botvidi told him the princess would come tonight, under cover of darkness, he knew he'd have his last chance to find the Maundifu flow today."

"Even if Deza were a witch, she wouldn't find Maundifu water; the City diverted it generations ago in favor of sweet water."

"He only knew that it used to flow near the karst, or under it, and he had to find it before the princess arrived. I wouldn't have known even this much, but he had to tell me to greet the princess if he doesn't get back in time. He's really angry with me, you know."

"Because you're going native?" Radi grinned. "I'm surprised your mother didn't give Deza away; she's got to be in a real dither over her son falling for a native."

"Mother wouldn't do that until she had her geodes," Edvar said. "They were supposed to be marked, weren't they?" When Radi nodded, Edvar frowned. Radi supposed there was even more to Harubiki's treachery, but he was deeply concerned about Botvidi's involvement. Botvidi was a surface governor, a priest of sorts in the eyes of natives, but he came from a long line of military men, the very reason Radi had supported his selection in governing the region the foreign Tycoon was trying to usurp.

"Botvidi has actually been in the compound?"

"Yes. Many times. Most recently the night that Deza left, and of course again last night. The shuttle had landed with the weapons, and he came to inventory them. The landing maneuver lights the desert like day, and the hovercraft buzzing around are hardly silent. How could you have missed it?"

Radi grimaced. Remembering how he'd over-looked so much activity was an exciting memory, but hardly one that would endear him to Edvar if he told him about it. "So now you're afraid Botvidi will see Deza tonight, and your father, having no further use of her, won't care. That's why you're telling me all this, eh? To get me to help you to save Deza?"

Edvar nodded. "My father hasn't really harmed anyone, but your princess hasn't hesi-tated to take lives. It will be bad enough if Botvidi sees Deza, but your princess could act immediately if she chose. So yes, there's Deza to be saved, and, I fear, my father as well. He's never done this sort of thing before," Edvar said rapidly. "He's . . ."

". . . a businessman, right?" When the boy nodded, Radi nodded, too.

"She refused to give him the Maundifu ground water unless he pays with the shipload of weapons. He hadn't expected that, but by now he's so far in debt that, when he realizes Deza can't help him, he'll believe it's the only way. Sheria is coming to the compound tonight to take possession of the weapons. I'm afraid of what will happen when she has them."

Well he might be, Radi thought, remembering Harubiki's prediction that the guns would be turned on the foreigners themselves. Finally the boy had uncovered Radi enough to slit the bonds on his wrists, but Edvar hesitated, the blade gleaming in the moonlight.

"Before I free you, you must promise that you'll help me save Deza and my father."

If Edvar deserted him now, Radi was pretty sure he could finish getting loose on his own; he didn't believe the boy had it in him to kill him outright. But there was a sincerity in Edvar that touched Radi, even though the love he bore for Deza was an annoying factor. And how would Edvar feel when he learned that Deza loved Radi? Did Deza love Radi? Like Sheria loved him? The thought made his head spin. "Give me more wine," Radi said, feeling unreasonably hot in the cool of the night.

"First your answer," Edvar said sternly.

"I'll help you save Deza. We'll get her away from the compound tonight. But I'll be honest with you; I can't tell what if anything I can do for your father. If what you say is true about Sheria, if she truly plans to supply him with ground water from the source, the City in the Red Cave will be in grave danger. The Maundifu river once flowed through the cavern where the City itself now rests, and it cannot fill your father's reservoir without flowing through the same caverns again. My loyalty to the City comes before aiding a foreign . . . businessman."

"He's just confused because everything that is his is invested in those mbuzim. He'd face ruin and to him that's worse than death," Edvar said, a plea for understanding in his voice.

"Perhaps that's your answer then," Radi said gently. "Best tell me everything, Edvar, or I'll be trapped by lack of information. If there's any way to save your father from his own folly, I promise I'll do it, but not if it threatens the City in the Red Cave. Now, cut me loose."

Again Edvar hesitated, but finally the blade sliced through the coils, and Radi was free.

Edvar explained as they hurried back through the darkness to the compound on Edvar's pony. It must be nearly midnight. The moon was high overhead, shedding more light than Radi would have wished for, but at least it speeded their journey.

The situation was much what Radi suspected, but happening much sooner than he believed was possible. Not only did the Tycoon know he could force premature fossilization of mbuzim hooves and bones with ground water, he'd already invested enough of his resources in building herds that he kept in secret underground pens to become desperate for ground water to make the mbuzim profitable. The Tycoon was right to believe the source would provide that ground water; the flow from the Maundifu could easily fill the reservoir above the compound and water any number of beasts. The question in his mind was no longer if Sheria would provide water from the source — he'd heard too much to believe any longer that she was as guileless as she'd seemed — but if she understood the consequences when she did it. Sheria was not a water witch, and she understood less about the intricate checks and balances of the water tables above the city that were monitored by the computers. Yet, she was not so stupid that she couldn't understand the danger if Botvidi explained it to her. So the only question remaining was just how far her treachery went: Did she merely desire to increase her power by arming more troops of marines for herself? Or did she plan to wipe out the entire City deliberately, the only place where there would be any organized opposition to her absolute rule over Mahali? The former was bad enough, but the latter was unthinkable . . . nearly as unthinkable as her *pretending* to love him, making a sham of his own noble dreams of sharing the throne with her. Oh, yes, Edvar had told all, even more than Harubiki, and it hurt every bit as much. Sheria had bragged to the Tycoon of Radi's blind love for her, assuring him that her own power was quite enough to consummate their deal. Well, he had been blind . . . or stupid enough to provide his innocent bride-to-be with a trained bodyguard, only to have Harubiki turned into a trained assassin.

It was impossible to approach the compound without being seen, so Edvar whipped the pony that was carrying the two of them into a full gallop, not reining up until they were at the door of the house. It was none too soon. Before they hurried into the foyer, Radi saw a fleet of hovercraft broaching the dunes from the sea approach, their metal hulls glittering in the garish green moonlight. The foreign craft were, he was certain, carrying Sheria's entourage from the bay where the troop carrier, freshly arrived from Sindra at last, would be anchored. There was room aplenty for her entire household guard in that many hovercraft, and a number of Botvidi's crack troops as well. Hardly the number to form a simple caravan that would transport the goods. Edvar's fears for his father were well grounded.

In the foyer of the house, their entrance startled an alert guard, who drew his laser and aimed it at Radi.

"That's right," Edvar said, "hold him."

Radi didn't even have a weapon to reach for, and the long sojourn in the grave must have slowed his reflexes, for Edvar's sudden treachery took him by complete surprise. But even as Radi cursed himself for trusting the boy, Edvar walked around the unsuspecting guard, drew a desert hunter's mallet from his belt, and brought it down on the guard's skull with a solid blow. As the guard crumpled silently to the floor, Edvar wrapped his burnoose around the wounded head; not a drop of blood touched the woolen carpet.

"First a singing snake, and now a guardsman. They teach self-reliance quite well on Kalmar," Radi said.

Edvar shook his head. "It was your countrymen who taught me. The nomads grow bored very quickly with stalking stupid mbuzim, however great the rewards my father heaped on them. It amused them to see me try to keep up with them when they diverted themselves with more clever prey."

"Bet they were surprised when you did keep up."

Edvar grinned openly. "People have a tendency to underestimate me."

"Did the nomads also teach you not to crow over a kill when another predator might be around?"

"Ah, yes, the princess. I'll have to be her host until my father returns. You must watch for him and Deza, get Deza away before anyone sees her. Hide her in the stable until I can come for her."

Radi shook his head. "I'll keep her in the slipspaces with me. Now, hurry, help me get this man into the priest's room before someone else comes along."

Edvar helped him, but when they got to the priest's room, he surveyed it as if he'd never seen it before. Then he walked to the wall and touched a panel with his fingers, as if he expected it to move. It was the wrong panel. "We had them in the old house on Kalmar . . ."

Radi laughed. "You didn't know about the slipspaces, did you? Of course not, or you'd have bothered Deza long ago."

Edvar flushed, but his fingers finally found the right panel, and it slid open. "Don't think for a minute that my father doesn't know about them. He came to Mahali to supervise the construction of the compound. It's like him to do this, if only to enable him to move about beyond my mother's watchful eye." He looked at Radi dolefully. "He didn't tell me about them. I wish he trusted me more."

Radi shook his head, wondering at the boy's loyalty. He couldn't fault him it, but he found it difficult to sympathize. "Go do whatever it is that a Kalmarran host does when a princess arrives. This time I *can* hear the hovercraft; they must be just about in the compound green."

Edvar nodded and leaped for the door, already on the run for whatever he needed. Radi rolled the downed guard into the slipspace, then waited for the arrival of Sheria's entourage, wishing he had thought to grab up a flask of wine while he waited. It was quick in coming, and unmistakable. The sound of hard-soled cave boots on the wooden hall floors was distinctive, as was the clink of sidearms against decorative mail. He left the upper slipspaces for the lower to watch for the Tycoon's return with Deza. A peek into the dark stable told him that the Tycoon had already returned, either a moment before or a moment after his and Edvar's arrival, for his mount stood crosstied, heaving for breath. Edvar's pony was there, too, but there was no sign of another mount. Hastily he retraced his steps to the upper slipspaces, dashing to Deza's room and taking the dark steps two by two. He opened the slipspace carefully, hoping to see Deza within. Only when he saw that the room was empty did he realize how eager he had been to see her again, how alarmed by her absence. Had she evaded the Tycoon somewhere out on the karst, discovered a chance to run and taken it? He hoped that was what happened, for otherwise, he could only guess that she'd walked straight into Botvidi and Sheria.

Radi returned to the slipspace, intent on following the sounds of Sheria's noisy entourage when his foot rolled over something soft and his ears were filled by the sound of a belligerent bawl. Deza's stupid mbuzi, its pupilless eyes glowed now where a second ago there had been nothing but darkness. It probably had been sleeping, and only his taking the stairs two by two had prevented his stepping on the beast earlier. He picked it up and tucked the thing in a turn in the passageway beyond Deza's bedroom. This time he made his way back down the steep stairs uneventfully.

The first sounds of activity in the lower levels of the house that Radi stopped to investigate turned out to be the result of City technicians in a little used hall. They had carried in a computer communication console and now were uncoiling leads to the Tycoon's power sources. The technicians were dressed in Sheria's blue, not the City's scarlet as they should have been. The console they were installing was not the kind ordinarily used. This was a big console, the kind with memory banks of its own, so that bits of the grid data would be instantly available to the operator. Years ago this kind of console had regularly been used by water witches whose power had in some mysterious way comprehended the vast amounts of data about the grids while they worked the sluice gates that controlled the water. Much of what they had been able to do was lost now, or perhaps locked in the computer banks. But the console could be used, even if less effectively, by those without water gifts. Radi had used it himself, and Sheria used it often. It was painful to remember her sitting in the high-backed control seat, with her face almost surrounded by the curving headrest of the chair, looking as if she were a child with a new toy. There were no landlines between the compound and the City to achieve communication between the console and the computer, but there was a big receiving antenna on the surface above the cave. If the Tycoon could arrange a shuttle filled with weapons, he could arrange an orbital relay of signals to that antenna. Radi had hoped there'd be some time, that Sheria would have to work her treachery in the City itself. It was obvious now there'd be no delay, no time or chance to forestall her anywhere but here in the compound. It was scant consolation to have it cross his mind that the Tycoon might gain some advantage over Sheria if she remained in the compound. He was, after all, first a businessman, and if Edvar was right, only recently a desperate juggler of realms and light-fingered gentry. It'd be luck if he were able to use his advantage. He passed on, still hoping to find some sign of Deza.

Sheria's voice made him pause. He couldn't hear her words, but he was certain it was she. Unable to restrain himself, he opened the nearest slipspace panel a hairline crack, and peered through. Yes, it was Sheria, seated on the largest and most comfortable cushions in the great room. Harubiki sat crosslegged by the princess's feet, amid the folds of Sheria's silk travelling cloak, carelessly discarded. Behind Sheria's blonde braids, and a bit to her right, stood Botvidi, priestly garb set aside in favor of more impressive military clothes. Edvar was pouring wine for all of them, doing his best to keep the native robe's sweeping sleeves out of the goblets; the garment did at least hide the desert dirt clinging to his regular clothes. Radi tried to press closer to hear what was being said. Instead he heard a noise behind him. He turned swiftly and silently, staring into the dim passage. *Click-click, click-click.* Inwardly he sighed; the mbuzi again. He licked his dry lips, wishing he'd kept Edvar's wine flagon with him. Then he turned back to look and listen through the slipspace. That was his undoing, for the next thing he heard was the sound of himself and someone much larger crashing through the panel, and then he was flung at Sheria's feet atop the very robe where Harubiki had sat only seconds ago. Now his one-time henchwoman's dagger was at his throat and the big foot in his back could be only the Tycoon's.

"Ssss," Harubiki raged. "Will you not die?"

"Try again, Harubiki," the Tycoon said. "Perhaps you can get it right if I hold him down with my foot."

"Oh, no, not here," Sheria said, hastily drawing back the hem of her gown from where Radi lay. She got up and stepped away, a distasteful expression on her face.

The Tycoon laughed loudly. "I followed a trail of priest's robes and unconscious guards; had to be this one again. Is this another example of your City efficiency?" He jeered at Harubiki. "My young son follows orders better than you."

Radi felt the steel across his neck begin to move as Harubiki took insult. But again Sheria said, "No!" All looked at her, Radi the quickest of all. Her lovely face was distorted with horror. "It would be . . . disgusting," she said lamely. It wasn't the compassion he'd hoped for, but it stayed Harubiki's hand. The assassin stepped away and gestured for Radi to get up. He did so slowly.

"I know what you are about to do, Sheria," he said. "You must not go through with it."

"Did you really think I'd share my throne with you?"

"You had my complete loyalty, until today. We could have ruled well together," Radi said.

"Over a dark cave," Sheria snapped. "Alone I shall rule the entire planet."

"Sheria, my dear," Botvidi said, stepping around the silken cushions. "There's no need to converse at all with this rebel, not here, not now.

I'm certain the Tycoon has excellent accommodations for his kind."

"Better listen to him, Sheria," Radi said. "He's cautioning you not to open your mouth in front of the Tycoon. The foreigner is not the ally you believe him to be, nor quite as big a fool, either. Isn't that right, Botvidi?"

"I meant nothing of the sort," Botvidi said, straightening to his full height. "Our host has provided us a great assistance in putting a dangerous rebel into our hands, but we would not wish to strain his hospitality, would we, Sheria?"

She had completely composed herself. "Of course not; you're absolutely right. This rebel is the City's problem and none of the Tycoon's." She smiled gratefully at the big foreigner. "If you'll but hold him until we're ready to leave," she suggested.

"My dungeons are large; I'll do that with pleasure," the Tycoon said, but Radi hoped that he had sowed a seed or two of mistrust in the man. He didn't dare look at Edvar straight on, but from the corner of his eyes he could see the boy was tense. "I'll summon my guards," the Tycoon said, stepping toward the door.

"Hold a moment," Harubiki commanded. "He didn't escape the grave I left him in without aid, which means he still has an accomplice at large."

"She's right," Botvidi said, suddenly concerned. "It can't be Chappa; he's been dead since last night. Who helped you, Radi?"

Radi straightened his spine, inwardly surprised at how much effort that took. "She tied
the bonds poorly. She's careless and stupid."

"A lie!" Harubiki said, but Radi could tell she
was terribly embarrassed at having failed in her
task, for whatever reason. Her dagger was in
hand again and she stepped menacingly toward
him. "Tell me, Radi." The blade flashed and he
knew his earlobe was nicked. It was only a
warning; she could have taken the whole ear, just
as easily. Despite his will not to, Radi was
sweating profusely. "Tell me who, Radi, or I'll
design a special set of tortures for you . . . perhaps one finger at a time? Or maybe chop off a
little something more important?"

"Deza," Edvar said, speaking up for the first
time. "It must have been Deza."

Radi looked at Edvar; he looked frantic.

"Who else but the trollop?" Edvar said
coarsely. "Why, I'll bet she's been working with
him all along. Tell me where she is, father, and
I'll fetch her in here right away. We'll settle this
matter of who we can trust once and for all."

Radi frowned. The boy was throwing him to
the wolves for a chance to save Deza, yet, he
couldn't blame him. He might have done the
same if their circumstances were reversed. Deza
would need help in getting away safely; Edvar, as
the Tycoon's son, might be the only person
capable of doing it now. Radi had few illusions
about his own fate; Harubiki would lose too
much face if she failed again. Nothing worse

195

than a prideful assassin.

"Yes," Radi said at last. "It was Deza who rescued me. She followed us into the desert and dug me out just as soon as it was dark." The boy looked immensely relieved.

"Deza?" The Tycoon laughed. "Deza? Oh, that's very good. Tell me, can water witches fly? Because that's what she'd have had to do to get out of the sinkhole, assuming she could survive a thousand foot fall."

"What?" Edvar said, stunned but alert. "What are you saying. Where is she? Where is Deza?"

"Dead," the Tycoon said, glowering at his son. "I threw the useless wench into a sinkhole in the karst."

Edvar gasped and moved, perhaps as if to reach for his knife, perhaps only a gesture of recoiled horror. Whatever the reason, Harubiki grabbed his hand.

"Look at his fingernails," she said. "There's dirt under his nails." In a single movement she slashed the sash on the boy's robe and pulled it from his shoulders. The knees of his breeches were badly stained from kneeling so long over Radi's grave. "Here's your accomplice," Harubiki said, relieving Edvar of his knife.

The Tycoon stopped laughing, staring at his dirty son. "Edvar, is this true?"

Edvar's lips pursed belligerently, then he said, "You don't know what you're doing. You might have pulled it off if all they wanted was gold, but guns, Father. What do you think they are going to do with the guns?"

"Oh, my dear friend," Sheria said, gently touching the Tycoon's arm with her slender fingers. "Your son is young and has time in which to learn. Perhaps he'll learn more quickly if he spends a night in the dungeon with a real criminal. I think the morning light will bring him to his senses."

Radi caught Sheria's wink, as did the Tycoon. The big man hesitated, but his anger overcame him. "Guard!" he bellowed. Household guards burst into the room. "Take these two to the dungeons." He pushed his son into Radi with the heel of his boot so that the guards would have no doubt of which two he meant.

"I'm sorry," Edvar said under his breath, and Radi couldn't tell whether the remark was meant for him or the Tycoon. He watched almost with detachment as Edvar was dragged out of the room. Then he allowed himself to be half-carried downstairs, wishing irrationally for a drink of the wine still in the flagon dangling from Edvar's belt.

CHAPTER FOURTEEN

What finally woke her was the sound of dripping water. Deza opened her eyes and looked up. At first she could see nothing, and that and the steady sound of water on rock made her think she was underground. She was lying, not on rock, but on sand, and she did not feel cold at all, even though desert nights were treacherously chill. She turned onto her side and went to sleep.

When she woke again, she could see degrees of darkness, the flat black of rock against the clearer black of an edge of night sky and a few stars. She was lying under an overhang of rock on smooth sand, perhaps under the shelter of the cliff where she had fallen off her pony. She was not underground after all. She had been dreaming she was lost underground, wandering endlessly through dark caverns and winding passages, looking for her father, but it was only a dream. She wrapped her cloak about her and slept without dreams.

Morning woke her fully, and she saw that she had been both right and wrong. The overhang above her head was not one of the heavy cliffs of the karst, and although it was sand she slept on, it was not the prickly desert sand, but the smooth bed of a river that no longer flowed here, carving out the rock above and below till its roof was narrower and more fragile and collapsed finally under its own weight. She was, in fact, underground, halfway down a sinkhole.

The Tycoon must have made good his threat, Deza thought. He said he'd throw me down one if I didn't lead him to his source. She wondered lazily how she had managed to survive the fall and crawled out from under the edge of the overhang to see. Her tracks in the deep sand were easy to see — the underground river had poured through this ruined passage and past it perhaps ten feet before plummeting straight down into the underground lake that formed the body of the sinkhole. From above, the Tycoon would have seen nothing but shadows. When he had kicked her in (not pushed, she decided) she had fallen not even on her hands and knees but like a sack of orbs. She could read that record in the sand. Totally helpless, unconscious perhaps, and he threw me down a hole. Very nice. With any luck I would have gone all the way to the bottom.

Deza stood up, her head nearly touching the low rock roof. She felt a little dizzy. I'd better not go too near the edge, she thought, or the Tycoon will get his wish after all. Using the sides and roof to keep her shaky balance, she edged out into the sunlight. The overhang sloped downward near the opening and then cut off sharply, part of the general collapse, forming a straight-fractured cliff that extended straight up a good twenty feet. Deza inspected the east-facing rock face in the morning light, but could see no footholds that would help her climb out, even in the full sunlight. The rock had fractured smoothly, leaving an almost perfectly flat face.

Deza stared up at it awhile, blinking against the bright sunlight, and then crawled back under the overhang. There didn't seem to be any way out of the sinkhole, but oddly she did not feel particularly worried by that realization. She did not feel hungry, and if she was beginning to be a little thirsty, there was that comforting sound of nearby water to be explored. In fact, considering that she had had heat prostration or something and then fallen twenty feet or so, she felt remarkably well.

She sat down cross-legged in the sand. The sand still felt warm, abnormally so. Out of the sunlight permanently, it should be clammy and cold. Deza wondered if there were a hot spring somewhere farther underground. She could take a bath, if she could find her way to it. If she could find a way out of this comfortable but cramped hideyhole.

— You know the way, Deza, — she heard her father say so clearly in her head that she was certain he had spoken to her from the slipspace.

She was instantly on her feet, nearly cracking her head on the rock. "Father!" she shouted, not caring what avalanches she brought on. "Where are you? Talk to me!"

There was no answer. No flicker of one. She

sat back down and went over the voice in her head till it was clear it had not been her father's voice, but an extraordinarily sharp memory.

"He said that to me when we were escaping from the Red City," she said aloud, and the karst dreams came back to her, not in fevered pieces, as they had forced their way physically into Deza's conscious mind, but as connected memory now. She wondered why the remembering had been so violent. It nearly killed me, she thought, and found that she remembered that part of it, too, the fever and the dizziness, falling off her pony, the final blackness. The Tycoon didn't even have to finish me off, she thought, I was already gone. Which made his rolling her over a cliff a little more understandable, but not much. Her father must have kept those memories clamped down tight — post-hypnotic commands, repressive synapses, maybe — so tightly only the scene of the crime was strong enough to force them out, nearly destroying Deza in the process. But why?

Because I am the princess of the Red City, she thought, and knew it was true. The memory was there, Deza knew, complete now, jumbled forward and then put in access by her hours of exhausted sleep. She had only to sit here in this warm place with her back against the comforting rock and put it all in order.

There had been trouble for a long time. Deza was too young to understand the meaning behind her father's unpredictable actions, but she could sense the tension, the uncertainty of each day's activities, which before had always been so planned. Now Deza might be allowed to go down to the computer grids with Vira or she might be kept at home, and no reasons given. No reason was given either for the sudden move out of their high, balconied apartments to the far darker rooms down on the floor of the canyon and against the overhanging walls. And all the whispered conferences between her father and his lieutenants, between her father and Vira, the bundle of blue cloak, extra clothes and food kept under Deza's bed, the sound of panic in Vira's voice when Deza sneaked over to the computer center to play. Certain words floated through the conversation and sometimes Deza's own name. Her father's voice was always kind and patient when he spoke to her, but when talking to the others he was abrupt and even unreasonable. And he was gone all the time.

And then she had found Vira dead, her throat cut in Deza's bedroom, the cloak and extra clothes scattered around her, ripped and slashed as though the murderers had thought the bundle she carried was Deza herself. Deza's headlong flight through the darkened rooms, the cold hand reaching out to draw her back into the darkness. Her memories were jumbled, muddied, and Deza sensed they would never be completely clear.

Only when she had realized the terrifying hand belonged to Chuma, her father's faithful lieutenant, had her memory taken on any kind of clarity, and by then they were far underground. She must have been handed through some kind of secret passage in the apartment into the solid rock of the canyon behind, which must have been the reason for her father's moving them there.

She remembered a long dark stairway down which she held onto Chuma's hand with one hand and a smooth wall with the other, and then her father's voice, and she had somehow managed in spite of the dark to wriggle out of Chuma's grasp and fling herself into her father's arms.

He gave way completely. She could not, from all her conscious memories, remember any time, no matter how filled with emotion, when her father was not sardonic, almost offhand with her. But then he had been nearly hysterical. He blubbered out something only half-intelligible about Vira and the open door, and the grown Deza realized he must have thought it was she that had been murdered and not her nurse.

Of course! It had to have been the little girl Deza they were after. She had assumed for some reason through all the trauma of the visions she'd had on the karst that it had been her father in danger, she escaping with him. But it was the other way around. Children's nurses are not murdered in order to find out where the father is. And Vira had not told — Deza wondered if the game of hide-and-seek had been a last

203

minute hopeless attempt to get the little girl to hide. She shuddered at how close her cheerful playing had brought her to Vira's murderers. And Vira, cruelly murdered to save her. She had always thought (correction: had been carefully taught by her father) that she must trust no one, that she must rely only on her own wits in trouble because ALL men could be bought if the price were high enough. What about Vira? she asked silently. What about Chuma, who led me to you?

Deza's father had seemed almost unable to speak, and when Deza had patted his shoulder in the dark, her hand had felt as it had when she touched Vira. She had started to cry, and her father had squeezed her hand and whispered to her not to say anything about the wound.

After that, her memories were not so much unclear as unformed. With no light to make touchstones for the mind to remember, the long trip underground was like time spent in a closet. Chuma led the way. Deza remembered that once he suggested lighting a torch that he had brought along. Her father had objected strongly, saying there was too much risk while they were still so close to the Red City. Deza, remembering, wondered if the wound he had not mentioned was the reason. Chuma had not pressed the point, and had begun a stream of quiet conversation with Deza as they felt their way along the passages.

Deza sat up, hunching against the rock for

warmth against a sudden change in the air outside. Trust nobody, her father had said, because everybody can be bought. What about Chuma, Deza thought, did he betray us, too? Then she was drawn back into the memory almost against her wishes because she knew now what was coming.

Chuma had offered to carry her at some point in the endless blackness, and her father had said no, so that she was very angry with her father because she was so tired and to be carried piggyback by Chuma was just what she had been wanting. Even when he explained that Chuma needed to keep his hands free for sudden drop-offs, that she might hit her head on an overhanging rock, that soon they would need to crawl and possibly even swim and Chuma was not to be burdened with her, she had sulked over it, and her legs had seemed as if they wouldn't hold her up.

She had dragged behind, whining, and her father had come back and given her a swat on the rump that had echoed like a terrible beating against the rock. She had cried, an awful sound underground, and then trudged on between Chuma and her father, with an occasional hiccupping sob that was supposed to elicit pity.

It did. Her father gave her a stick of something sweet to suck on, and Chuma began a comforting monologue that cheered her immensely. He told her about the dark passages they were travelling through and about the wonderful places they would be coming to, silver steps and rooms filled with stone snow and glittering ice, a lake so deep and clear no one knew its bottom except the flashing fish, pale as ghosts, that swam in it.

Once or twice her father interrupted the narrative, concerned that they had taken a wrong turning. "We should be coming to the steps soon."

"Of course," Chuma said. "We have not come as far as you think. The long corridor comes first."

"But it should have narrowed by now."

The arguments led nowhere. Her father was not willing to risk a light, which was the only way to determine their location, and Chuma was unwilling to waste valuable time by turning back. He maintained angrily that he knew where he was, and finally Deza's father gave in, and they trudged ahead through the impenetrable dark.

"Soon we will reach the great crystal lake, little Deza," Chuma said, "where stone flowers bloom beneath the clear surface like a garden of jewels. It is a great lake, so far across that we must take a little boat with a bottom as clear as the lake so that it is like sailing on air."

"No," the sturdy little girl said and stopped so short her father nearly crashed into her.

"Deza!" her father said irritably. "This is no time to be naughty. We're almost there."

"No," Deza said stubbornly, and folded her

arms across her chest. 'Don't say anything more,' the remembering Deza cautioned, but she already knew that the little girl, by some incredible luck, had thought that by saying 'no' she was being perfectly clear. And by some even more amazing coincidence, her father had done exactly the right thing.

"Go on ahead, Chuma," he said. "See if the boat's there. Deza and I are going to have a little talk." He had said it with just the right touch of exasperation, and Chuma had no argument for not moving ahead, his steps echoing on the loose pebbles of the passage.

Deza's father took the little girl by the shoulders and said, "You are heading for a spanking, young lady, unless you get moving immediately. Don't you want to get to the lake?"

"We're not going to the lake," Deza said, and felt her father's hands tense on her shoulders. "It isn't this way."

"How do you know?" her father said in a deadly whisper.

"There isn't any water. There has to be water for a lake, doesn't there?"

"You can feel the water?" her father said in disbelief. "How long have you been able to feel it?"

Deza frowned. "Always. Can't you?"

"Where is water?" her father asked, fumbling for something in a pocket.

"Behind us," Deza said, and her father felt the direction she was pointing along the length of her outstretched arm.

The passage flared suddenly into light and as suddenly went dark again. Deza had only the briefest impression of rock walls with a high ceiling before her father had put the tiny pocket flare out again. Then her father's hands were on her shoulders again, clutching at her. "Deza," he whispered urgently. "You must stay here and you must be very quiet."

"I'm afraid," said Deza, answering him in that same terrible whisper that echoed ominously from the rock. He lifted her into a niche in the rock. "Wait for me," he said, and went to kill Chuma.

That's me now, Deza thought. Surely I didn't know that as a child. She tried to remember what she must have felt, huddling in the high narrow niche, but she could not separate it from the truth of what her older mind could make of the memories. The brief moment of light had shown her father all he needed to know. Even though the little girl had never been in this vast labyrinth of underground rooms and passages, she was able to glimpse that the corridor they were in was manmade. It looked no different from any of a hundred corridors Deza had played in in the Red City. Chuma was not leading them to safety. He was simply marking time until the soldiers arrived, or worse, leading them straight into the arms of Vira's murderers. One memory was definite: even at age three, the little girl knew exactly what was going to happen next. She was not shivering at being abandoned or left to shapeless monsters in the dark. She was only afraid that her father might not be able to kill Chuma and that the hands that lifted her out of the niche would smother her again with their immenseness.

I was a very smart little girl, Deza thought. She wondered momentarily at her father's shock when she told him she could feel the water through her cheeks. It must have been the first time she'd told him about it, though she could not reach farther back to remember a time when the water-readings had not been a part of her. Her father had seemed inordinately excited, as if her gift were something extraordinary. He had always told her later that it was the result of her Red City ancestry, that everyone from the Red City had it, hinting that it was through her mother that her inheritance came and not her father. He had always given her the impression that he had never even been there. These memories contradicted that. And Radi and the others from the Red City had shown no aptitude for waterwitching, though Radi was posing as a priest.

Radi. Deza had not thought of him since that last urgent message to Edvar. The Tycoon had said he'd left the compound with Harubiki, and Deza had known that was a dangerous thing for him to do, that Harubiki was his enemy as well as hers. But, oddly, she could not feel any panic now, even though he might at this moment be more helplessly trapped than she was.

"There is a way out of this," her father seemed to say, though now she knew she was not really hearing his present voice, "and you can find it." She felt no urgency for anything except the memories which she was ravelling like a long string with some treasure at the end of it.

CHAPTER FIFTEEN

Something was wrong. More wrong than his being captured by Sheria and her accomplice the Tycoon.

The echoes from the guards' boots had been sharp and close, and flambeau light glinted off flecks of quartz in the limestone walls instead of being gobbled by darkness as happened in the caverns of home, but even though these caverns beneath the Tycoon's compound were not so immense, they were as cool as a wine cave under the Red City. Too cool, cold. The manacles they clamped to his wrists were made of Kalmarran steel, but they felt like ice and their touch wracked his body with painful shivers. The smell of mbuzim was strong in the chilled air and sometimes Radi could hear the distant bawl of a lonesome kid, or was it the sounds of his own moans he heard?

"Radi! Radi, wake up!"

I wasn't asleep, he thought, then knew that he had been asleep for a moment, just like a babe who didn't have a care in the world. This was no way for a soldier from the Red City to behave. He struggled to sit up, wondering when he'd lain down, or fallen.

"Drink." Edvar was forcing the vinegary wine

from his flagon into Radi's mouth. "More," the boy commanded. "Every drop. There's a peketa wound on your neck."

Finally Radi understood. He was cold in cave air temperatures he should be accustomed to because he was sweating away his body's moisture, his sweat glands running amok from the peketa's poison. The treachery of the little devils' bites was that they were not painful. Deza had played her little swindle at the compound gate just right. He hadn't felt the bite at all, though he must have gotten the bite while he was buried. But the drilling tail didn't even sting, and if the victim's mind were preoccupied with other matters like treason and a faithless woman who was also princess as Radi had been, he did not stop to wonder that he needed to urinate frequently. Now he realized that his bladder ached, as if he'd been drinking beer all night. He hadn't had enough of Edvar's wine to make him feel that way. The peketa's poison had stimulated his kidneys like adrenalin stimulated the heart. Radi drained Edvar's flagon. Better his innards worked hard on liquid he could afford to lose than sponge it from his already thirsting tissues.

"You'll need more," Edvar said. His chains rattled as he shook the last drop into Radi's mouth.

"They're not likely to bring us more," Radi said.

Edvar nodded glumly. "I think my father will make them let me go in the morning, but . . ."

"I won't last that long without more to drink," Radi finished for him. Again Edvar nodded. "Don't look so sad, my young friend," Radi said. "We'll just have to recycle what we do have."

"Pardon?" Edvar said.

"You heard me. If you did indeed travel with the desert hunters, you must know how they manage to survive a peketa bite."

Edvar frowned. "I saw a man bitten. They gave him mbuzi blood to drink. That was bad enough."

Radi grunted. "Well, this is worse, but it works. Hand me the empty flagon."

Edvar did as he was bade, but turned his back while Radi filled it. For awhile his bladder would cause no discomfort but filling the flagon did nothing to slake the sweat, nor did it ease the pain in his lower back. A soft cushion would be nice for the pain, but there wasn't so much as a rag to comfort him in these deep caves. At least they had left a round flambeau behind. Radi was no stranger to the utter black of caves, but that would have been small comfort. It worried him, too, that any enemy would be thoughtful enough to light a dungeon. Maybe prisoners were allowed to see their surroundings to convince them there was no hope of escape. The heavy manacles were chained to the limestone by bolts burrowed deeply into the limestone, their grip expanded by explosives, and as if that were not enough to hold them on their tiny ledge, an impossible crevasse separated the cell from the main tunnel. A bridge of waffled metal had been drawn to the other side and lay there tantalizingly. Edvar followed his gaze.

"Even if the chains were long enough to allow it, neither of us could possibly jump that far," he said. "Can't climb down either. But I'm sure Father will let me go in the morning. He's just trying to frighten me. Sometimes he thinks that's more effective than punishment. It's like the time he sent me out into the desert with the hunters because I spoke up for a native servant. He . . ."

"He murdered Deza," Radi said. The wine he'd drunk was beginning to clear his head of the fever throb, but remembering that Deza was dead almost made him wish the fever would rise and burn out the ache in his mind that was Deza. Thinking of her was more painful than any physical ills could be.

"No. No. He's never murdered anyone. I thought it over while you were sleeping. He's just trying to frighten me again. He can be that way. He doesn't know how to control without fear."

Radi would have liked to believe Edvar, but he'd seen the Tycoon's face when he'd announced he'd pushed Deza down the sinkhole. He'd looked triumphant and satisfied, and Radi knew the sinkholes in the karst were virtual abysses, for the Maundifu had run deep there hundreds of years ago before the Red City had diverted it for its own purposes.

"I'll have to find Deza first," Edvar was mumbling. "As soon as I get back into the compound, I'll sneak away to find Deza. Then we'll go to your friends in the City and tell them what has happened."

"Even if I told you the sea route and how to find the hidden harbor, you'd never get through the shoals without signal lights, and Sheria's not likely to arrange that for you."

"We'll go overland. Deza has been in the mountains. I'm sure she'll be willing. I can get sure-footed ponies from my father's stable and we'll go overland."

"Too long," Radi said. "Even if you don't get lost in the mountains, it's a ten day trip." He didn't bother to mention how long it would take to search every sinkhole in the karst for Deza's body. "The City will be underwater just as soon as Sheria has taken possession of the armaments."

"I have to stop them," Edvar said fiercely. "I have to save Deza."

"You are willing to take a lot on yourself, my young friend, and I do admire your courage. But this is real life. Deza is dead and the whole world is doomed, and there is nothing that you or I can do about it."

Edvar fell silent and Radi knew he was grieving. It was likely that the boy had never lost anyone he loved, and certainly he'd never been so close to affecting millions of lives before. But heroic intentions wouldn't change anything, and Radi had to get Edvar to stop fantasizing and to deal with what little they might control. The kindness of the light still bothered Radi. He looked up at it now. It was a foreign device that looked like a gob of molten metal in a heavier metal sconce. "Who placed that flambeau?" Radi asked Edvar. "Was it Harubiki?"

Edvar frowned, apparently trying to remember. "It could have been. I think the others were carrying pocket flares, but she took that from the sconce in the foyer."

"I thought so," Radi said, still staring at the light. "We need to put it out. She left it deliberately."

"We won't be able to see our hands in front of our faces if we do that," Edvar said.

"But we will be able to see Harubiki when she returns. She'll have to carry some kind of light to make her way through these caves. If we wait in the dark, we'll be able to spot her light, and we can at least put up a fight."

Edvar shook his head. "Why should she want to? We're no threat to her or to what's going on up there."

"You don't know Harubiki. My being alive is an insult to her, a terrible blow to her pride, especially after so many attempts. She'll return to finish me off just as soon as she can break away from Sheria."

"What about me?" Edvar said.

"She won't leave any witnesses."

It seemed that Radi had merely confirmed what Edvar had already guessed. He nodded, stood up, and tried to lift the globular light out of the rough niche in the wall. It was out of reach, but he quickly took off his shirt and snapped the fabric at the bright globe. Radi smiled, wondering if he'd have thought of that technique as quickly through the fuzz in his brain. It took several tries, but finally the fabric picked up enough of the light's weight to knock it out of the sconce. The light dropped and rolled, gathering momentum on the downslope of the ledge. Edvar dived, trying to grab the ball of light, but his chains brought him up short, and the light dropped over the edge, swiftly leaving them in blackness. Edvar cried out in dismay.

"Ah, well," Radi said. "It would have been a comfort to have something solid to throw at her, but at least we're not well-lighted targets any longer. Feel around for rocks. Perhaps there's something we can work loose."

"You want to throw stones at her?"

In the darkness, Radi heard Edvar laugh. It was ludicrous. Harubiki carried a throwing knife and a laser hand gun. Their chains gave them a little maneuverability, but not enough to make any difference in the end. Harubiki could stand across the chasm and fire at will. She could even use a crossbow and get the job done. But luck had saved Radi from a watery death, lust from

Harubiki's knife. Nothing but his exhenchman's wanton need for revenge had left him alive long enough for Edvar to save him from the singing snake. Was it so unreasonable to hope that something would give him an edge just long enough to put out Harubiki's eyes with stones?

"I'll be damned before I lie here and just let her shoot me," Radi muttered angrily. "Come on, Edvar, help me find something to throw."

"Radi, look no further. I have something much better than stones."

"A knife?" Radi said, choking on the word with hope. He felt the boy touch his knee.

"Better than a knife. I have the snake, Radi. The singing snake. I can pitch it across that chasm as easily as I can throw a stone. It can't even turn on us because of the precipice, and it ought to be angry enough to strike quickly."

Maybe not quickly enough, Radi thought, but it would be sure. Harubiki would never escape the frenzied snake in the confines of the tunnels. He squeezed Edvar's shoulder. "That bit of good news almost makes me eager for her to arrive," he said. "But how . . . ?"

"With a lure," Edvar said. "The hunters showed me how. The song-fangs bring good luck. The natives catch them all the time."

"And a lot of them get killed in the process, too," Radi said.

"They do?"

"They do," Radi assured him.

Momentarily there was silence and blackness. Then Edvar said, "Where's the flagon? I think I need to contribute to the contents."

Radi handed it over.

CHAPTER SIXTEEN

"There is a way out of this," her father was saying to the little girl, speaking to her out of the darkness before he reached up to lift her out of the niche into his arms so she would not be frightened. "You can find the way, Deza."

"Is he dead?" the little girl said.

"Yes. Now listen carefully to me, Deza. Can you find the underground lake that Chuma told you about? With the little boat made of glass?"

It was an extraordinary conversation. He mentioned Chuma as casually as if he had not just come upon him silently in the dark and murdered him, but Deza was not surprised by it. She accepted it with the straightforwardness of a small child and was worried only by the pressure of the water, seeming to come at her from all directions, even from overhead, now that she focused on it. She concentrated inward, trying to separate water from water.

No, that was not what she was doing. That was what Deza had to do now, sorting the water pressures out patiently, fighting at the same time to stave off the panic she always felt that the water would somehow overwhelm her. The little girl Deza felt none of that panic. There was water all around her, even bearing down with incredible power through the mazelike structure that criss-crossed the entire cliff they were now under. Not only that, but the little girl could do more than feel the pressure. She could identify it unerringly from a dozen sources.

"The lake is that way," she said, her father holding onto her hand again like a blind man as she pointed first in this direction, now that. "There's water between us and the lake."

"How much?" her father said.

"This high," Deza said, pointing to her stomach.

"Wadeable then," her father said, and they had plunged into the darkness in the direction they had come. Deza's father led for awhile, but he kept getting them off into side tunnels. Then the little girl would dig in her heels, and he would retrace their steps back to the main tunnel. After two episodes of that, he had exploded, "You lead! You're the one who knows where we're going!" and pushed her ahead of him. She had whacked her head a couple of times on rocks jutting suddenly from the ceiling or walls, and once her father got stuck where she had squeezed through easily. But she had made no wrong turns. She had led them straight to the lake.

She was not so much heading blindly toward the water, Deza realized, as visualizing the entire network, tracing a mental finger along the inter-secting natural tunnels and manmade viaducts to find the most direct path to the lake. Now, why can't I do that? Deza thought, annoyed. I could have found the Tycoon's source for him.

Her father strapped their lanterns to their wrists and they lit like magic when they reached the lake. Deza was so astonished by what she saw in their light she almost got them lost.

"Pay attention, Deza," her father said as the boat bumped into the solid rock end of a cul-de-sac.

"But it's so pretty," Deza protested, and her father let the oars rest a moment so Deza could look her fill. The lake was crystal clear under a high domed ceiling the lanterns only caught glimpses of. Deza lowered her hand over the edge of the boat to look at the delicate stone flowers growing under the water and along the shores like clusters of snow. Her father was not looking. His head was cocked to one side for the sound of pursuers.

After a few minutes, he said quietly, "Which way, Deza?" She pointed and then pointed again and they rowed silently out of the deadend and into the main current of the Maundifu. Their oars made rippling, overlapping echoes that crossed each other into a kind of music. Once Deza started to say something, and the effect of her own voice, multiplied and diminished till it sounded like a bird's trill, so unnerved her she didn't speak the rest of the trip down the long dark river.

After a very long time the river widened and smoothed out to a surface of glass. Deza's eyes, almost closed in sleep against her father's chest, suddenly widened. She sat up, her whole body stiff, and her father steered the boat immediately into a sandy cove and left it there, lifting Deza out onto the soft sand and setting off on foot in the direction she pointed, into a dark passage that turned and turned again into the open, to the spot where the water of the Maundifu plunged straight down into blackness.

From there on the trip was harder. Her father knew where he needed to go, but their destination did not end in water, in fact needed above all to get away from the Maundifu, which was the route their pursuers would follow. He had to take the lead again, using what landmarks he could remember and consulting Deza as to what lay between. It was not so much that he didn't know the way as that the landscape changed constantly with the computer's shifting of the water table, flooding a chamber here, leaving a usually drowned passage dry, opening and closing the sluices and dams that kept the delicate interstices of the water table from drowning the Red City or cities on the surface. The Maundifu had been a roaring flood on Mahali's surface, pouring through canyons, tumbling underground to carve and destroy, spilling Mahali's very life into the poisoned sea so that she was a true desert planet, uninhabitable at all except along the shores. The people of the Red City had changed something more important than the face of the planet. They had changed its very foundation, subduing the Maundifu to their own wills, to the wills of their computers, claiming its deepest canyon for itself, and once entrenched there, using its impenetrable position as a base for ruling the planet: diverting the water of the Maundifu into a complicated network that crisscrossed under nearly the entire continent, creating oases all across the land with rich wells of sweet water for the nomads and even richer wells of mineral-laden ground water for the mbuzim.

They had had an extraordinary gift for water. Much of the technology that had been able to do that had been lost over the years, replaced by superstition and politics until the originally water-sensitive witches became formalized priests who were forced to consult their computers on every decision, and the men of the Red City no longer travelled through the complicated underground they had created. Except to escape.

At first Deza's father had led her haphazardly from pool to tributary to waterfall, but the landscape had changed so since he had last explored the vast underground kingdom, that he had led them from deadend to rock wall and finally to a trap cave, a sloping passage that ended in a hundred foot drop that would have killed them both had not Deza cried out in warning. The trap cave was one choice, the other was going back the way they had come, the third a flooded sluice that Deza's father refused to tamper with, even though a terminal stood near where it would have opened onto the trap pit. "Any change in computer instructions will show up immediately on the main terminal. It would be like shouting, 'Here we are, come and get us!' " he told Deza.

He sat the little girl down at the junction of the three equally bad routes and said, "I am going to try something, Deza. Close your eyes."

He must have used telepathy, Deza thought. It was not a complex process, just a simple visualizing of the karst where she had just been with the Tycoon — a picture of the yellow cliffs, the blue-gem lake, the sinkhole she was in now, the ledge. The ledge. Deza was excited, distracted by that knowledge, but she did not have time for it. She needed to finish remembering the journey, all of it, the wading down dark airless passages in slimy mud, climbing up long-forgotten human-carved stairways and down natural stairs made over the years by the slow spilling of minerals, till they were pulling themselves up the long last slope into the stunning daylight of the karst. She remembered it all, not in order any more, but plunging out of her like the Maundifu plunging over the edge of an abyss.

Here! Deza thought, standing up, we came here. Only it wasn't chopped off like this. The slope went on up — in her mind she visualized how the truncated ledge had been part of the longer slope she and her father had climbed, gradually widening into the climb that brought them to the end of their journey farther up the sinkhole's side. That had caved in, and perhaps the recesses below Deza had caved in when it collapsed, but if it was blocked only by a layer of rubble, Deza knew not only where she was but where she was going.

Deza hurried as far back in the cave as she could get, then dropped to her knees and crawled into the recess, testing the walls to see if they were solid. The back of the recess was piled with rubble, gravel and chunks of rock that Deza was able to brush easily aside. It was easy to see where the opening had been. There was one large rock wedged between two smaller ones in the opening, and Deza searched momentarily for a long sharp rock to use as a wedge in freeing the smallest of the rocks.

She was thinking very clearly, undisturbed by outside thoughts, fears, or distractions, as she had when she was three years old, too young to read terrifying implications into the actions of others, when her own actions had been simple and direct. Deza was not thinking of the Tycoon, or of Radi, even of the astonishing meanings of what she now remembered about her own past. She thought only about the problem at hand, which was enlarging the opening and descending into the underground world she and her father had explored.

The small rock came free, tumbling the other two down to where she could roll them out of the way with her hands. The passage was very narrow at this point, but Deza squeezed through, only to encounter more rubble. She backed out and searched for a different stone, a flattish rock she could use as a scoop. The red scarf the Tycoon had tied her with still hung on her wrist. She put it across her lap and leaned far into the hole she had made, scooping the rubble into the scarf and then, when the scarf was full, dumping it to the side on the sand. She worked steadily until she suddenly broke through dirt and emerged into emptiness on the other side. Then she abandoned the rock scoop and scrabbled with both hands to widen the hole.

Her cloak was in the way. She folded it into a flat packet and stuffed it into her blouse. Then, unencumbered, she wriggled through the hole. When she stood up on the other side, she was in complete darkness. Her effort to pull herself through the hole had loosened more dirt and rocks and blocked the opening again. The sound of dripping water was louder ahead and below her a little.

She had changed from the child Deza in one important way. She was no longer afraid of the dark. And she knew exactly where she was. She did not even hesitate — the warm spring was ahead of her and drinkable. She and her father had filled their canteens at it.

She stopped to drink at the spring and then moved, surefooted, down the gentle slope, vaguely aware that she was in utter darkness but seeing that other journey vividly now. The

227

spring, and beyond it a steepening slope, winding down to the floor of the sinkhole. It was not only the memory that was guiding her, she realized so suddenly it stopped her cold for a moment in her blind descent. It was the water, mapped clearly in her head, the spring just behind her, the shallow pool at the base of the sinkhole, the network of thermal vents that had warmed her hideyhole, farther away but as clear as if she were reading a grid, the blue hanging lake on the karst, the oasis where she and the Tycoon had stopped, the sea.

— Father, — she thought, forgetting she could not make contact with him. — When you repressed those memories of our escape, you repressed a lot of other things, too. No wonder you had trouble passing me off as a water witch. —

— It seemed the best thing to do under the circumstances, — her father said. — Where are you, Deza? —

— You wouldn't believe me if I told you, but I'm on familiar ground now. Why didn't you tell me I was a princess of the Red City. —

— You might have believed me. —

— And tried to claim my birthright? Tried to get revenge for all those who were murdered for me? You bet I would have. —

— That would have been a mistake. All those who deserved revenge are dead. Sheria rules. She was no older than you during the coup. An innocent child. Revenge is a dangerous thing. —

— How dangerous, Father? So dangerous a wandering con man and his daughter are not safe from it? —

— Our safety lay in our anonymity. —

— And my ignorance. I'm at the bottom of a sinkhole, Father, and you're being eaten by buis on the desert. How safe were we, Father, from the innocent babe Sheria? She caused the hovercraft accident, didn't she, just on the offchance we were still alive. —

He didn't answer.

— The Tycoon said she was coming to the compound to sell the Red City's secrets, your innocent Sheria. Well, I'm coming too, Father. From a direction no one expects. —

She did not wait for him to argue with her. At the next turning she could see light, and she half-walked, half-ran to the sinkhole pool and the open sky above it. The water was nearly all gone, evaporated into the dry air of the karst, the pool no longer being fed by the Maundifu, which Deza could feel now, farther underground and to the south.

Tycoon, Deza thought, I could show you your source now if you hadn't been so hasty. Sheria can't find it for you. I'll wager she's no true water witch. And the two of you were so bent on my murder I don't think I shall grace either of you with the knowledge. I will come to see you, though.

There was a limp bundle on the far side of the pool. Deza skirted the smooth, carved-rock

229

shore and bent to pick it up. It was the Tycoon's pack, thrown after her body, no doubt, as being useless. All his hopeful equipment for finding the underground river: carbide lanterns, ropes, climbing pitons, magnesium pocket flares, and an ample supply of food and waterskins. Good, Deza thought, now I won't have to skulk through the dark on my way back to the compound.

She put her cloak into the pack, strapped one of the carbide lanterns to her wrist, and slung the pack onto her back. The warmth of her body activated the lantern, though its light had little effect here in the sunlight. Its beam shone dimly across the pool onto a narrow opening marked by two squat stalagmites. She felt a sudden longing to enter that door, retrace their journey. To go home, she thought, but not yet. I have business to settle at the compound first.

She turned determinedly and looked behind her. The little girl and her father had not followed the underground passages to their ending at the sea, probably because there were native settlements along the shore, though the compound had not been built yet. They had left the underground regions here, climbing onto the karst by the route she had just descended. It didn't matter. The water and the lack of it and all the dark passages between formed a pattern in Deza's mind. She was not even sure she needed the lantern at her wrist to find her way back to the compound, so confident of her new powers did she feel.

She plunged into the shadow at the edge of the sinkhole and unerringly into the passage that would lead her through the surrounding bluffs of the karst and under the compound's plain, ending, Deza supposed, in the mbuzim pens she had seen before. From there it would be an easy matter to get into the house.

— I'm coming to get you, Father, — she thought jubilantly.

— And who else, Deza? — he said.

She closed her mind stubbornly. — Do you know where Radi is? — she said.

— Is it Radi you are longing to see, or the Tycoon? And Sheria? Revenge is a pointless exercise, Deza. —

She didn't answer. The lantern let her make quick work of the two miles to the edge of the karst. The tunnel she was in took a sharp downward turn and the walls began to take on the dustiness of the mbuzi caverns. She began to move more cautiously.

She heard a faint echo of voices and a soft thud as of something small falling. She switched off the lantern with a flick of her wrist and waited listening in the dark. No sound. She switched on the lantern again, this time shielding it with her other hand so it gave off only enough light for her to walk by, and rounded a corner.

She was not at the pens. The narrow row of shallow caves cut into the rock had not been built for mbuzim, but for men. The low openings were effectively cut off from the tunnel by a deep wide chasm. Dungeons, she thought. It's a wonder I didn't end up here before this.

She heard the sound again, a sliding, and swung her light to the left, close to the wall. At her ear, very close, she heard the sudden trill of a singing snake.

CHAPTER SEVENTEEN

It was so dark Radi couldn't tell if his eyes were open or closed. He only knew that it took extraordinary strength to raise his eyelids to see nothing at all. Even so, he tried to keep them open and watch for the telltale glow of Harubiki's light when she came creeping down the stone corridors to assassinate them.

"It's moving around, Radi," the boy had whispered hours, or only minutes, ago. Edvar, sitting beside him, had put the sack with the singing snake in it on his belly to keep the reptile warm so it wouldn't become torpid in the cool cave air. Radi had no idea how much time had gone by since he and Edvar had been chained in the dungeon. There was nothing by which to measure time's passing, and the fever in his body distorted any natural rhythms he might have judged by.

"Radi!" Edvar whispered.

"Shhh," Radi cautioned. For an instant he thought it was the fever making phosphenes in his eyes, but the glow he saw bobbed and brightened in a fashion that could only indicate someone quickly approaching with a carbide lantern. There were no boot sounds like those the Tycoon's guards would have made, so it had to be Harubiki in her soft leather cave boots. "Throw the snake the instant the light touches us," Radi whispered to the boy.

Edvar was so silent in changing his stance that Radi seemed to feel him moving about rather than hear him. As he watched the light grow, he imagined Edvar poised to throw, arm drawn back, muscles tense as he held the snake's fangs and tail. When the light struck them, it momentarily blinded Radi, but he knew the snake was away, for he heard its song behind his ear, where he knew the snake could not be.

He watched the light halt, hoped that it would never move again. Suddenly the beam of light streaked upwards, flashing off crystals in the limestone walls and just briefly catching on red wool pants.

"Who's there?" Radi said hoarsely, worried that some innocent servant had been sent with rations to feed the prisoners, perhaps even one with keys to free Edvar.

"Radi, is that you?" It was Deza's voice.

"Deza, run!" Edvar shouted. "There's a singing snake . . ." Before Edvar could finish his warning, the light dived to the floor of the cave and stayed there, radiating out across the chasm. "It got her," Edvar shouted. "Radi, the snake got Deza."

Radi struggled to his feet while he stared at the motionless light. The brilliance after so long in the darkness was making him blink, or was it tears that blurred his vision? He groaned, sick to raging that his sick body could make his wits so sluggish that he couldn't distinguish the footsteps of the woman he loved from the ones of the woman who would murder him. No matter that he thought Deza was already dead and that he was taken by surprise. He'd killed her with his signal just as surely as if he'd drawn his knife across her throat. "Oh, Deza," he said, groaning again.

"What?"

Radi blinked and rubbed dust, not tears, from his eyes just in time to see Deza step into the light, struggling to put something in her pants pocket.

"Deza?" Edvar's query sounded with his own.

"Yes, just a moment." It was the singing snake she was struggling with, and she had no snake hook with which to maneuver the serpent the way the native hunters did. "They're so wiggly . . . there." She looked up at them. Her curly red hair was matted and tangled and her yellow shirt was dirty and torn, but she was very much alive. She put her hands on her hips. "What are the two of you doing down here . . . and in chains?"

"It's a long story," Radi said, leaning back against the wall of the dungeon. His knees were getting weak.

"Deza, do you have any water?" Edvar said urgently. "Radi has a peketa bite and we've run out of . . . liquids."

"Peketa bite? Down here?" she said, stepping back into the shadow. When she returned she had the carbide lantern by its wrist strap and was holding a pack from which she withdrew a dripping waterskin.

"Careful, Deza, there's a chasm between us and you," Radi said. But Deza had already seen it or knew it was there, for she was pushing the metal bridge out onto its track with her foot. When she ran across, Edvar caught her in his arms.

"Deza," he said joyfully. "Thank the stars you are alive. I knew my father wouldn't kill you, but then the snake . . . Deza, Deza . . ."

Radi could only stare up at the boy as he continued to crush Deza against him, and envy the pleasure of feeling her heart beat against him. But as he looked, her sparkling eyes met his, her attention totally on him in spite of Edvar's strong grip. Finally Edvar seemed to realize that Deza was responding as much as a rag doll might, and he released her and stepped back.

Without even a glance at Edvar, Deza knelt by Radi and opened the waterskin. Her strong hands supported his head as she put the waterskin to his lips.

"Drink all of it," she commanded gently. "Four or five skinsful and we'll have the poison flushed out of you." She sounded confident, but Radi could see that she was biting her lower lip to keep from saying more, and now her eyes were flashing with worry, too. He must look terrible. He felt her fingers pushing aside his clothing as she looked for the peketa wound. She barely paused when she found it on his neck, continued looking.

"There's only the one," Radi said, pushing away the water skin.

Deza sighed, relieved. Radi knew what she was thinking. One peketa bite was dangerous enough without sufficient water to treat it, but two or more would have been a death warrant unless there was a lake full of water to drink, which was clearly impossible here. "Were you out on the desert looking for me?" Deza said. "Is that how you got bitten?"

"Yes and no," Radi said. "I was out in the desert with Harubiki. She tried to kill me."

"Oh, no. I should have warned you. Radi, she never sent the water message. She was disobeying you right from the start."

"How could you know the message was not sent?" Radi said.

"I just know. I can feel such signals in the water for hours. There was nothing."

"Why didn't you tell me?"

Deza looked chagrined. "I thought you were a pirate."

Radi shook his head regretfully. "Nothing was as it seemed, was it, my dear? So much has happened to make me understand how ingrained this treachery has become. But it's me who is to blame for your troubles with the Tycoon out on the karst. If I'd paid attention to business that night instead of . . . other things, I'd have known that the Tycoon meant harm to both of us. I counted too much on marines that never came, marines that Harubiki never sent for. Your instincts were more reliable than mine. You had good reason to be frightened. At least he didn't try to kill you."

"Yes, he did. He just didn't succeed. And he may never understand how, but he did me a favor when he threw me down that sinkhole. I couldn't get up, but I remembered how to get out through the caves."

"What do you mean?" Radi said, frowning. "Are you trying to tell me you came to these dungeons under the compound all the way from the karst?"

"Yes," Deza said. "I probably wouldn't have remembered how to travel through the caves or who I am if he hadn't taken me out onto the karst. Radi, do you know who I am?"

Deza the con artist was not the answer, of that much he was certain. Radi remembered the delicate gembone cheek insets, perfect to the last detail in looking like genuine insets. He remembered Deza wet and shivering, awed by the vast ocean. And Radi knew that only a true water witch could handle a singing snake without fear. He shook his head. "There is only one true water witch that I know of. Can it be that Akida and the princess Deshenaza did not die so long ago?"

"Deshenaza," she whispered. "No one has called me that for a very long time. I had almost forgotten the true form of my name. But there is another princess. Your Sheria."

Radi shook his head. "My allegiance is to the Red City first, and she has betrayed the City. She's going to fill the Tycoon's reservoir with water from the Maundifu. I fear she will drown the City in the Red Cave during the process. All in exchange for a shipload of arms, with which she thinks to rule the surface world."

"Sheria's not a true witch. She cannot unleash the Maundifu," Deza said, looking royally indignant in spite of her tattered clothes and tangled hair. "She wouldn't know how."

"Not how to do it safely, but she can do it. When your father left the City with you, there were no more witches. Sheria's father ruled by computer and he taught Sheria what he knew. She thinks she controls the computer, but it may well control her. She has brought terminals with her to the Tycoon's compound, and by her command, the computer can release the waters of the Maundifu."

"Sheria's here? In the compound?" Deza looked wild and excited. "I thought I'd have to go through the caves to the City to find her. But she's here!"

"Yes, she's here. But so what?"

Deza let go of his hand and stood up. "Don't you understand, Radi? She forced me out of my home, and she tried to kill me twice! She succeeded in killing my father. I won't let her kill all my people in the Red City as well. I've got to stop her. I've got to go home, and when I go I want my home to be there."

She turned and ran toward the bridge.

"Deza, no. You can't do this alone. Get the keys to our chains and free us. We'll go to the City by the underground trail." She hesitated, staring at him. "Deza, you don't fully understand what you're getting involved in. You must let me help."

Deza shook her head. "She killed my father. She murdered him, just like her father murdered Vira."

"Deza!" The sharpness of his voice stopped her again. "Deza, I am the commander in chief of the defense forces of the City in the Red Cave. I am a minor prince, but one loyal to the true line. I pledge my oath of loyalty to you, Deshenaza, and I beg you to allow me to come with you." But she ran, her soft-soled sandals flashing in the light of the lantern. "Deza, I love you!" he shouted. And then she was gone.

"I pledge my oath of loyalty to you," Edvar mocked. "Throwing kisses. You would have done better to tell her to throw her pack at us. Look at what's over there."

Radi shook himself, trying not to fear what Deza was running to, and looked where Edvar was pointing. There were ropes and pitons, and sturdy picks that could have chopped at the bolts in the limestone walls, if only they had them in their hands. Worse still, the carbide lantern was beyond their reach and staining in their eyes. If Harubiki came now, she'd have easy prey, and there'd be no singing snake to stop her.

CHAPTER EIGHTEEN

Deza was nearly to the level of the pens where the mbuzi had been kept before she slowed her headlong ascent and leaned against the rock wall to catch her breath. The caverns where she had left Radi and Edvar helpless prisoners were far below her, almost on the level of the Maundifu. She wondered if they had originally been part of the underground network of the Red City.

Deza tried to call her father. She had had some sort of fixed idea that her father had to be where she had left him, but the sight of the pens above her had brought her to her senses. Her opinion of the Tycoon had changed drastically out on the karst, and now she had to keep that change clearly in mind or she would find herself a prisoner, too. The Tycoon had to have known about the slipspaces. He already knew about the mbuzi and Deza's attachment to it. Deza had no idea what she might have said in her delirium. She might easily have betrayed her father, and if so, she was walking into a trap with the mbuzi as bait. No, that was wrong. Even the Tycoon would not set a trap for a dead person. Then where was her father? Asleep? Sulking?

— I don't have time for this foolishness, Father. —

— I quite agree, — he said suddenly, so suddenly he had to have been listening for some time. — Foolishness is a luxury we cannot afford with time so short. So come and get me and we'll be off to the Red City. Your Red City. —

— There are things I have to do first, — Deza said.

— Yes, — he said, — I know what things. There isn't time. If I had allowed myself the time to revenge Vira's death, you would not be here to argue with me. —

— Vira? — Deza said, the anguish in his voice jerking her back to the image of the woman whose blood had flowed from her throat onto Deza's hands. — My nurse? —

— My beloved, my betrothed, your new stepmother. —

Deza did not answer. She pressed her face against the rock, trying to absorb this new staggering piece of information. Finally, she said, — You did not take any revenge. —

— You cannot help the dead, and they are past caring for revenge. The living are worth saving, and the time to do it is now. I'm in the slipspace, — he said, and she realized from his unbidden admission that he must think he had convinced her of something.

But he hasn't, she thought, keeping the thought carefully concealed. I will revenge my father's death. She moved carefully up to the level of the pens and was almost instantly rewarded for her stealth because the narrow

242

space she squeezed into to reconnoitre turned out to be the place where the keepers of the pens stored their belongings. Including the keys to the dungeons. Including spare water skins hanging from the wall. She pocketed the keys and took a moment to sling two of the full water skins down the steep path she had just ascended. She could pick them up on her way back. Then she started her careful way across the pens, keeping to the walls and watching for the servants who would be tending the bleating mbuzim.

She stopped halfway across. It had taken her far too long to get even this close. She had still half the distance of the pens and then the stables to cross before she could reach the back staircase she had followed the servant down on her first trip to the pens.

— Father, — she said, — do the slipspaces extend into the mbuzi pens? — She did not think he would know, but it was worth a try.

He was slow in answering, but his voice was strong, as if he were very near. — Deza, — he said, and his voice faded a little. — Come and get me. I'm in the slipspace. —

— What's the matter? —

— Between Radi's room and yours. Come. —

The message was not cut off. It trailed away in a manner that was more frightening than if it had abruptly stopped.

— I'm coming, — she said, and shot from her cover, straight across the center of the cavern. The pens themselves afforded her some cover, though her flashing red pants were bound to attract attention from the men feeding the mbuzim. She saw no one. Her luck held all the way through the mbuzi pens and into the narrow defile that led to the barns.

A guard was blocking the way, facing outward. He turned around, his mouth open in surprise, his hand hesitating near his laser hand gun.

"Let me pass," Deza said, flinging her head. "I have a message for the Tycoon."

"You're dead," the soldier blurted.

"No," Deza said imperiously. "I am here. Let me through."

"I'll conduct you to the Tycoon," he said, turning slightly as if he were confused.

Deza took advantage of his confusion. "You are not a very good guard. I hope you can guard the compound better than you guard this passage. I came into the pens without you seeing me and now I nearly passed you again. Like a whisper. Like a ghost. You will not conduct me anywhere. I know the way. You alert the guard at the gate. I came from the desert, where the danger is. Hurry."

She was not sure she had buffaloed him into heading for the outer edges of the compound. If she had, she would have succeeded at least in putting the attention of the guards where it would least hinder her. If not, she had implanted the idea of her being a ghost, which was surely easier for the guard to take than the idea that she had appeared out of solid rock, and it might give the Tycoon a few minutes' uneasiness before he realized she had to be alive.

As soon as she was out of sight of the guard, Deza took the back stair. Halfway up, she stopped where she had heard the faint noise before and felt for the familiar slipspace device. It was there, and just in time. She heard hurrying footsteps and the soldier's voice talking about the girl who had passed through his body like air.

"You're crazy," another voice said. "She came this way, you say. We'll catch her on the stairs. The Tycoon has them closed off at the top."

"That won't stop her."

Indeed it won't, thought Deza, then she stepped back and let the darkness of the slip-space swallow her. She was sorry for a moment that she had left her carbide lantern back in the dungeons with Radi and Edvar, but the darkness was so like that of the caves she felt herself relax and her excellent sense of direction take over. Even without any water to witch, she was very good at finding her way in the dark, and she moved ahead quickly down the slightly slanting slipspace, visualizing the rooms she was passing — the kitchens, the servants' rooms, a slight slant up, the priest's room. She felt with her hand for the connection up to her own room. Her hand passed into emptiness, and she pulled herself up into the steep familiar passage between their rooms.

— Father, I'm here. —

She heard a faint sound that she thought might

be a poor connection with her father, and then realized it was the even hum of machinery from somewhere close. Her own room. Radi had said Sheria had brought her terminals and was operating them from Deza's room.

Deza felt her way almost to the door of her room, where the sound was definitely coming from, then retraced her steps. Halfway down she found what she thought was a connecting slipspace and the key to her father's disappearance, but it ended after only a few feet. The mbuzi was not here.

The door to Deza's room opened, glaring light into the slipspace, and Harubiki's voice said, "I'll check the slipspaces again. There's one that connects to the stair."

A voice said something Deza could not hear, and the light went out. Deza pressed back against the wall of the deadend, wishing she had some kind of weapon, and tried to still her breathing for the sound of Harubiki in the slipspace.

There was no sound, and after a few moments, Deza heard two voices from the room, both muffled, but one unmistakably Harubiki's. Whoever had spoken, he or she had stopped Harubiki from exploring the slipspace that led to the back stair. The soldier had gotten the word out fast, and Harubiki was not buying the ghost story.

Deza tried calling her father, but there was no answer. She had not expected any. Harubiki's familiarity with all the slipspaces meant that they had been through here many times before, and except for this little cul-de-sac, which they had surely stumbled into as Deza had, thinking it was a passage, there was no place for the helpless mbuzi to hide. Her father could not be here. Then why had he told her he was? No matter. Harubiki was in that room up there, and perhaps the Tycoon and Sheria with her. Deza could have her revenge on all of them.

— And then what? — her father said drily. — All those murders will take a week, especially since you'll have to do them with your bare hands, and personally I don't think you're much of a match for Harubiki or the Tycoon. By that time the Red City will be full of fish and not much else. You will make a fine princess then, ruler of the cretins and the featherfish. —

— Where are you? — she demanded. — Are you all right? —

— I'm in the pens, — her father said placidly. — You went flying past me. The last pen on the right. I saw your little business with the guard. Not bad, but not too well thought out either. He is bound to have told the Tycoon. —

— Why did you send me up here to the slipspace? I thought you said there was no time to waste. —

— I had an idea it might do you good to hear what is going on in your room. A great deal has gone on in your room, but nothing like this. —

— I have no intention . . . —

— They're all there. Sheria and the Tycoon *and* Harubiki. If you so choose, you can go tearing in and crack their heads together, but I'd suggest you listen at the door first. Only a fool would not take advantage of such an opportunity to eavesdrop. —

Deza cut her father off sharply and dropped to her hands and knees. She thought she had kicked something when she first came into the cul-de-sac, and she wanted to find it now. She crept toward the main tunnel, hoping the stick or broom or whatever it was was something she could wedge the door with. She was not about to be caught with an opening door, a glare of light, and Harubiki looking down at her. The whole idea was to catch *them*.

No matter what Radi said, the time and place to stop them was now. All thoughts of revenge aside, it was still the most practical way to put an end to the threat to the Red City. Once on their way to the Red City, she and Radi would have no way to control what was happening here. The Tycoon and Sheria might take a notion to flood the very caverns they were passing through or to blow the City to smithereens. Radi might have some silly idea of erupting out of the earth with a full-blown army, but Sheria would still be sitting at the computer. She could manage to push the crucial buttons before they killed her, of that Deza was certain. Still, she was not about to barge in with no idea of the situation on the other side of the door.

248

Her hand touched a length of wood and followed it to its tip. A pole, no, a spear. Just what she needed, and don't think about who had waited outside her door with such a weapon. She crept to the end of the slipspace and inserted the end of the spear in the depression next to the door's opening mechanism. The metal would break the contact and keep the door from opening. She wedged the blunt wooden end firmly in the corner. Only then did she put her ear to the door and listen.

"I thought you said she was dead," Harubiki said.

My, my, Father, word travels fast. If you hadn't pulled that stunt about being in the slipspace, Father, nobody would have seen me. Now the whole world knows I'm back.

"I heard her fall," the Tycoon answered her angrily.

"But did you hear her hit?" Harubiki again. "She's a tricky little bitch. Maybe she managed to hang onto the edge and didn't fall at all."

"She was unconscious," the Tycoon said. "She may already have been dead when I threw her in. And how could she have gotten into the pens without passing the guard? The stables are locked."

"Perhaps she had an accomplice," Harubiki said, and added slyly, "as the priest Radi did. A helper. A guide."

"No." That was a new voice, imperious and used to making statements that were never questioned. Sheria. "No accomplice. I had the little servant girl who attended her killed."

There was a silence. Deza leaned her forehead against the door. Oh, Radi, even you would want revenge for this. The servant girl did nothing. How many others has she killed or tried to kill? Father, you, Edvar, and her father before her murdered Vira and tried to murder me.

"This Deza person is dead. The servants are making up ghost stories to frighten themselves with," the voice went on. "Or are you, Tycoon? To distract me? To delay delivering your part of the bargain? There will be no water for your precious mbuzim until I get my shipment of arms."

"I will show you where they are just as soon as we talk," said the Tycoon.

"About what?" Sheria said, too sweetly. Like a singing snake would sound before it took a chunk out of you. Radi, really, your taste in women is hardly flattering.

"About my son Edvar," the Tycoon said, his old manner returning. "I want him out of that dungeon."

"I suppose you want to release Radi, too. You're a very forgiving person."

"Edvar is my son. I do not know what you intend to do with them."

"Nothing," Sheria said.

"Nothing?" The Tycoon's voice rose on a note of hope, and then dropped suspiciously. "You don't mean just leave them there to starve?"

"Starvation is too cruel a way for even traitors

to die, and they are not traitors, only . . . obstacles."

Deza could hear the Tycoon's sigh of relief. "Then you'll leave them there until our purpose is accomplished and then let them go?"

"I'll leave them there until our purpose is accomplished." There was another silence, accompanied by slight sounds of movement and then the slam of the outside door to Deza's room. The machinery hum became louder, muffling the voices.

Sheria said something Deza did not catch, and then Harubiki said, "How long will it take?"

"Half an hour at the most," Sheria said. "The dungeons are well below the level of the sluices. They'll fill like a cup."

"It won't give the Tycoon his water, will it?"

"No, that's why I waited till now, to get a simulation on the grids of what effect the localized flooding will have. The dungeon is porous sandstone. All the water will soak back to the level of the water table before the Tycoon can trap it. But it won't soak in fast enough to save our friends. 'Edvar is my son,' indeed."

Deza stood up with such speed that she knocked the spear's tip to the edge of the depression. She paid no attention. Her mind was operating at high speed. She raced down the slipspace to the pens, calling to her father and finding him where he had said, wobbling onto his spindly legs to greet her. There was not a soul in the pens. They were either guarding against the danger from the desert or frightened of Deza's ghost.

She skidded down the steep stairs to the dungeons, grabbing up the waterskins where she had thrown them, unlocking Radi and Edvar with such urgency that they followed her without a word into the darkness. She stopped a few feet into the rock, the heavy pack on her back and the carbide lantern dangling from her hand, reading her own private grids at almost the speed of Sheria's computer. It was not enough to get them out. She had to get them up, above the level of the sluices that were being released, before the water poured across their route. She switched the lantern on.

"Come on," she said sharply, taking in everything at once, Edvar's reluctant sullenness, Radi's dried skin and stiff gait, the chasm beyond already half-full of water, her conscious mind clicking along at super-speed, while in another part of her mind, moving in slow motion, she saw the metal-tipped spear fall and fall, slowly, slowly, till it clattered down the slipspace with a noise Harubiki would hear.

CHAPTER NINETEEN

Deza, Deshenaza, true princess of the City in the Red Cave had led Edvar and Radi from captivity. She had seemed like a flame, red and gold, standing there with the key. Her commands had been quick, urgent, and once he was free of the chains, somehow he'd forced his clumsy feet to follow Deshenaza. On the upgrade, she had taken his hand to pull him along faster, walking, nearly trotting while balancing the mbuzi and the pack until Edvar had wrested him away from her.

She had let Edvar take over helping Radi, but only long enough for her to run ahead a few steps to a split in the passageway. She lifted her arm to let the lantern fill the passage and, trancelike, seemed to peer far beyond its light, looking first to the left and then to the right. Then she returned to Radi and Edvar to lead them up the right-hand passage, up, ever upward.

Radi's knees quivered and he stumbled heavily against Edvar. Deza looked at him worriedly and pulled harder at his hand. Radi wanted to tell her to stop and rest for a moment, but he couldn't summon the extra strength needed to speak.

The peketa poison level was high again, for he'd been without liquids too long. Deshenaza was carrying water in her pack, of that Radi was certain. He could hear the water like a roar in his ears. A drink of it would begin to help him within minutes. If there was enough, he could be feeling quite well in just a few hours. But he would not ask for the water. In the garbled depths of his mind was the single clear thought that Deshenaza would need the water for herself to make it through the caves to the City. Less clear was the hope that if she could make it there in time, if she could find his friends, if she could convince them that treachery had taken place, if . . . Radi's right foot refused to move, then his left, and he would have fallen onto the limestone cave floor were it not for Edvar's strong grip.

"Go," Radi said. "Leave me. Save the City."

"Put him down," Deza said to Edvar as she unslung the pack. "Drink, Radi. We'll rest a few minutes and then you must try to walk." Her hands were cool on his feverish skin. The rustle of her silken blouse sounded like water in a fast-rushing stream.

He tried to push away the waterskin. "Save the City. Keep the water for . . . long way."

"Drink," she said. "What do you think will happen if I arrive at the City with the Tycoon's son and no one else to substantiate my claim to the throne? By the time they find out it's true, it will be too late."

"We may never make it at all with me along," Radi said.

"Drink," Deza said again. "The fever's

clouding your thinking. Trust me. I know what I'm doing. If I can't witch water out of these rocks, nobody can."

She did not speak in the imperious tone Sheria always used, yet he obeyed. He emptied the waterskin. He imagined that his parched and poisoned innards leached moisture from the new reservoir just as quickly as he filled it, and he wished for more. Strange how his mind kept hearing that which he desired.

"It has started," Deza said, pressing her fingers against her cheekbones and smoothing a line to her temples.

"What has?" Edvar said, an edge of curiosity in his voice overcoming the gruffness Radi was certain he intended. The boy had followed along only because he didn't know what else to do, of that Radi was certain. Deza seemed unaware that she'd hurt Edvar with her open display of affection for Radi.

"Sheria has opened some of the ancient sluice gates. She means to fill your father's reservoirs. She knows she'll flood these lower caverns in the process. The computer will have told her that much, I'm sure." She looked to Radi for confirmation.

He nodded. "This part of the karstlands is thoroughly surveyed. Supplying water here along the coast in exchange for tithes is the City's lifeblood."

"And the witches like my mother and father had plotted all the grid levels around the City and put the information into the computers for all to use," Deza said. "But that which lies inland . . ." Her voice trailed off and she shook her head. "I'm the only one who knows, aren't I?" Again she looked at Radi.

"There's nothing between," Radi said. He sat up, surprised and pleased that he could do so. "A few caves left where the Maundifu used to run, but mostly it's solid metamorphic rock."

Deza shook her head. "That's all they can see, the marble caves, the schist riverbed. But there are places where the mountains are still soft shales and clays and salt. Oh, there's lots and lots of salt, all porous and half-dissolved from the City's sending water this way and that to places where water shouldn't be."

While Radi and Edvar looked on, Deshenaza pressed her temples with her fingertips until her hands turned white. She swayed, and the mbuzi on her shoulders bawled softly. It was not a trance, Radi knew. It was the strange empathy that water witches had with the waters of the world. She was fighting to keep it from overpowering her, and he had not seen anyone struggle in that way since he was a boy. The water's power was strong in Deshenaza, she who was the only child of the City's most powerful water witches. Her fingers trembled, and she breathed deeply as she fought against the flow in her mind. The pattern of the grids there would be more complete than if the surveyors of the City fed data into the computer for another hundred years. Radi had heard that the powers of the water could drive a person mad if the individual were not witch enough to stay in control. He believed that was true, for the number of witches had declined to a mere handful by the time he was born. The power was a dominant trait, but many who had the power never lived long enough to pass along the genes.

Finally Deshenaza took her hands away from her face, and it was Deza, looking pale and frightened, standing before him again. "We have to hurry," she said, her voice sounding shaky. "The water is rising quickly. Too quickly."

Only now did Radi realize that it was not delirium causing him to hear the sounds of water. The sounds were real. Water was rushing somewhere in the dark caves behind him, and the sounds were quite real. He grunted and tried to stand. Quickly Deza's strong arms were around him, helping him.

"She tried to drown us," Edvar said, looking back down the dark passageway from which they had come. "She tried to drown us, and he let her!"

"No," Deza said briskly. "Your father didn't know. He bargained for your release, but she betrayed him, too, as she's betrayed us all."

"And you've saved us all!" he said bitterly, and Deza seemed to become aware of his mood for the first time.

"It seems to me you've done your share of

saving, too," she said gently. "I'm very grateful to you."

"I didn't know I was saving your boyfriend for you or I might not have been so willing to dig him up."

"I don't believe that," she said firmly. "You were helping me. You were the one I turned to for help, the only one I could trust."

"I was a lot of help to you on the karst," he said, sounding more sad than bitter now. "I couldn't believe he'd try to kill you. My own father."

"He thought I was already dead when he threw me down that sinkhole. He was just disposing of a body, not killing someone," she said, telling him the one thing he needed to hear most. Radi knew what an effort it must have been to tell that particular lie. "Your father's not the enemy, Edvar. Sheria is. Your father may end up a victim of her treachery like the rest of us if we don't get to the Red City in time to stop her."

"Will we be in time to stop her?" Edvar asked.

"Not if we stand here," Radi said, throwing an arm around the Tycoon's whelp. "So let's get moving."

Edvar said, "Just a minute. There's something I want to say. I don't know how to make an oath of loyalty like a prince, but I just want you to know you can count on me, Deza."

"I already knew that," Deza said, and shouldered her pack again.

"At least we'll have clear passage," Radi said.

He cocked his head toward the mounting sounds of rushing water. "No one can follow us through that."

"I wish that were true," Deza said. "Harubiki may be past the water and right behind us. If she heard me in the slipspace, she would have had enough time to get through the dungeons before they were flooded."

"*If* she heard you? Did she? Did you make a noise?" Radi demanded.

Deza grimaced. "I was in a hurry, but . . . yes, the spear must have fallen."

"Then we can bet she's behind us. No maybe about it. When she realizes that I've escaped her again, she won't even consider turning back. She'd swim the Maundifu if she had to to finish me off."

Still weak, feeling grim, Radi leaned onto Edvar's strong shoulder and tried to walk faster. In an hour, he'd be stronger. But they didn't have an hour, not with Harubiki lurking nearby.

CHAPTER TWENTY

Deza stopped uncertainly, started forward, and then stopped again before the men had a chance to follow. She didn't sign to them for silence. She didn't have to. She had already heard the sound she was waiting for. Deza didn't know what she had heard, the scrabble of sliding pebbles, perhaps, the scrape of a knife along a sluice wall. Harubiki was behind them.

She leaned tiredly against the wall for a moment, wishing she had the power to feel where Harubiki was as easily as she could feel the water. Sound underground was wildly deceptive. Harubiki could be miles behind them or only a few yards. Deza wondered what kind of weapons she would be carrying.

"Radi," she said, and then wished she hadn't. He still looked dazed, even though she'd given him the last of the water twenty minutes ago, and it should have taken effect by now. If he had gotten more than one peketa bite, as she was beginning to fear, waterskins would not be enough to revive him, and they were a long way from the Maundifu.

"What is it, Deza?" Edvar said. He didn't look much better than Radi. The effort of climbing and half-carrying Radi through this nightmare terrain had almost done him in. She thought momentarily of lying to him in some misplaced idea of protecting him. All that was likely to get him was an unexpected knife in the back.

"Harubiki's following us," she said. "I heard her."

"I know," he said quietly. She wondered how long he had been keeping it from her.

"We have to get through to the Red City," Radi said groggily. "We have to get to the computers. Forget about me. Take Deshenaza, the princess of the Red City, and go. She will know what to do. Take her to the computer."

"And do what?" Deza snapped. "I don't know anything about computers. Neither does Edvar. Just exactly what do you expect us to do without you?" Her voice caught.

"Deshenaza knows. Go with her," Radi said and sank back into the half-sleep in which Edvar half-dragged, half-carried him. They would never make it.

Edvar shifted Radi to a better position over his shoulder. "We'll all get there, Radi my man. Don't worry. Just concentrate on putting one foot in front of the other and we'll be there in no time." In exactly the same tone he said to Deza, "We'll never make it. He's past hearing you. We've got to get him to water, Harubiki or no. It's our only chance. How far are we from this underground river?"

"About a half a mile, I think," Deza said. "I couldn't risk leading us back the way my father and I came. They've flooded half the sluices, and the rest of the approaches to the Maundifu are riddled with cave traps. We could all end up going over a cliff."

"We'll have to risk it. Can't you tell a dead end with your . . . abilities?" His tone was hurried, almost impatient. How far behind us is she, Deza wondered. She plunged into the explanation.

"All I can tell is whether there's water and where it's flowing. I can't tell if the opening is a slope down to a beach or a drop of hundreds of feet unless there's water in the passage. The cave traps look like they're safe, and before you know it, you're over the edge."

— Ah, yes, the cave trap, — her father said suddenly. — A useful device. —

— How is something that can kill us useful? I've got a sick man here and an enemy right on our heels. —

— If it can kill you, it can kill your enemy. She is, I understand, an excellent tracker. She would surely follow wherever you lead. —

"I'll get us to the Maundifu," Deza said. Edvar perked up, as if he thought she had witched the answer out of their dilemma. "This will have to be trial and error. I can only tell if there's water, not if it's safe."

"Let's get on with it," Edvar said and urged Radi, now totally unaware of what was happening, down the narrow slope.

It was more than the half-mile to the river's

edge, and Deza had to stop every few feet to recheck their position. They moved ahead without turning off their lanterns or trying to step soundlessly. She had not been quite truthful with Edvar. She could sometimes detect a cave trap from the water going over the edge. That was what she was doing now as they went. She could probably more easily find a deadend by poking her head into one passage after another, but it would do no good to lead Harubiki into a trap if they were trapped in it with her. What Deza needed was a combination of a real opening to the river and a false one, close enough to one another that Harubiki would be deceived. At last she thought she had it and moved rapidly down a twisting sluice newly emptied of water. The floor of it was slick under her feet, and she went back to help Edvar, but he waved her on ahead.

The sluice branched to right and upward, left and downward. The roar of the Maundifu was audible even to the men here, and Radi lifted his head like an animal sniffing a water hole. She halted them at the branching, handing Edvar her knife before she took off into the upward-branching corridor. As she had divined, the path climbed only for a few yards and then went down in wide easy steps to the river's edge. She went only far enough to be sure of the path's trueness, then raced back to get Edvar and Radi and start them into the corridor. Edvar tried to give her back her knife, but she pulled the mbuzi from around her neck instead and stuck it, unresisting, under Edvar's arm, and waved them on.

As soon as they were safely out of sight, she headed into the lower corridor, sure with a sudden frightening certainty that Harubiki was hard on her heels. She turned off her lamp and crept forward on her hands and knees down to where the corridor began to twist in on itself, rising almost imperceptibly.

There were a few inches of water on the floor, seeping slowly down from some higher point in the corridor, not enough to read her path by, and the corridor was rising rapidly now and becoming narrower.

Her intention was to go to the last possible safe point before the cave trap started its descent, then make enough noise that Harubiki could get a fix on her, and get back out of the sluice before Harubiki showed up. If that didn't work, she had felt a narrow alcove, hardly a slash in the rock, that she could fit into if worse came to worst.

Deza could feel the water plummeting over the edge of the cave trap only a few yards further on, though the passage was still climbing steadily and she could not hear any sound of water at all. She took another climbing step, letting go of the sluice wall to steady the pack on her back, and put her foot down onto emptiness.

Deza screamed. Her foot connected with the cave floor, but she was already into a careening descent, skidding as she had fallen, half on her shoulder and with the pack twisted helplessly across her arm. It was like a water slide, but she knew it would end in sudden death. The roar of the water was suddenly, violently loud. She could not hear the end of her own scream. She flung her free arm out to brace herself, but the tunnel wall was smooth, and she was sliding faster as new waters poured in from overhead sources and plunged her to the falls.

— Put your arm up — her father said, an island of calm inside her head.

She reached up, the pack constraining her, and grabbed onto a strong bar. She gripped it and felt almost jerked apart by her sudden stop. She pulled herself to a sitting position and latched onto the bar with her other hand. She had thought the bars were metal, part of some ancient pipes of the Red City, but she realized now they must be tubular crystals of galena, formed by intrusion of the lead into the volcanic roof of the passage. They would not bear her full weight, but she could use them to break her slide and guide her ascent back to the point at which she had fallen into the trap. She began a cautious hand-over-hand retreat up the tunnel to where she had been trapped.

The sound of water lessened to the trickle she had heard at first, one of the tricks of the passage. It cushioned its own sounds so that the luckless traveller could not hear his doom just ahead. The latticework of crystals faded, too, to an occasional spur of rock. Deza heaved herself the last few feet, praying she wouldn't start to slide again. And heard Harubiki.

It was the sound of a footstep, a footstep in water deep enough that Harubiki was far into the tunnel and moving fast, perhaps with a light. There was no time to waste. She fumbled out of her pack and slung it over into the cave trap. Then she counted her steps rapidly back to the niche and squeezed herself in. In the darkness she had no way of telling if one flash of Harubiki's lantern would expose a foot or a hand. She pulled herself in as tightly as she could, and stopped breathing.

Harubiki went by almost immediately. She had a light, but it was only a pocket flare that pinpointed the corridor. She also had a laser. She was as unlikely as Deza to see the treacherous trap. Deza listened to her progress, the deepening of the water slowing her steps a little, and then the sound that must have drawn Harubiki so unerringly. Harubiki screamed. It was a strange sound, thinned and muffled by the acoustic properties of the passage, and yet oddly naked. Deza had not been able to hear herself over the roar of the waters. Harubiki would not either. Deza closed her eyes.

The scream died away, and there was no answering sound, but Deza felt it and put her hands involuntarily up to her cheeks: the sudden displacing of water as something fell into the endless depths.

She found her way rapidly out of the passage and into the branch that would lead her to the

Maundifu. The men weren't by the river, but she turned on her lamp, and used it to find one of the lights embedded in the rock. With its even light, she could see their footprints in the soft sand, heading upstream to the lake.

Edvar was standing by the lake, the lantern on his wrist casting rings of light on the lake. Radi sat at the water's edge cupping his hands to fill them with water, and raising his hands to his mouth. He seemed to be drinking absently, his attention on the gleaming surface of the lake until he heard Deza's nearly soundless approach. Radi turned abruptly.

"Deza," he said, getting shakily to his feet. "Deza, are you all right?"

"Are *you* all right?" she said, taking his hand and raising her lantern to look at him.

"He may be too bloated to move," Edvar said, looking at Radi's distended belly critically, "but I think his head's clearing."

There were terrible circles under Radi's eyes, and his flesh still seemed drawn and pinched, but his eyes were not so glassy as they had been. "Good," Deza said, feeling some measure of relief. She squeezed Radi's hand, then knelt in the sand to take a drink from the lake. Edvar was looking down at her inquiringly. She scooped up water and drank before she answered. "Harubiki's dead," she said.

Edvar nodded. Radi seemed stunned.

"You're sure?" Radi said. "Harubiki is not an easy one to dispatch."

"I'm sure," Deza said, feeling slightly irritated. "I did so well that I almost fell into the trap myself, and *I* knew it was coming. She's no witch. She couldn't have known, so she's dead."

Radi threw a sharp look at Edvar, but the boy just shook his head.

"He's angry that I let you endanger yourself. He's being more reasonable about it now. You should have seen him twenty minutes ago. He got just strong enough to really be mad. It was all I could do to keep him here."

"Some of that was the peketa poison," Radi said apologetically, "but you must understand that Deza is the princess. The salvation of the City lies in the continuation of the water witch line."

Deza looked at him, feeling strange inside. "There's no salvation in computers," she said, knowing somehow that was true, yet wondering how she knew. She must have seen the City's computers as a child, but she would not have known their importance or their limitations at that age.

Radi smiled slightly at her and extended his hand to help her up. She took his hand, but did not lean into it. Even so, she sensed there was some strength in him now.

"You are without question your father's daughter. Akida's child," Radi said. "Do you know that I was charged with your safety when I was merely a boy myself? I've bungled the job badly. It has been a case of mistaken identity for years. I thought he meant any princess of the City should be kept safe and in a position to continue the line. I always thought that princess was Sheria. She had the genes even if she didn't have the gifts. But now I know he meant you. If there's salvation for the City, it'll be yours to give."

"When you talk like that, it's hard to tell if you really care for me, or just for the City."

Radi smiled again. "Deza, Princess Deshenaza, there is no difference. You may not realize it now, but you *are* the City."

"Akida," Deza said, musing. "He used many names, but never that one and yet I know it's right. I can hear Vira my nurse calling him." For just a moment, Deza felt overwhelmed, her head reeling. — Father, — she said. — Father, I know so much, and yet I know so little. How did you make me forget? Won't you help me fill in the rest? Please, Father. Father? — Deza took a deep breath, caught her balance even as Radi was reaching for her in alarm. Deza looked around wildly. "The mbuzi," she said. "Where is the mbuzi?"

"We were looking for it when you came," Edvar said, raising the lantern to cast its light on the waters again. "It got away when I was dealing with Radi. It's in the water, drunk as a pirate."

"How could you let it go?" Deza said, stepping out into the water to add her own lantern light to Edvar's. "You know what happens to them when they drink too much groundwater. This is the Maundifu. It's got to be out of its mind with . . ."

— Delight, — she heard. — You oughta try it, Deza old girl. This is much better than the pools of Sindra. Come on in. —

"Where?" Deza said frantically, then caught a glimmer of ripples off to her left. She ran through the shallow water, Edvar and Radi at her heels.

The mbuzi was swimming strongly in tight circles, nostrils flaring, eyes wild. It saw Deza and dived, no mean feat for a four-legged beast, but its head and body were suddenly submerged, and only the tips of its ears were visible.

Deza tried to walk to it, but by now the water was up to her waist. Her wool pants dragged heavily against her legs. — Father, come out of there at once, — she said. The mbuzi surfaced and bawled, and the sound echoed endlessly off the cave walls.

"Deza, leave it. We have to hurry," she heard Radi say. "The City needs you, Deza."

"It will swim until it dies," Deza said. "It won't have enough sense to come out before it's too tired to make the shore." She took a few more steps toward the mbuzi, which was now swimming in a line parallel to the shore. It was one step too many, and Deza went down. Her lantern went out, but this time she remembered to stand up. She'd barely regained her feet when she felt Radi's and Edvar's hands on her, both of them pulling her back to the shore.

"No," Deza said stubbornly. "I won't leave without him." — Father, — she shouted silently. — Come out of that water or I'll leave you here to drown. —

— No, you won't, Deza old girl. You need me in the Red City. Who's gonna unlock the computers if I'm not there? —

— What are you talking about? —

— The keys to the City. Ha. That's a good one. The keys to Mahali. You can't leave me. I'm inspedensible, spindemensible, . . . —

— You're not indispensable, you great lummox. I should have left you in the desert to begin with. — She was trying to wade back into the water, but Radi bad too firm a grip on her. "Radi, please," she said, trying to struggle out of his grasp.

Suddenly her arm was free, and Radi was gone from her side, leaving her and Edvar in water up to their hips. Edvar was still holding their last working lantern.

— That's right. Send your ape of a boyfriend after me. You'd better not let him hurt me. I'm . . . —

— I know. Indispensable. What makes you think that? — There was no point in talking to a drunk, but maybe she could distract her father long enough for Radi to be able to catch the mbuzi.

— I remembered the insets, didn't I? Even when Vira was lying there, all bloody. Poor Vira! Poor bloody Vira! — Her father began to

271

blubber, but his drunken emotions didn't seem to be having any effect on the mbuzi, which was paddling steadily toward the edge of the light. Now Deza could see Radi swimming after the beast, not as fast as he might have if he were well, but the water seemed to give him strength. The mbuzi hadn't been weakened by peketa poison. It hadn't even been tired by the long trek through the caves of the karst. It had gone the whole way on Deza's shoulders, so it was full of energy. It saw Radi coming and let out a gurgling bleat.

— You're no match for me, you ape, — her father said. — And don't think I'll let you marry my daughter, either. I deserve respeck. —

Radi lunged for the animal and went down in a violent splashing of water. The mbuzi continued swimming.

— No respeck at all. —

"I wish I'd never given you the little beast," Edvar said anxiously. "We need to get going."

"I know, but . . ." Deza said, on the verge of telling him the mbuzi contained her father's spirit. But what would she say? That old goat out there is my father?

Radi's head disappeared from view. Deza gasped, and Edvar went a few steps deeper to cast the light farther over the water. The mbuzi was swimming at the farthest edge of the light, and then they couldn't see it anymore, only the ripples of its wake. Deza held her breath, and Edvar lifted his arm high to flood the cavern with light. Nothing, not even the ripples now.

"He's gone under," Edvar said. "I'd better go after him." Edvar unstrapped his lantern and handed it to Deza. She saw a splash at the edge of the ring of light.

"Wait," she said. The two of them stared for a moment, then Radi's head surfaced. Within seconds they heard the mbuzi bawl again, as if in pain.

— Ow! Make him let go of my tail! — her father said.

— You're lucky it's not the ears he caught hold of, though I think it's the brain end of you he's got hold of, — Deza said, at once angry and relieved.

Her father seemed to burp, or something like it, in her mind, then said indignantly, — You always were a brat. —

When Radi was close enough, Edvar reached out and grabbed the mbuzi by the scruff of its neck, picking it out of the water. The little beast sagged down to the bottom of its skin, dripping and still trying to swim, pupilless eyes half-closed. Deza took the lime beast and draped it over her shoulders, wanting to admonish it, but knowing that anything she said or did would be useless in its present condition.

"Can we go now?" Radi said, also dripping and bedraggled. She noticed, however, that despite his exertion in going after the mbuzi, he did not reach for Edvar's shoulder to lean on.

Deza nodded. "Akida may thank you personally for this some day," she said. "But until then, I will have to thank you on his behalf."

Radi shrugged, accepting but not really understanding. She didn't try to enlighten him. No one really believed in spirits in gembone, not until it was a personal experience. And how could she tell him the truth of the matter when she didn't know it herself? Had her desperate need for her father's advice made her create his ghost? Or had he been born out of the hypnotic blocks her father had placed in his child's mind? The revelations of her past might have driven her insane if she hadn't found a logical way to let it out, bit by bit, in the form of her father's advice. From an mbuzi.

— Reedicklus, — her father said. — I'm not a figment of anyone's mijajination . . . gimazination. Give me another drink of the Maundifu and we'll see who's a figment. —

— Oh, shut up, Father, — Deza said, and stepped out of the water.

CHAPTER TWENTY-ONE

Radi walked behind Edvar and Deza as they followed the shore of the lake. There were lots of old sluices here, cutting through the sand, but they were empty or just trickling a bit of water, and he knew that they ought to be full. It had begun, then. The water was being diverted from its natural path, and was pooling somewhere above the City. Every minute was precious, and he had wasted an unknown number of them on the cursed mbuzi. He looked bitterly at the black lump across Deza's shoulders. Its head lolled and it bawled incessantly, lamenting its abrupt rescue from the intoxicating lake.

Yet Radi knew he could not have done otherwise. Deza held an odd attachment for the little creature, and it was hard not to remember that Sheria had no room in her heart to love anyone, not him, and certainly not a stupid animal. The difference between the two women was important. The crowned queen of the Red City must have compassion for all in her domain, even the natives on the planet surface and their beasts.

"Can you walk faster, Radi?" Deza said, not breaking her stride to look back at him.

In response, he quickened his pace. It was not an easy thing for him to do. His muscles were stiff from poison and abuse, and his stomach felt as if it were full of lead. But he could move now, for the effect of the peketa bite was losing its grip on him with this last gorging of water to wash it through. Yes, he w as thinking more clearly, and his muscles responded to his will, albeit painfully.

Deza turned from the beach and led them into a narrow tunnel, part natural cave but widened in places by the old machines to allow more water to flow. So much time had gone by and so much water had flowed through them over the years that the travertine had built up and clogged the old scars in the rocks. There was no water here now except that which was pooled in the depressions in the travertine under his feet. The way was slick, and he walked carefully.

"How far, Deza?" he asked.

"It can't be much farther," Deza said, putting her hands to her cheeks. Radi thought she must be aching nearly as much as he, though from a different cause. Great amounts of water could distress water witches if they didn't constantly strive to keep it under control, and in times of stress, he knew that might be difficult.

"Perhaps we should rest," Radi said.

"No," Edvar said flatly. "We have to hurry."

"Deza may need a minute . . ." Radi said. She looked at him gratefully, but she shook her head.

"I'm all right."

"Only now," Radi said, "am I realizing how difficult it must have been for you to pull me out of the sea. You are untrained."

Deza shook her head and walked on grimly clutching the mbuzi. "No, he trained me. He threw me into the pools at Sindra, he never let me skip a bath. It never became easy for me, but I managed."

"It will," Radi said.

"Will what?" Deza asked.

"Become easy, just as easy as eating and breathing. Witches who have no fear to conquer don't usually live to adulthood."

"Well, this one won't make it to old age if we don't hurry."

"What's that?" Edvar said suddenly. The mbuzi had bawled again, but Radi knew he was not referring to the beast's noise, for between bawling and snuffling it had rarely been quiet the entire trek along the lake. They stood silently, and heard a scraping noise.

"A sluice gate," Deza said. "They're opening or closing one ahead."

She half ran down the passage, wondering, Radi supposed, if they were about to find themselves shut into this tunnel by one of the sluice gates. His own heart was pounding, but he did not run on with his companions. It had been the sound of a sluice gate ahead that they had just heard, but he wasn't entirely certain the first noise had been from the same direction. He peered back the way they had come, saw nothing, heard nothing. Still, he was not convinced. Sound was deceptive in the caves, turning corners and ricocheting from above. But he could tell the difference between the scrape of a metal gate over limestone rocks and the thud of someone catching a fall as feet slid away on the slick travertine. He reached for his dagger and realized he had none. He had no light either, and Deza's and Edvar's light was rapidly getting smaller.

Perhaps he should wait here in the dark. Any pursuers would betray themselves by their lights, whether it was the Tycoon's soldiers or Harubiki, not so dead as Deza believed. Then he thought better of it. The dangers still ahead were more certain than the dangers behind. He did not expect a royal welcome for Deza in the City and certainly none for himself. He hurried after Deza and Edvar, following their bobbing light through the hollow earth.

The sluice gate at the top of the water run was open, and Deza led them across an empty manmade canal to a natural cave that sloped sharply down. The way was filled with loose rock and so steep that only the narrowness of the passage prevented them from falling a long way. As it was, they could deliberately jam their bodies against the wall to prevent headlong plunges, and wriggle through when the way caught their clothes and flesh.

"Where are we?" Radi said. They had to be close to the City by now, but he'd never seen anything resembling this passage on the grids. He thought he would have remembered one this close to the City.

"We're climbing down to the City," Deza said, slipping through yet another crack in the rock. The mbuzi bawled indignantly as its fanny scraped along behind her. "The galleries are right through this wall," she said, giving the rock a slap with the flat of her hand, "but we have to enter from below. The water is flowing over the City, in the old bed. The sluice gates up there won't hold." Her voice sounded anxious, but she was not frightened. She lowered herself, ledge to protrusion, moving steadily down.

Finally the tiny chimney they'd been climbing through widened into a sloping wall, down which they half-climbed, half-fell. At the bottom was a small natural chamber, formed of the same red rock as the City itself, limestone heavily laden with iron and oxidized to a brilliant rust. A staircase had been carved in the stone. It spiralled up to a wall.

"We made it," Deza said, taking the steps two at a time. "There's a door. It's tons of stone, but it's counter-balanced . . . if we can just find the lever." She was groping along the rock face at the top of the stairs, feeling along the smooth red rock for a lever Radi was sure must be hidden. Edvar was halfway up the stairs, ready to help.

As Radi went to join them, a stone tumbled down the slope from above. It was a tiny stone, its noise almost insignificant compared to the noise the two on the stairs were making. Any one of them could have jarred it loose during their downward plunge, left it precariously balanced until a grain or two of debris had shifted and upset the delicate balance. Perhaps. But all his soldier's instincts warned him that a foot could just as easily have upset that stone. His best course of action was to stand back in the shadows and wait to see who emerged from the overhead chimney. But that course of action was not open to him. He heard Deza shout in triumph as the stone door swung wide.

"Wait," Radi said. He dashed for the staircase. "Deza, you can't just go running into the City. Edvar may pass for a native, but you're wearing the royal insets. You'll never get past the guards. Take off your insets."

Deza started to unsnap the filigreed gembone from her cheeks, and then stopped. "No," she said. She bent swiftly, rummaged through her pack, and triumphantly pulled out her blue cloak. "What about this?" she said, tying it around her neck and pulling the hood far forward to hide her face.

"Blue is Sheria's color," Radi said doubtfully. "It will only . . . well, it's better than nothing. But keep your face hidden. And carry the mbuzi under your arm. They'll never believe you're Sheria with that thing draped around your neck."

They ducked through the door into near darkness and swung it shut. "Can you lock it?" Radi asked Deza.

"I don't think so. I can close it, though." She pressed her hand into a wide flat space in the rock and the door swung slowly shut. Radi could see no means of locking it now that it was shut. Invisibility was its protection on this side of the wall. But the other side was a stairway leading to solid rock, and Harubiki would have no trouble figuring out where they had gone.

Deza, he noticed now, had stopped and was looking around the narrow hallway in which they found themselves. There was a little light coming in from farther down the corridor, and Edvar switched off his carbide lantern and stuck it in his pocket. The hallway had once been opulently furnished, but the dark blue wallhangings hung in shreds, and there was a smell of must about the place. "I think we go this way," Radi said. "This was one of the old apartments on the lower level of the computer center. I think this hall leads to the outside."

"No," Deza said. She had flung the hood back. "I know where I am. I hid in this hall, waiting for my murderers. I know this very well."

She pulled the hood forward with one hand and brushed past them, striding rapidly through the adjoining room and to the foot of a wide stairway. Radi hurried after her and grabbed at her arm. "Deza!" he said furiously. "You can't just run up there like you own the place. We've got to have a plan.

"Edvar, the stairway will be heavily guarded. I

don't know if they will let us through or not. They must know by now that something is going on, but she wouldn't have warned them that they were about to be sacrificed. We may have to fight our way through."

Edvar nodded grimly and withdrew the knife Deza had given him from his belt. He kept it nearly out of sight as they started up the stairs.

"Deza," Radi said. "You see your chance and take it. Don't wait for us. Go straight to the main computer terminal."

"But I've never worked a computer before."

"I'll be right behind you. And keep that gorgeous face hidden."

She flashed a sudden smile and started up the stairs ahead of Radi. He followed, hoping there wouldn't be more than two guards. There were seven of them, guards in full regalia, standing two to a step but for the captain who stood a few steps above them. Their swords were sheathed, and they stood at easy attention, watching but making no move as Radi, Edvar, and Deza approached. The captain was staring. Radi recognized him as a young captain who'd trained under him a few years ago. Now the young soldier recognized Radi. He made no move, gave no shout, but Radi had seen the shock of recognition on his face. He'd been a good man, Radi remembered. Maybe he could . . .

"Do nothing," Edvar whispered, and Radi felt the blade of Edvar's knife pressing into his ribs at the same moment that the young captain spoke.

"Seize them!"

"No need," Edvar said, stepping around to show his knife. "I've got him in hand."

But Radi knew that trick would not work here, not in the Red City. These guards were not the Tycoon's men. They had no reason to trust a native if that was what they believed Edvar was. Radi leaped away as the first guard approached and lunged for the half-drawn sword. Others fell on Edvar behind him.

Radi disposed of the first man by kicking him soundly in the head, only to have two more appear from each side. He went for the closest first, wrenching the sword away and then turning on the second, feeling slightly better now that he was armed. The swords crossed, and the cave was filled with the noise of their fighting. Radi became aware that more guards were coming from the piazza above, and he shouted to be heard above the noise.

He pinned the captain against the railing. "Listen to me. We've been betrayed. The princess Sheria means to kill us all." The captain leaped free.

He wouldn't have listened either if he'd been in their places. Now he was fighting two swordsmen, and though he could see that Edvar was managing to hold his own, he knew they'd be hopelessly outnumbered in seconds. He looked wildly around for Deza, but saw her nowhere. He did, however, see Harubiki, racing up the stairs past the fight.

"No!" Radi shouted, and turned to follow her. He hadn't taken two steps before the rest of the guards barred his way.

CHAPTER TWENTY-TWO

At the top of the stairs Deza turned to the left and ran into the maze of water grids. She was not using her waterwitching powers here. She knew the way well from all the trips to the computer center with her father and the forbidden games of hide-and-seek with Vira.

The grids cut her off completely from Radi and Edvar and the soldiers. When she looked back all she could see were the banks of upright computer grids with their tortuous map-like tracings and their endless lists of coordinates that made no sense.

— Why are you stopping here? — her father said. He sounded fairly sober, and the mbuzi had stopped bawling, but it was still kicking feebly under her cloak. — You know the way to the main terminal from here. —

— I'm waiting for Radi. —

— He told you to go on, — her father said, mildly enough, but the mbuzi flailed against the blue cloth as if it were being smothered.

— I have to wait for him, — Deza said stubbornly. — He knows how to work the computer. —

— So do you. —

— How can you say that? — Deza said, but she

285

started forward again between the grids that marched like walls on either side of them. — Even these grids mean nothing, and they're simple compared to the controls of the terminal. And don't tell me you taught me how to run the computer and then made me forget that, too. I was only three years old. The only thing I did in here was play hide-and-seek. —

— Indeed, — her father said thoughtfully. — And you may need to play that game again. I hear someone. —

— I don't, — Deza said, but she hurried through the rest of the maze, cutting a zigzag course that brought her out onto the computer floor where all the auxiliary terminals were.

The main terminal was up another flight of very steep steps that rose free of everything and ended in a platform scarcely wide enough for the throne-like chair and the complex main terminal, high atop the red rock pinnacle. Deza had called it "the tower" when she was little. Her father had let her run up and down the steep steps when he was working there.

She could not run now, not with the struggling mbuzi under her arm. Halfway up she stopped and laid him gently on the narrow step.

— You'd better mean what you say, Father, — she said, clambering to the top. She had put him down just in time. The stairs got not only steeper, but shallower, till at the top there was barely room for her to stand facing the terminal. The dark blue cushioned chair with its high back

286

and curving headrest filled almost all the space.

She had almost believed her father, almost believed that she would look at the controls and magically understand them, but the board remained as undecipherable as the grids. There was no light behind the controls and no image on the screen. She put her hands on the touch panels, pressing randomly, but she could not get any response at all.

In exasperation, she looked back at where she had left the mbuzi. — I told you so, Father. Now look at all the time I've wasted. —

— You don't need to know how to work the computer, — her father said. — Deza, wait. —

— I don't want to hear another word. I'm going to go get Radi like I should have done in the first place. — She plummeted down the steps and out across the floor into the forest of grids. She did not even try to obscure her course this time. She went straight for the stairs.

The hand snaked out with such terrible suddenness from behind a grid that Deza gasped, "Chuma!" and flung herself out of the hand's grasp, reeling against the facing grid, choking with an old childhood fear.

"We meet again, Deza," Harubiki said. She had a knife. If Deza had not acted from pure reflex, from the remembered childhood nightmare, her throat would be cut by now and her blood spilling across the rock floor between them. She faced Harubiki silently, struggling to even her ragged breathing, to think. To think.

"Are you surprised to see me?" Harubiki said. She was wet and dirty, her sallow face bruised. "Of course you are. After you arranged my murder. You should have stayed to make sure it had been executed."

There were no weapons here, only the meaningless grids, and she had no knife to defend herself with against the knife in Harubiki's hand, against the dagger she was sure she had, and the laser handgun she had carried when they marched to the compound. No weapon at all, not even anything in her pocket she could make into a weapon. Her pocket.

"I heard you fall," she said, turning slightly so that her side would be away from Harubiki. The cloak would shield her movements when she put her hand in her pocket.

"That was your pack falling. You shouldn't have abandoned it there. It prevented my fall. And deceived you. What did you plan, with me safely murdered? To rule the Red City?"

"To save the Red City," Deza said. She slid her hand up her side to her belt. She has the laser, Deza thought desperately. I don't have a prayer. "Sheria will drown the City. She'll drown you with it."

She could not see Harubiki properly. She wondered if her fear were somehow blurring her vision. Then she realized what it was — a fine mist obscuring the space between them, dampening the stone floor.

"It's begun," Deza said. Harubiki looked up.

I must get the snake, Deza thought, and her hand went into her pocket and folded around the wriggling snake. She dropped her hand to her side under cover of her cloak, but then she could not think what to do. Should she throw the snake at Harubiki or would Harubiki blast it in mid-air? Deza was almost certain she was carrying the laser handgun. The snake, once released, would strike very fast, but would it be fast enough? She could not think clearly. It's the water, she realized suddenly, piling up in the empty salt domes behind the City, but she was afraid to focus in on the water and control its effect on her, in fear that Harubiki would catch her off guard.

She concentrated only on Harubiki and the snake. Everything depended on Harubiki not seeing the singing snake, which meant Deza must not look at the snake even though its song would tell her exactly where it was. She opened her hand and let the snake drop with a soft sound onto the stone floor. "It's begun!" she screamed, jerking her arm toward the ceiling. "We'll all drown!"

"No," Harubiki said. "You won't drown, water witch. I'll kill you first." She did have a laser. She leveled it at Deza.

"The water!" Deza shrieked, and then cut off her scream. In the silence, the snake sang very close to Deza.

Harubiki went white, her bruises standing out in dark purple against her frightened face. "Where is it?" she said breathlessly.

"I don't know," Deza said. "It's you it's after. Not me." She was careful to keep her eyes on Harubiki and not look down to where she knew the snake had to be, only a few feet from Harubiki. It was hard to concentrate now. The water was pouring into the salt domes un-checked, pressing on the last line of water gates separating it from the City. The water pressed against her cheekbones with a devastating pres-sure that threatened to break through and destroy her.

"Tell me where it is or I'll kill you where you stand," Harubiki said, her voice shaking. The laser wavered in her hand. Deza should jump for her and knock it out of her hand. The snake sang again, off to the side, and Harubiki swerved to face where the song had come from. I must jump her now, Deza thought. She'll turn back in an instant. But why is the snake over there? Why doesn't it strike? It's behaving as if it doesn't know where to strike.

It sang again, from far across the open space. Deza looked down. The tiny snake was at her feet and moving behind her. Why was it doing that? There was no one else here. "What's wrong?" Deza said dreamily, vaguely aware that the nearness of the water was influencing her more than her immediate danger. She saw a flash, and the snake was suddenly only a charred black mark on the red rock paving. She looked up blankly at Harubiki.

"You're apparently no water witch," Harubiki

said. "The snake was coming after you. And I want the pleasure of killing you myself." She was holding the laser only inches from Deza's face, but Deza couldn't focus on her. The water behind the City was pushing against the gates with tremendous pressure. One of the gates, imbedded in artificial limestone, was beginning to give way. And the snake would not have hurt her. He was slithering past her, toward somebody else. There had to be some other human here. She half turned.

Radi and Edvar skidded into the space between two grids and stopped cold. Harubiki raised the handgun slightly to include them. The gate shuddered on its dissolving limestone base and water began coming through. The base shifted and the gatepost cracked.

"All my enemies together," Harubiki said, and Deza collapsed against her.

The gun went off, startling Deza back to her senses. She grabbed for it, still holding Harubiki down with the weight of her body. She couldn't quite reach it, but she shook Harubiki's arm violently and knocked it free. The gun slid across the floor to the charred spot that had been the snake and went off again with a searing flash.

Harubiki rolled out from under Deza and regained her feet almost instantly, the knife in her hand and going for Radi. Deza grabbed for her foot and got a kick in the chin that set her bones vibrating. It was seconds before she could see clearly enough through the steadily increasing drizzle to see them: Radi and Harubiki, faced off like crouching animals and circling one another cautiously. Radi held a sword he must have gotten off one of the guards, Harubiki her knife. Radi's forehead was cut and bleeding, and he was having trouble keeping his footing on the wet floor. Deza began inching on her hands and knees toward the laser.

"No, Deza," Radi said sharply. "She's my enemy. This isn't your fight," and Harubiki lunged.

Deza scrambled for the gun and got it, then backed against one of the grids, waiting for a chance to fire. Radi and Harubiki were locked together for a moment, and Deza could see the glitter of the knife, but then Radi wrenched free of her. He came away without his sword, breathing heavily, supporting himself against the grid as if it alone were holding him up.

Deza fired the laser, squinting against the shock of light. Nothing happened. Harubiki darted forward again with her knife, going straight for Radi's throat.

"No!" Deza said, and lunged for her. She skidded on the damp polished rock floor and slammed into Harubiki with a force that sent the two of them pitching forward. Deza could feel Harubiki curl to roll free as she fell, but Deza was too close atop her. They hit the stone together, Deza's fall cushioned by Harubiki.

Before Deza could even gather her feet beneath her, Radi pulled her off and straddled

Harubiki. His former henchwoman remained still. Cautiously, Radi turned her over. The deadly knife was plunged hilt-deep in Harubiki's breast. She was still breathing, but shallowly, with a gurgling sound. Radi pulled out the knife and stepped back. "Edvar's hurt," he said to Deza. "He got hit by a laser blast. Go see to him."

Deza looked around, alarmed. She had not even seen Edvar since that first moment. He was slumped against the grid on the far side. He must have been going for Harubiki's laser, too. She stood up.

Harubiki grabbed the hem of her cloak almost pitifully. "Please don't let me die," she said. Deza bent over her. "I believe you're the real princess. Help me." The dagger that Deza had known was there flashed up, and Deza struggled frantically to pull away, but Harubiki held the cloak in a grip like iron, and the dagger lashed up at her.

Radi plunged Harubiki's own knife into her throat. Her arm dropped, and the dagger clattered to the floor. "Go see to Edvar," Radi said grimly, tucking the dagger in his belt. She ran across the slick floor, flinging the horrid cloak from her as she went.

"Hello, Deza," Edvar said. "I take it Harubiki's dead. I couldn't quite see from here." He was lying awkwardly against the grid, almost hidden from view. His arm dangled by his side. The sleeve of his shirt was charred and smoking.

Deza ripped the sleeve away. The laser had cut cleanly through his arm, missing the bone but not much else.

"Look," she said. "You're going to be fine. Laser wounds cauterize themselves so you can't bleed to death." She ripped the sleeve off and tied it around the wound. "Radi and I are going to leave you here while we get the computer to stop the water. We'll be right back. All right?"

Edvar nodded, and she stood up. There was a rumble like distant water, but when Deza put her hands up to her insets, she felt nothing more than the pressure she had been experiencing all along. In fact, the gates were holding so long as no more water was brought against them.

"Soldiers," Edvar hissed, struggling to his feet. "Hide, Deza." She pulled him quickly behind the grid, reluctant to leave him.

"There he is!" she heard a loud voice say, and the open space filled with soldiers.

"Radi's caught," Edvar whispered. "They'll never listen to him now that he's killed the princess's bodyguard."

"I can't work the computer without him," she whispered back. "I don't know how."

"You have to try. Radi's caught. I'll try to help him get free. You have to go or you'll be caught, too. Now!"

She hesitated for a second, and then darted down the long labyrinth of grids, away from the soldiers and toward the tower, crying sound-

294

lessly, — Father, you have to help me!

— Of course I'll help you, — he said as she reached the foot of the tower and began to climb. — I would have helped you before if you'd have listened to me. Climb to the top and sit down in the chair. —

She had reached the top and stood before the console, out of breath. — I don't have time to sit down. Just tell me how to run this thing. —

— You don't need to know how to run it. Sit down. —

He was still drunk. Radi and Edvar could not help her, nobody could help her, and all her father could say was, "Sit down."

— Tell me how to work the controls, — she said as patiently as she could. — Maybe you taught me how, but I don't remember. —

— Sit down, — her father said.

— What good will that do? — Deza said, unable to restrain her frustration any longer. — Radi and Edvar are fighting off half the city so you can lie there giving me useless orders. This is hopeless. I'm going to go help them. At least we can all die together. —

— SIT DOWN! — her father shouted, so loudly it echoed in her mind. — All your life you have refused to follow the simplest commands. You will not disobey me now. SIT DOWN. —

Deza sat. She hunched forward on the seat of the highbacked chair, looking at the unfamiliar controls. If her father thought he could jar loose more of her memories by his shouting, he had failed. She was certain she had never sat here before.

— Lean back, — her father said, more quietly but still with the tone of command that Deza had never, in spite of what he had said, disobeyed.

She leaned back gingerly into the curve of the headrest, supporting herself on her elbows. If she leaned all the way back she would be almost completely encompassed by the chair, unable to see the controls, let alone reach them.

— All the way, — her father said. — And sit still. —

All the way. Her head rested against the cushioned headrest. The curving sides moved slightly inward, shaping themselves to the contours of her face. Deza fought the feeling of smothering as they moved inward to press against her cheeks and sat very still. The sides touched her insets, pressed against them.

Deza sucked in her breath. No wonder her father had told her she didn't need to know how to work the computer. She was the computer. She had thought her mind was working at top speed in the caves, reading and sorting the water. It was nothing compared to this. She could see the entire water network of the planet, from the seacoast, across the great Tegati Desert to the far mountains, a vast network of underground sluices and passages no one alive had ever guessed at. All this in less than a second, and more. The way they had just come, already changed, the banks of the lake rising to fill the tunnels, the sluices filling, water streaming through the chimney and flooding the stairway, and at the Tycoon's compound, the other terminal.

"Hello, Sheria," Deza said, and felt the shock of recognition from the other end as the princess's hand must have hesitated above the touch panel. If Sheria spoke, Deza couldn't hear it, because Sheria couldn't speak through the computer as Deza did, but she could imagine what she said. "I'm taking over now," Deza said, and even before she said it, she had taken control, was already starting the actions that would save the Red City. She punched no buttons, did not even attempt to reach the controls. She could do it all in her head.

She closed off the sluices nearest the City, diverted the water below and east of the canyon, allowing it to flow down across the paths they had just come. She opened every passage along the Maundifu, letting them fill with the overflow and slow the massive rush of the river that Sheria had unknowingly started when she flooded the caverns where Radi and Edvar were imprisoned. She had come close to unloosing the Maundifu, which must not happen. It would destroy the City, the compound, the vast underground network between. She had no idea of the power she was dealing with, thinking she could fill the Tycoon's reservoir like one dips a cup into a well, never realizing the force that lay in the water.

The level of the lake was still rising. Deza opened more sluices between the lake and the City, and saw instantly that that was the wrong thing to do. The overflow pushed back into the salt domes behind the City, where the gates were already severely overworked. She slammed those sluices shut as rapidly as possible, but water had still come through and was pooling behind the City like a vast sea. She diverted water below the City, letting the old tributary that flowed next to the City fill to its banks. That was dangerous, but it stopped the rain that was falling on the City.

Now the water she had shut out of the salt domes had nowhere to go. It could not go back to the lake without threatening to break through to the Maundifu. It could not go anywhere that would not endanger the City, and the thought that had been with her from the beginning, the thought she had suppressed even as the insets linked her to the computer and she flared into complete awareness, spread over her consciousness with the overwhelming wash of despair. She had not been in time.

She shot an anxious glance at the ceiling. The drizzle had stopped, but water was still dripping from cracks that had not been there before, pooling on the computer center's floor. The mbuzi lay in a puddle. Deza made a move as if to go rescue him and was instantly disconnected.

— Sit down, — her father said. — A little water won't hurt me. —

— I can't save the City, — Deza said help-lessly. — It's too late. —

— How ridiculous! Of course it's not too late. Unloose the Maundifu. —

— Edvar, — she said, and sank back against the headrest.

She could see him and Radi, as if they were there before her, not grainy images on a monitor, but them. They had come out onto the main floor of the computer center, all the way to the terminals, but the soldiers had caught them there. The soldiers had them cornered between the grids and the terminals, but they were not fighting. They were looking up. Radi, Edvar, the soldiers, everyone was looking up. The leaks were worse there, a steady rain, muddy with the rock it was dissolving.

"Now will you listen to me?" Radi said. "Sheria will drown this City and all of you with it. I must get to the computer."

"No one gets near the main terminal but the princess," one of the soldiers said. He glanced at the tower and registered the shock and surprise that must mean he could see Deza. "No one. Stop that girl."

Edvar was holding his arm. He stepped, swaying a little, in front of the soldier. "She's the princess. The real princess. Only she can save this City from being swept away." The soldier put out his hand to brush past Edvar, but he never even touched him. Edvar slumped forward onto the wet floor.

Radi moved convulsively toward Edvar and was stopped by the soldier's sword. "Get that girl away from the computer," he said, and the other soldiers ran forward across the floor.

— There's no time for anything else, — her father said. — Besides, it will give you the revenge you have been wanting all along. —

— The Maundifu will destroy half my kingdom. Who will it take revenge on but me? — she said, and was surprised to realize that was true. She had a kingdom to protect, a kingdom that she alone could see and understand, that she alone could save or destroy.

— It's the only answer. The soldiers will be here in a moment. The second they pull you out of this chair your chance will be lost. No one can help you. You have to choose. —

— Father . . . —

— Your father is dead. —

Deza closed her eyes, but she could not shut out any of it. It would be with her always. The mbuzi on the lower steps, Radi arguing frantically with the soldiers to delay them, Edvar in the pool of water on the floor, all the vast honeycombing of rock and water. Her kingdom.

She unloosed the Maundifu. The mighty gates of the river, shut — how many years? — opened all at once, allowing the Maundifu back into its natural bed from all the countless taming sluices, channels, dams. It lunged forward like a chuma cat set free, plunging through its dry bed, filling the lake's cavern to the roof and then

300

rushing in a mighty wall through the channels, carrying crystals, rock, and the beautiful work of years with it. Toward the karst. Toward the compound, where Sheria sat at her console, not even understanding yet what was coming.

"Close sluices," came a message from Sheria's console, followed by a long string of coordinates. Deza didn't try to stop her. The command was meaningless. There were no sluice gates to close. The Maundifu had torn them away.

"Divert to secondary channels," Sheria commanded, and Deza could imagine the Tycoon leaning anxiously over her shoulder, saying, "What is it? What's happening?"

Would Sheria answer him, would she say, "Take your fat wife and head for higher ground!" or did she, like Harubiki, not even care for death as long as she could take others with her?

There was no higher ground. The Maundifu swept through the karst, the last long passage she and her father had climbed together on their journey of flight. It obliterated the warm, sandy hideyhole she had fallen into and swept on through the caverns, filling every channel, gathering strength with every mile it went.

Closer and closer to the compound, to the sea.

"Override," Sheria commanded. "Redirect Maundifu," as if it were not a raging chuma cat almost upon her. "Open sluice gates," her fingers told the computer through the touch panel. Deza did not recognize the coordinates for a moment. Then she did. The salt caverns behind the City. Deza slammed them shut again, but two, no, three of them were swept away in the shock of the water.

Deza darted out of the chair and down the stairs. The soldiers were at the foot of the stairs and starting up. "Run!" she said, thinking frantically that they would not believe her. "Get your people to higher ground. Get them above the second balconies. On the east side. Hurry."

She saw their look of disbelief, and then they scattered. She did not understand it at first, and then she heard with her ears what she had been hearing in her head. The sound of water. She ran down the remainder of the stairs and over to Radi, who was dragging Edvar over the wet floor.

"How high will the water come?" Radi said.

"We'll be safe at the top of the tower," Deza said, pulling on his body because she was afraid of hurting his arm. An alarm started ringing, its echoes pealing like a great bell in the cavern.

Radi lifted Edvar and slung him over his shoulder, and they started up the steps, Deza behind trying to balance Edvar so they wouldn't fall. "It's coming," she said in anguish, and stopped. "The water's coming."

Radi had put Edvar down. "I can't carry him any farther. The steps are too shallow. We'll have to drag him." Deza came up beside him and they each took an arm. Edvar cried out, but it was the only way to get him above the level of the water. They backed up the narrow steps.

The Maundifu roared through the dungeons like an enraged animal. It paused at the mbuzi caverns, filling the great hall almost slowly while the helpless animals bawled and were silent, and exploded into the compound, crushing the building, the animals, the fleeing natives, and carrying them before it in its last mighty leap into the sea.

"Deza," Radi said. "Don't stop. We're almost to the top."

"I killed Sheria," she said numbly. "I killed the Tycoon. All of them. And half my kingdom."

"But you saved the City," Radi said. "And now you have to help me save Edvar."

"Yes," Deza said, and the water broke through the western wall of the City.

"Here it comes," Radi said, and gave a mighty pull on Edvar's arm that almost yanked it out of the socket. The water swirled around the base of the tower, rising above the terminals, the grids, climbing the stairs like a relentless enemy. Deza tugged on Edvar's body, trying to lift him into the chair, going down two steps to push him from behind. The water reached her feet.

Even though she was ankle deep in the water and struggling to keep her balance, the water seemed to have no more of its terrifying power over her. It was only water. Radi gave her a hand to pull her up, but she rejected it, watching almost fascinatedly as the water came to the top step and then began to subside, flowing steadily toward the river. It doesn't hurt, she thought wonderingly.

— Of course not, — her father said. — A little water never hurt anybody. —

She dived for the mbuzi, which was already floating away from the tower, bawling and struggling to keep its head up in the powerful current, but Radi had her by the back of the neck.

"Father!" she shouted aloud, and Radi heaved her back out of the water and onto the top step.

— Deza old girl, — he said faintly, and then was gone.

CHAPTER TWENTY-THREE

Radi held Deza for a long time while she cried quietly. "I can't lose him now, not after all this," she had said. "I never should have left him."

He'd tried to comfort her over the loss of the mbuzi, wondering all the while how she could carry on over a beast when half the City was under water. Then she'd shaken her head bitterly; "It was my father, Radi. His spirit has been in the mbuzi's gembone ever since the hovercraft crash." Through her tears she'd told him the rest, how she'd escaped through the caves with her father so long ago but had not remembered the ordeal until she'd gone to the karst with the Tycoon. How the old man had guarded his daughter by keeping her in ignorance with hypnotic blocks; how even after death he'd tried to keep Deza from being discovered by her enemies in the City. But after death, Akida's control had been indirect, a mind-talking mbuzi at best, and maybe nothing more than suggestions he'd planted in Deza's mind years before. It wasn't enough to prevent her from heading straight for the nearest body of water she could sense, the sea. She'd saved Radi from drowning there, and he thought that if he had not been so caught up with concern over his ill-fated mission, he might have paid more attention to her uneasiness at the sea instead of dismissing her peculiar behavior because he thought she planned to rob him. He was certain from the story Deza told that the hypnotic blocks her father had placed hid the truth from Deza better than it did from the rest of the world, for her nature and natural gifts must have given her away a thousand times. Only the brilliant scheme of Deza posing as a water witch could have saved them all these years. When people got close to the truth, Akida no doubt saw to it that close inquiry revealed a couple of surface natives engaged in a swindle. Since no one liked admitting being duped, their worst punishment probably had been to be sent packing. Even so, Radi wondered how many people had seen Deza's insets and recognized them as genuine. Deep down Radi remembered now that he'd known a stolen pair could not meld against her cheeks so perfectly, that they'd been fashioned for her by a master craftsman, Akida. She'd lost her father in the flesh days ago on the desert, but in Deza's mind she'd carried him with her until she saved the City. To Radi's way of thinking, that was somehow appropriate.

Someone silenced the alarm. Its disappearance was as much a signal for activity as its onset had been. People began poking their heads out over the rails of the upper balconies to peer at the mess below. Looking down, Radi saw that the water had nearly stopped flowing. Only a final sluggish wash remained in the lowest reaches of the cave floor. Broken furnishings and chunks of red rock clotted gutters and corners, and bits of foliage from the gardens floated where the water had pooled. Mercifully, there were no bodies to be seen, which made Radi hope that the alarm had been sounded in time. Deza sat up, wiping her cheeks with a fist while she looked around.

"Radi," Edvar said. "What's going on over there?"

Radi looked up at Edvar, still sitting on Deza's throne, looking wet, dirty, and terribly pale with pain. With his good arm he was pointing to the other side of the computer floor. When Radi turned, he could see soldiers entering the computer's archive building. "They're going to check the monitors, maybe do a playback," Radi said. "That's good. There won't be any doubt in their minds that Deza saved the City. It will save us a lot of explanation."

"More soldiers," Edvar said.

Many more, swarming toward the tower, surrounding the base of the stairs.

"What shall we do now?" Deza said, her hand clasping Radi's. "They will know that I . . . I killed Sheria." For just an instant Deza's frightened eyes met Radi's, looking frightened as they had when she first realized she couldn't control the con she was working back at the compound. But the fear was brief, giving way to sorrow when she looked up at Edvar. "Edvar, your father.

307

I . . . There was no way to . . ."

The Tycoon's whelp reached out and touched Deza's damp and matted curls. "Don't," he said. "You did what had to be done, and it was right for Mahali."

"They're waiting," Radi said.

"What?" came Deza's reply.

Radi gestured to the landing below the tower stairs. A ring of soldiers stood shoulder to shoulder, hands on the hilts of their swords, the officers with their lasers drawn. "They're waiting to hear from the people checking the monitors. They know you sat at the main control console; but they don't know what you did . . . yet." He grinned at her, but his smile faded involuntarily when he saw that she was holding Edvar's hand against her face. He just couldn't help the stab of jealousy.

"Better help me down," Edvar said quickly. "When they find out for certain that she saved them and realize who she is, I don't want them to think they have a usurper to deal with."

Radi let go of Deza's other hand to help Edvar. The young man put his good arm all the way around Radi's shoulders and slipped off the throne, whispering, "It's still nice, even knowing she doesn't mean anything by it."

"What are you two whispering about?" Deza said, helping Radi settle Edvar on the steps with them.

"I was just telling Radi that the people will adore their new princess, and that he'd better get used to sharing your affection."

"There's so much to do. I wish they'd hurry," Deza said absently. She sat down and stared at the soldiers. Civilians were gathering behind them, looking up at them with open curiosity, whispering among themselves.

They would love Deza. She was everything Sheria was not and never could be. She was courageous, intelligent, and had her marvelous witching gifts, but of the greatest importance was her genuine ability to love people and be lovable in return. She had not seen these people since she was three years old, yet she had risked her life to save them all. She was the princess the City needed, and the woman Radi wanted.

"Why don't they come?" Deza said nervously, her eyes fixed on the doorway of the tall archive building.

"It takes time, Deza. The water couldn't have gotten to the top and damaged anything important, but they'll want to be sure. They may run it through two or three . . . yes, look," Radi said, pointing. "Some of the elders are going in. They'll run it through for them, too."

Deza groaned and wiped the palms of her hands on her damp and dirty pants. "I want to get started," she said, glancing back up at the throne. Then she turned suddenly to Edvar. "You must be my ambassador to the foreigners from Kalmar."

Edvar smiled with pleasure. "They'll be clamoring for ground water rights and buying up mbuzim. Word must have gotten out on Kalmar by now about the gembone circuitry in the water message devices. You're putting a lot of power in my hands, Deza."

"It's safe in them," Deza said confidently. She touched his hand again and looked at his injured arm with concern. "Does it hurt terribly?"

"Not so much," Edvar said with a wink at Radi. He had to be in agony, but was not quite aware of it for ecstacy of Deza's touch.

"And we'll have to rebuild the City, of course," she said to Radi, "but I think it's time we stopped hiding down here and we simply must dispense with this mumbo-jumbo those bogus priests give the surface natives. A fair price for water, and it will be high for a while because we're going to have to work very hard after this fiasco to deliver it. But we're not going to make them think there are ghosts poisoning their wells when they can't pay the price."

"You don't believe in spirits?" Radi said, faintly amused, then regretted immediately alluding to the mbuzi and Deza's father, for her resolve seemed to waver and she bit her lip.

"It seems so unfair," she said, "for him to be deprived of seeing what must have been his fondest hope for Mahali coming true."

"And for you," Radi added. Deza just nodded, apparently unaware that as sovereign of the Red City she'd control immense personal wealth and be able to have comforts and luxuries she'd probably only thought about in her dreams.

"I just wish he were here," Deza said.

Radi took her in his arms, holding her closely and feeling fiercely protective. "It was fitting, sweetheart," he said quietly. "I was only seven years old when Akida charged me with protecting the princess, but I didn't understand what he meant until now. He kept you safe until he could deliver you to me. I love you, Deza."

"And I love you, Radi."

"They're coming out," Edvar said.

Radi and Deza looked over at the archive building; soldiers and elders were coming out the door, walking steadily across the computer floor, seemingly oblivious to the thick red silt deposited there by the flood. The people on the stairs let them through until they reached the upper landing and the head of the guard. They stood talking quietly for a few minutes, the people nearby crowding close to hear. Before they were finished, a whisper was rising from the crowd, faint and barely discemable at first: "Deshenaza . . . Deshenaza . . . Deshenaza," becoming louder as the rest of the crowd caught up the rhythm: "Deshenaza, Deshenaza, Deshenaza."

"Your people are calling you, Deza," Radi said, giving her a final squeeze.

She took a deep breath and nodded, then stood up. Her long hair was a tangled mat of damp curls, her clothes wet and dirty. But her shoulders were squared and her back was straight, and perhaps from years of practice at behaving like a princess or just from instinct, she stepped forward with a grace that made the people cheer. To the sounds of their happy voices she started down the steps, ready to begin her royal duties.

Radi helped Edvar up so they could follow her. Akida, Radi thought, I will do everything within my power to hold her and the City safe for all time.

— It's about time. Where were you fifteen years ago? —

"What?" Radi said.

Edvar looked at him, shook his head with a smile, indicating that he couldn't hear what Radi had said above the noise from the shouting, cheering crowd.

— Muscle and sinew. I thought you were going to take care of her, — Radi heard clearly despite the muttering tone. — Get down there and make a path for her before they love her to death, you great lummox! —

Half carrying Edvar, Radi rushed down the steps. The crowds were gathering close to Deza, threatening to crush her in their enthusiasm. He draped Edvar's arm over a cheering guard and dived into the crowd. "Make way," he said authoritatively. "Make way." He got to Deza and continued making a path for her, as he would have done in any case, he was sure, even if he had not heard the voice of Akida telling him to do it. It was just the tenseness of the moment, the emotional high of talking about the once great man . . .

— Once great? —

Always great, Radi thought. He was getting as bad as Deza, imagining Akida's spirit talking to him. Where would his soul have leaped to this time when it felt itself being washed to death with the mbuzi? There was no gembone around except for Deza's insets, which were surely inviolate, or he would have made use of them after the hovercraft crash instead of saddling her with that smelling beast for all those long miles. Radi touched his gembone medallion thoughtfully. Surely he wouldn't have . . . It was Deza he wanted to talk to, to give advice to.

— She may be a little hard to advise now that she's the princess. She always did think she knew how to handle things better than anyone else. All this cheering will go straight to her head. But with our help she won't make a total fool of herself. —

— Our help? — Radi said silently, and then aloud, "*Our* help?"

— That's right, you big lummox. And don't you start in with any figment of the imagination arguments. I've had enough of that from my own daughter. —

With a prickling feeling along his scalp, Radi stopped and looked back at Deza. She smiled at him. Surely she hadn't really been talking to the ghost of Akida all this time. Surely this voice he was hearing was only an aberration brought on by adrenalin. Once the excitement was over, the

voice would fade to what it really was, his boy-
hood memory of the great man.

— I wouldn't count on that, — the voice said.
— Anyway, what are you griping about? Edvar
could have given you a pet mbuzi, too. Then
where would you be? —